PATHWAYS IN
THE DARK

Also by Lou Paduano

Signs of Portents

Tales from Portents

The Medusa Coin

PATHWAYS IN THE DARK

Greystone Book Four

Lou Paduano

Eleven Ten Publishing LLC

GRAND ISLAND, NEW YORK

Eleven Ten Publishing LLC
282 Fareway Lane
Grand Island, NY 14072

Publisher's note: This is a work of fiction. Names, characters, places, and incidents either are the product of the author's imagination or are used fictitiously. Any resemblance to actual events, locales, or persons, living or dead, is entirely coincidental.

Printed in the United States of America
Edited, formatted, and interior design by Kristen Corrects, Inc.
Cover art design by Kit Foster Design

First edition published 2018

Library of Congress Cataloguing in Publication Data
Paduano, Lou
Pathways in the Dark / Lou Paduano

LCCN: 2017917319
ISBN-13: 978-1-944965-53-2 (hardcover)
ISBN-13: 978-1-944965-08-2 (paperback)
ISBN-13: 978-1-944965-09-9 (eBook)

For Parker Rose, who always lights my way.

TABLE OF CONTENTS

COLLATERAL

CHAPTER ONE

Gina Fisher entered the office, the same as every other day. Same parking spot, three blocks over in an overpriced downtown structure. Same cup of coffee—dark roast with three sugars. Just another Thursday in the city for the twelve-year collections veteran.

Except today was completely different, like seeing the world again for the first time. Gina felt refreshed, awake beyond the caffeine-laden beverage in her grip. Colors were more vibrant, her smile a permanent fixture.

She strode into the office on the seventh floor of the downtown high-rise, excited for the day ahead. No matter the calls to angry clients unable or unwilling to meet their minimum payments, she was happy to talk with them today. Nothing stood in her way. And nothing would. Not when destiny was in reach.

Cubicles stretched across the floor as the elevators opened. Gina made a beeline for her desk, placing her purse in the top drawer. Becky rushed over from the end of the row, a quizzical stare on her face.

"Gina," she called, tucking in close to lower her voice. "You disappeared last night at the bar. Figured you'd be planning a mental health day."

"Not today," Gina replied, her smile unabated.

Becky pointed, tilting her head. "What's with the grin?"

Gina stared off down the wide aisles of desks. Phones blared. The day had barely begun but the lines were already filling with requests and urgent payments to process. They faded like the questions from her closest friend. Her focus fell on the small group gathered along the floor around a single man.

Walter.

He stood tall and proud, wearing the same button-down he always wore on Thursday—navy blue, his favorite color. He thought no one noticed but she had for years. Too long without a word.

Until today.

Becky was still beside her, gazing wistfully. "Something in that coffee you should be sharing?"

Gina handed her the cup. "Sure. Here you go."

Becky scarcely managed to catch it as Gina let the travel mug loose before heading briskly down the aisle. She split a pair of curious colleagues, unable to take her eyes off the man, who was the reason for her being at the office this morning. The reason she came to work every day for the last seven years, if she was being honest.

Becky called after her. "Girl, what are you doing?"

Gina tossed her a wave and kept walking. "Something I should have done years ago."

They almost had, too. There was a moment at the start of their working relationship when a romantic interlude was only a matter of time. But they let it slip away, whether it was the social stigma of the situation or something more. The two of them simply fell into friend mode, a routine they enjoyed.

Gina married soon after and filed for divorce almost as fast. Walter never married and rarely dated, content with his lifestyle. Or so he said, though never convincingly. Not to her.

"No," Walter said, his voice low but his confidence high, surrounded by two of his cubicle neighbors. "I think if we bring this to her as a team, she can't dismiss it."

"What have you been smoking, Walt?" Andre asked, sipping his coffee. "Have you even had a meeting with the ice queen?"

"That's the issue, isn't it? You can't supervise people by e-mail."

Richard patted his shoulder. "I'll pack your box for you."

The pair started for their desks, leaving Walter the lone man standing. "Cowards."

Gina glided between the departing pair. Walter brightened at her arrival. "Gina, what do you think about—?"

She pulled him close and kissed him. His hands flailed in surprise then settled along her back. Even with her eyes closed she could feel the stares on them. Her smile returned as the kiss broke and she stepped back.

"Gina?"

"I've wanted to do that for a long time."

"What?" Walter rubbed his neck, his cheeks flushed. "You have? With me? I mean—"

Gina fixed an undone button on his shirt. "You're cute when you're flustered, Walter. Very cute."

He ran a hand through her hair, seeing her for the first time. "And you're hot. I mean really hot. Are you feeling all right?"

"Perfect. I'm perfect." She laughed, pulling away from his touch. "Be right back."

She moved for the stairs. Walter followed, the eyes of the entire seventh-floor staff enthralled. He reached for her. "Gina?"

Her lips fell on his once more. A quick peck, then she closed the door to the stairs.

Heat billowed from her chest, filling her every cell. She pushed through it, climbing the three stories to the rooftop. The wind cooled her, the air a calm refresher.

She did it—she kissed him. Walter. The man she always wanted in her life, yet fear kept them apart. Hers more often than not. But there was no more need for fear. No more need for anything. Their kiss released her from the prison she had created.

Gina let the moment wash over her. The heat returned, burning hotter and brighter, building in waves from her chest and spreading. It swelled in every breath and every step toward the edge of the ten-story high-rise in downtown Portents.

"Perfect," she whispered, her smile spread ear to ear. She looked out over the city, letting the sounds of the traffic below surround her like a symphony. The vibrant colors of the world filling her with light. "I'm perfect."

Then Gina Fisher jumped.

CHAPTER TWO

Greg Loren set down his half-eaten bowl of cereal, wondering if he should consider a cooking class or ten. Meals were never a priority in his mind; the diner down the block was more than able to handle his dietary needs with some over-easy eggs and buttered rye toast. Still, how hard could it be to grill up a burger every now and then?

Pushing aside his less-than-satisfying meal, Loren shifted away from the coffee table for the window. Rain dripped along the pane of glass. Even the weather couldn't be bothered to put in a major effort.

His arm ached. His chest burned. Two weeks since his extended visit to the hospital and Loren was still struggling through decreasing amounts of pain meds and a terminal lack of sleep. The time off from work didn't help matters.

He was tired. Tired of the pain. Tired of pacing the apartment. Tired of pretty much everything, especially not being at work. He needed to feel useful after everything that happened during the Erikson case. His visit to the precinct, seeing Myers and Pratchett, helped.

Until he learned about the photo.

It sat beside the soggy cereal, the image burned into his every thought. Soriya Greystone in his apartment the day he lost his wife. The shadow in the window.

The missing person's cases offered a distraction—a much-needed one. Too many secrets in the city, too many factions hidden in darkness.

A Circle of Shadows.

Loren needed to be involved. He needed to be out there, even in the rain-filled night, looking for the answers to his questions instead of stewing in his own agony.

The police scanner propped on the arm of the couch assisted in his need. For the longest time he never considered it an option. When his shift ended, his personal life took hold—two separate entities. The separation was a necessity for his sanity. He refused to fall into the same traps, lost in an endless spiral of cases and conspiracies.

And Beth, his wife, always at the center of everything.

But something was in Portents. Something no one else saw, no one else noticed, lost to the shadows. And he intended to find it—find *them*—and drag them into the light.

The police scanner had other ideas, the static flaring before a voice came through the line. "Wagon requested. We have a 10-54."

Loren pulled away from the rain and the cold pane of glass. He eyed the scanner, recognizing the voice. "Myers? Wait. A 10-54?"

"Address is 467 Falconer," Myers chirped through the box. "Traveler's Cove."

A 10-54. Bodies found. *And the address?* "I know that address."

He grabbed the scanner then reached for his coat resting on the floor instead of a hanger in the front closet. He shook the pocket to make sure the keys still rested inside then started for the door.

"Why the hell do I know that address?"

The cab dropped him off a block away, a silent word of thanks followed by condemnation at the increasing rain. His sneakers leaked like a sieve at the slightest drop of water caught along the flapping heels, soaking his socks.

Traveler's Cove ran along the edge of the city limits, undeveloped land to the north before the suburbs took over. Bidding wars were constant, with more and more people wanting to leave the heart of downtown for the scenic coves. Less crime, more space. Who wouldn't want that?

Falconer Avenue marked the northern border. Few homes dotted the street, the distance between them ranging from a hundred to a thousand feet. Ram-shackled properties mostly, but some plantation-style homes well-kept. Not the case with 467 Falconer. The shack leaned with the wind and whole sections of the roof were missing.

But then, no one had lived in the place for years.

Loren stopped outside the police cordon, a lone officer in a bright yellow poncho acting as gatekeeper. He towered over the scene and brought a grin to the dreary and aching detective's face.

"Pratchett."

John Pratchett offered a confused then surprised look to the newcomer. "Detective? How are you—?"

"Getting there," Loren said. He raised his busted wing under his coat for effect, wincing as it rubbed against the stitches down his chest. "Cordon duty?"

Pratchett shrugged. "She likes her space. From me."

"From everyone."

"She's getting better about it," Pratchett whispered, peering toward the abandoned home. He led Loren through the cordon, their steps slow across the mud-filled lawn. "Well, a little better anyway."

Myers stepped out from behind the property, hands outstretched in disbelief. "Dammit, Pratchett. You let anyone else in here I swear I will…do something to make your life worse than it is. Which will take incredible effort on my part to discover. Effort I would rather spend clearing my DVR."

Pratchett crooked his head. "Like I said…"

"Yeah." Loren smirked. "Definitely getting better. Less cursing at least."

"Have your bromance somewhere else please," Myers said, waving Pratchett back to position at the edge of the property. Loren remained and her eyes thinned. "Go home, Loren."

"How many?" he asked, ignoring her request.

She sighed, taking the lead around the property. Loren followed close, slipping along the soaked lawn until they reached the back. Woodlands covered the rear, a short, broken fence separating the confined yard from the vast forest.

"Listen, Loren…" Myers started, trying to deflect. She looked tired and irritated, obviously hating the rain as much as he did.

"You know who owned this place?"

"I do," she said. "We're looking through it now."

Officers dotted the edge of the tree line. They walked in pattern, K-9 units leading each pair deeper into the woods. Flashlight beams scurried against the brush. Like a reenactment from four years earlier.

The Kindly Killer. Walter Schriff. This was his home. This was where he killed eight people before he was caught.

"Won't find anything in the house," Loren admitted. The search through the property was extensive. He led it himself, though in those days his work was less than stellar. Hence his surprise at the discovery in the woods. "We should've searched more thoroughly. Dammit."

"You couldn't have known," Myers countered weakly. They both knew better. "Hell, we wouldn't have either. Lucky break we caught wind of this scumbag hiding out back there."

More details rang through the scanner on his way over. Probably why the cabbie was more than happy to peel away as quickly as possible. A daytime robbery went sideways, the shooter only fifteen years old.

"Williams?" Loren asked, recalling the name from the report. "Geoffrey Williams?"

Myers nodded. "Shot and killed three."

"Too young for that."

"Is there a good age?"

"True," Loren said. "He found the bodies?"

"Sinkhole," Myers replied. "Too much damn rain lately, I guess. He fell in during the chase. Stopped him at least."

"How many, Myers?"

She stepped in front of him, trying to block his view of the woods. Her five foot nothing height failed to get the job done but she made up for it in words. "Does it matter? Seriously, Loren. If I say one it's too many, isn't it?"

His head lowered and he turned back to the house. "The damn Kindly Killer."

"You caught the bastard."

"Not me."

"Right." Myers' hands went to her hips. "Her."

Myers was the one who found the photo of Soriya. Her distrust of the vigilante was well known, her experience during the Erikson case less than ideal. Still, Loren had tried his best to steer the conversation away from his partner and friend. Until he understood what the image truly meant. For Beth. For him. For everything.

Myers read his stare. "Five. We found five so far. One grave."

Breath left his body and he struggled with the figure. "Five. Christ. He hinted but I never thought it would be true. Not after all the searching we did. When he died, I figured it was over. Why is it never over?"

Myers led him around the house toward the road. "You should be resting, Loren."

"I get it, Myers." He pulled out his phone, hoping a taxi wasn't too far away. "Send me the names?"

"I will as soon as we have them."

"Thanks," Loren said. She turned for the woods but he stopped her once more. "Five more. What if—?"

"We're looking," she said. "All we can do. These guys, the real nuts of this city, have pasts too. Secrets they take to the grave."

She left him in the cold rain, his feet soaked and freezing. "And we pay for them," he muttered. "Every time."

CHAPTER THREE

Loren couldn't sleep. His arm ached and the couch was too lumpy, but he knew these were only excuses he created to justify that his mind was stuck in a whirlwind over the news. Five bodies. Five more innocent people lost at the hands of a madman dead three years now.

Yet still making headlines.

Not only that but the timing of it, what with the memorial for those lost at Saint Sebastian's and the bowling alley incident. Dozens died, the bodies piling up. Collateral damage to meet the needs of one sick, twisted soul.

It darkened the city, and the endless rain helped in that regard. Winds swept from the pier, a wave of cold shattering the summer season. It beat against Loren's windows, offering a backdrop to his depressing thoughts.

How many other secrets were out there, waiting to be discovered? Both mythical and man-made mysteries offered endless variables and incalculable threats. How many other lunatics had something in motion waiting to jump out at a moment's notice?

One, in particular, repeated on him.

Henry Erikson.

Henry Erikson spent the better part of three years looking for a cure for his cancer. Medical trials, chemotherapy, holistic endeavors—all concluded without success. Where medical science failed, his knowledge of the arcane took over. If the Medusa coin was the result after searching for so long, where had Erikson started his journey? What might have been unleashed with his research that no one knew about or thought to ask?

Fear of the unknown shook him from his apartment to the Victorian home along the Riverfront district. Loren ducked under the police tape barely hanging in place as the wind continued to swirl. Above, the shutters slammed against the home's edifice, the gusts warping them more with each blow.

His flashlight led the way through the dingy house. The place had been mostly cleared out in the aftermath of Erikson's death, the investigation to root out the cause of the mayhem affecting the streets of Portents thorough, though not enough to satisfy Loren.

It wasn't their fault. The police. The media. Even the damn blogosphere. No one understood the truth and he helped keep it that way. Finding out what was really happening in Portents gave Erikson the key to unleashing Death, literal Death, upon the city. No one else needed to have that kind of knowledge, that level of power, over the affairs of others.

Loren stopped at the study. Scuffmarks lined the hardwood floors. Movement, and quite a bit of it, most likely from the officers in their rush. Nothing appeared out of place. He recalled the photos Ruiz had shown him in the hospital. Everything seemed to match those images perfectly.

Except for a stray light coming from the corner behind a bookcase pushed away from the wall. The shift created a gap, razor thin, but noticeable thanks to a dim light shining from within.

Loren inched closer, flashlight held tight. He wished the handle was the grip of his sidearm but he left that useful tool at home. Why would he need it? Just a quick peek around a creepy old house where a psychopathic murderer with Death on speed dial happened to reside?

Yeah, no gun necessary there.

Deep, calming breaths filled his lungs. Each creak beneath his feet caused his heart to pound in his ears. Still, he reached for the bookcase. He threw the unit open and stepped inside, flashlight falling on a single occupant in the secret alcove.

She sat in the center, surrounded by candles and books. All four walls were a repository of knowledge, none of which was uncovered by the officers during their search. His arrival did nothing to startle her, her focus rapt in the texts covering the floor. When she finished, she snapped the closest one shut then turned to greet him with the same smirk she always displayed when they were together.

"Looks like we had the same thought," Soriya Greystone said. Loren sighed at her joy over his arrival. "Yeah. The worst kind."

CHAPTER FOUR

Soriya delicately placed the scattered texts back on the shelves. Her legs, cramped from being curled up on the floor for hours, popped at the sudden shifting. Thankful for the reprieve, her tight muscles loosened with each graceful step.

She was careful with the books, each one set exactly where it was found. The binding was handled with extreme care. Every action taken to keep the pages pristine and the manuscripts secured without incident. Screw-ups were not needed. She had seen enough of them in her previous trips to libraries.

Loren included.

Every stolen glance at the man in the doorway brought a slight grin to her face. After hours of solitude in the candlelight, the company was welcome. That it was Loren, seeing him standing upright and healing from his recent injuries, delighted her.

"A secret room, can you believe it?" She lifted another round of books and slipped them back on the shelves. "Like something out of one of those comic books you're always talking about. Never thought I'd actually stumble across one." She stopped, grinning at her partner. "Guess how."

Loren sighed, pulling his injured arm closer to his chest to tighten the sling. "Candlestick on the mantel?"

"Candlestick on the mantel!" Her laughter boomed in the small alcove.

Loren circled the room, wary of the shelves around the space. "You realize that you live in a secret underground cavern that holds the nexus of all time and space, right?"

"Point," she said. Tucking her hair behind her ear, she turned to her companion. "I moved, though."

"What?"

She shrugged. "I'm still trying to nail down an apartment but, yeah, it was time to stop living there. Away from everything. Didn't realize rent was astronomical downtown."

"Always has been," Loren said without looking at her. He scanned the titles against the wall.

Soriya smiled. Talking about something as normal as rent with Loren was definitely a first for them. She tried to be more than her job, to be connected to the city and the threats therein. The change had been a challenge. Weeks of living out of ratty hotels and hostels almost made her miss the cold comforts of the Bypass chamber.

But being before the floating orb was not the answer anymore. The city was her home and it was time to embrace it fully. The way she always dreamed. The way she always wanted. She hoped Loren would be glad for her, that he would see her growing and trusting more in those around her. But he displayed no satisfaction at her evolution. His face strained, carrying an edge that kept his eyes on the books instead of her.

"You should be resting, Loren," she said. "What you went through—"

"Shouldn't have happened."

"Right," she said, then fell silent with a slight nod. She felt the same. During the Erikson case, Soriya abandoned Loren at the Library of the Luminaries and in effect, abandoned their partnership. She failed to trust in him, to trust that they handled things better together than apart and now she paid for her error with his every word, his every glance. Disappointment and anger— both very much earned through her actions.

"The books?" Loren asked, trying to steer the conversation.

"I wouldn't..." It was reflex and one she immediately regretted. The caution. The worry.

Loren kept to the room's center, his hands open and away from the shelves. "I won't."

She bit her lip, moving beside him. "Demonology texts in this section. Erikson spent three years researching anything and everything to save his own skin."

"But nothing helped."

"Not until he found the coin." She paused and skirted to the other side of the room. She pulled a well-worn journal from the shelf, its pages dog-eared with numerous markings along the edge. "He was nice enough to take copious notes."

"Ever the professor."

She handed the notes to Loren, who thumbed through each page. No word of thanks. No questions about her presence in the room. She should have been there the second Erikson died. In the fallout, she became distracted. Too many threats and not enough hands on deck.

Her fault.

By the time she realized the implication of Erikson's searching, days had turned to weeks. Soriya rushed over to the home the instant she could. Not an excuse for inaction, simply the reality of her role in the city. Not that it did her any good in Loren's eyes— or would, if he bothered to ask.

Loren peered up from the notes. "What am I looking at here?"

"Summoning spells, blood sacrifice—his own, thankfully. Other rituals that put images in my head that will take years to remove."

"But no success?"

Soriya let out a deep breath. "I wish."

Loren passed the notebook over to her waiting hand. She thumbed through it until she landed on the remains of a number of pages torn along the spine. Turning back a few pages, she offered the text again to her partner.

"Came across this before you showed up. I was hoping there would be more in some of these other books but no such luck."

"Soriya?"

She hesitated, pinching the bridge of her nose to center herself. "While I'm grateful Erikson botched most of his attempts at eternal life, if even one of these things made its way into Portents—"

"But that's what you're saying, isn't it?" Loren pressed, cutting through her like a knife. "You're saying one did."

"Looks that way."

"What is it?" Loren flipped back and forth through the book, over the torn pages to images of a circular pattern of candles. Latin filled the outline. A ritual she had never considered before or learned about during her time with Mentor. "Where are his notes about it?"

She pointed to the torn pages. "Destroyed from the looks of it. For some reason, the only souvenir from his little experiment is this." Reaching into her back pocket, she retrieved a large feather and held it before Loren. His eyes washed over the feather, watching it spin between her fingertips. Deep reds blanketed the plumage, like a burning fire washing over its delicateness.

"Any ideas?"

"No," she answered, hating the admission. The question had to be asked. She wished there was a response more to both of their likings. She held the feather in front of her eyes. It ran the length of her forearm, thick and lush.

"It's damn big," Loren admitted.

"And loose in Portents."

CHAPTER FIVE

Buchanan Jessup parked at the stately manor on Frontier. He took off his glasses and placed them on the dash. He hated to wear them but driving at night was becoming more difficult. They were meant to be worn all day, every day, but he never allowed that, their presence always diminishing his capacity in a crowd.

Not that he performed much better, or with much more confidence, when they were off. Every advantage—mental or physical—helped, however.

He had been to the home many times over the years. Holiday parties. Big corporate announcements or product launches. It always amazed him—the comparison from his own Cape Cod in the coves to the home of Shawn Prentiss, his boss and owner of Tone Dynamics where Jessup had worked over a decade.

A guard rushed down the front steps at his arrival. Jessup sighed, holding his briefcase tight to his side as he exited the vehicle.

"Sir?" the guard called, recognizing him immediately. "You can't be here. You know this."

"I have to see him," Jessup said, the driver's side door a barrier between them.

The guard's eyes flared. "I need you to get back in your car and go home, Dr. Jessup. Can you do that?"

He hesitated, heat pooling in his chest and sweat beading along his brow. So many times he had come to this home, hoping to be heard. Never successfully.

"No," he snapped at the guard. "Not this time."

He swung the door out, knocking the guard back. He rushed up the front steps and into the home, the door slamming shut behind him.

"Mr. Prentiss," Jessup shouted from the foyer, frantically searching the opulent home for its owner. He found him in the living room to the left. "Mr. Prentiss!"

"Jessup?" Shawn Prentiss said. Shawn, half the doctor's age, was reading to his three children. He left the book with his kids, rushing to keep the doctor on the far side of the room.

The door opened again and the guard slipped into the room. "Sorry, sir."

Shawn shook his head, then peered angrily at the unwelcome visitor. "I'm with my kids, for Christ's sake."

Jessup stepped past him and placed his briefcase on the couch. The children shuffled away from the frantic doctor as he opened the case and pawed through the schematics within.

"I've done it, sir. It was so simple, really. Right there the whole time. I might have seen it sooner. I *did* see it sooner, but the implementation was wrong and I had to—"

"We can talk about it at the office, Jessup."

Shawn's voice was soft and calm, placating him. Always talking down to him instead of listening to him as a peer or a colleague. Or even close to an equal, despite Jessup's extensive knowledge of the field. Hearing aids weren't some fly by night moneymaker for Jessup—they were his life, and he was tired of being talked over and ignored.

"You always say that," Jessup growled. "Listen now."

"Sir?" the guard asked. Shawn waved him back.

"Jessup, I appreciate your work," Shawn started, his voice slow and measured. "But my time at home is important. You get that, don't you?"

Jessup slammed the briefcase down. "*This* is important. A way to change frequencies, to cut down ambient noise. Adjusting the amplifier to the right—"

"Not here, Jessup," Shawn interrupted, unwilling to listen further. His voice was sharp, his patience failing. "There is a time and a place."

"Make the time!" Jessup yelled, his eyes raging.

Shawn stepped away, concern rising for the uninvited guest. The guard read his reaction, inching closer, his hand reaching for the weapon holstered at his side.

"I'm afraid I can't do that, Jessup."

"All right, pal," the guard said. "Time to go."

"You're right," Jessup replied. He reached into his pocket and pulled out a revolver. "Goodbye."

The shot was deafening, echoing along the vaulted ceilings. The guard failed to consider the shot, let alone prepare for it, before the bullet slammed into his chest. He peered down to the gaping hole, then collapsed near the entrance, his gun still in its holster.

The kids screamed, their father hugging them close. All faced the crazed Jessup, who quickly turned the gun on them.

"I won't be ignored," he said, a fire caught in his eyes. "Not anymore."

CHAPTER SIX

Loren stood impatiently in the center of the secret alcove, careful not to disturb the circle of candles at his feet. He wanted to help, wanted to shove Soriya aside and paw through the manuscripts in the hopes of piecing together some semblance of an answer as to what they faced.

The feather offered little in the way of direction. Soriya's studies could not decipher its origins or hint at where it came from. If Loren could help cut down on the research, they would be that much closer to some resolution.

And he could be far, far away from her.

Instead, he waited—that was his role now. Myers took the lead uncovering the Kindly Killer's hidden victims. Soriya did the same here. What the hell was he doing? He should have been home resting. Thinking about the missing person's cases or the damn photo of the person he called partner and friend for the last four years.

A sharp bite of static filled the air followed by the squawk of a voice through a speaker. "Reports of a 246 at 11865 Frontier. Repeat, 246 at 11865 Frontier. Units are responding."

"Dammit," Loren hissed. He pulled the scanner from his pocket and turned it off. He forgot he was carrying it.

"What's that?" Soriya asked, slipping another text back in place.

"Shots fired."

She shook her head, giving him a knowing look. *Of course she knows what a 246 is.*

"Scanner," he answered, showing her the handheld device.

"Taking your work with you now, Loren?"

He tucked it away. "Trying to stay in the loop. I'd hate to be left behind."

The edge to his voice told the story but if Soriya heard it, she made no mention. Instead, she returned to the feather, slipping it in her back pocket before moving for the alcove's entrance.

"That address is only two blocks over."

"Don't even—" Loren stopped. She was gone. "—Think about it."

Loren glanced around the room. He moved for the shelf. This was more important. This was where they were needed. He could take a look, see where it led him, hopeful that answers existed, hidden away like the room itself. He sighed and started for the door only to find Soriya waiting for him.

"You coming or not?" she said with a smile.

He entered the study as she stepped back inside the alcove. The candles blew out with a sudden breeze and she returned, closing the bookcase to keep the secret intact. The pair moved for the exit, awkwardly trying to make room for the other along the narrow hallway.

Loren stopped, letting her lead. "The police can handle it, Soriya. Shouldn't we—?"

"I'm tired of reading and finding nothing, Loren," she admitted. "Erikson destroyed whatever evidence there had been."

"But why?"

The night air welcomed them and Soriya pushed ahead for the sidewalk, taking a sharp right. Frontier sat in the distance and her pace was brisk. "What do you mean?"

"Erikson. He had failures before and didn't act that rash."

"Maybe because it wasn't a failure."

The notion definitely held a certain amount of truth. Erikson's success at drawing whatever offered him the feather into this world never provided him what he desired most—immortality.

"Yet *was* a failure in the end," Loren finished with a nod.

He picked up the pace, regretting the act immediately. His sneakers squealed against the pavement. His arm sent blistering waves of pain through his body, his chest aching from the swing of the appendage against the line of stitches in syncopated rhythm.

"Whatever came through didn't help him," Soriya said. "Possibly couldn't help him."

"Or refused to."

Soriya cocked her head. "Would explain the temper tantrum behavior with his notes."

Loren paused with the street sign for Frontier less than a hundred feet away. Soriya looked back as he felt his pockets for his phone.

"What are you doing?" she said, while he paged through his news feed.

"Looking for anything out of the ordinary," he replied. "I set up some news alerts. Just in case."

"You sure there isn't more to it?"

There was. The actions that left him behind in the Library of the Luminaries were only the beginning. He needed to stay informed, and if Soriya refused to offer any answers he needed to think outside the box. He needed to be the one doing the digging, searching for the things no one noticed.

Or *wanted* to notice, at any rate.

There was much more to the simple set of news alerts. The missing person's cases on his coffee table for one. The mark hidden out of sight and the lack of any investigation into its meaning. *A Circle of Shadows.*

Unfortunately, Loren didn't want to share. Not with Soriya.

"I…"

A woman in stark black rounded the corner on Frontier as they arrived. She shifted between them, thick locks of red hair spilling from her hood.

"Excuse us," Loren offered, lowering his phone to track the woman with his gaze.

"Not a problem," she said, her ruby lips shining under the streetlights. She continued down the block and he watched her closely, listening to the dim clacking of her heels along the sidewalk.

"Loren?" A hand fell on his shoulder.

When he turned, he was met with concern on Soriya's face. "Hmm?"

"You were saying?"

He shook his head and the pair moved down Frontier, closing quickly on the property in question. Loren thumbed through his phone, landing on a news story that didn't add up after an expedient scan. He passed the phone to Soriya. "Check this out."

She looked over the screen, eyebrow cocked. "Gina Fisher? A suicide. Loren, I don't think—"

"It popped up for a reason. Keep reading."

"Happy people do sad things all the time."

He took the phone back. "She took a swan dive off a ten-story high-rise during the morning rush hour. Only problem? She never hit the ground."

"What?"

"She burst into flames."

Soriya stopped, unable to find the words to respond.

Loren smiled, satisfied at her reaction. "Now you know how I feel when you say crazy shit."

She grumbled under her breath and led them to the fenced lawn outside 11865 Frontier without another word. A car sat before the front steps, the driver's side door opened, matching the entrance to the home. Shouts echoed from inside.

"I'm going in."

"Like that," Loren said, his right arm blocking her. "The police are on their way."

"We're here, Loren. Are you really going to leave this to someone else?"

"I didn't—"

She slid past him, running for the front door. Loren bit his lip and cursed at his unspoken thought. *I didn't bring my gun.*

Then he followed her into the home.

CHAPTER SEVEN

Loren crept through the open front door. The shouting increased by tenfold and he ducked low along the foyer wall. His ribs joined the chorus of anger, the sudden shifting exasperating his injuries.

Soriya took up position on the opposite wall overlooking the expansive living room. A hallway behind her led to the kitchen.

From his vantage point, Loren saw two main players arguing in the room. The short, frumpy soul flashed a small revolver around as he yelled.

"I've worked for your company for the last decade of my life! Every moment dedicated to its success. Never my own. Always for others."

The apparent homeowner held tight to his three children, trying to block them from the crazed gunman. Soriya tilted her head toward the body near the living room's entrance. Loren took her meaning and scurried across the gap beside her.

"Is he...?"

Loren felt for a pulse and found none on the burly enforcer. Doorman? Security? He shook his head. "No."

"Loren." Her eyes burned at him. She reached for the stone and he stopped her.

"Let the police do it, Soriya."

She grimaced and he crouched next to her along the hall. The screaming resumed; the children sobbed.

"I stayed quiet," the gunman yelled. "Tucked my head down, letting others take credit for my work. For the sake of the work. Not this time. Not with what I have here. These designs will revolutionize the industry."

"They won't," the father replied. The gun inched for his face and the man closed his eyes in preparation, a soft prayer escaping his lips.

"They will," the gunman bellowed. "You won't even look at them!"

"That's not… Jessup, listen to me."

"Why? You never listen to me!"

Soriya's nails scraped along her jeans. Loren heard her teeth grinding. "Loren, I can't—"

"Go."

She was gone, rushing down the long hall like a wraith. Loren took a deep breath, shuffling back to the fallen security guard. And his holstered Glock.

"Here we go."

He cocked the hammer and stepped into the living room.

"POLICE! FREEZE!"

The armed man spun, weapon still pointed on the cowering man and his family. His eyes raged, his pupils dilated. "Don't move! I'll kill him! I will!"

Loren kept the gun steady. He was out of his depth. He knew nothing of the situation or the players involved other than the gunman's name—Jessup. All he knew was that no one had to die. And that Soriya had a chance to make this right with his help.

"Why?" Loren asked.

"For ten years I've been ignored. And I let it happen. Then it hit me. Like a cloud breaking or a sound never heard before. It was time to stand up for my passion. Do you understand?"

"No."

It came fast and sudden, stopping the raging gunman in his tracks. He couldn't believe the response after pouring his heart out to the detective. All Jessup wanted was understanding, commiseration over his predicament. Loren refused to give it to him.

Loren shrugged. "But I don't really care."

"What?"

"Ever hear of a distraction?"

Jessup turned to his captive audience only to see the father of three prodding his children into the hallway and the kitchen beyond. In their place stood Soriya Greystone, a wry smile across her face and her fist raised.

"Hi."

The fist slammed against his left cheek and sent Jessup reeling to the floor. The gun sailed out of his grasp, skidding toward Loren who promptly kicked it away.

"No!" Jessup cried. "No, no, no. Not this time. Not like this."

"I'm afraid so," Loren said, closing the gap between them. "You're under—"

Soriya waved him back. "Wait."

"What is it? What is he—?"

Jessup howled. Clutching his chest, he flopped around the room like a fish out of water. Smoke poured from his ears and rose from his chest, his eyes screaming for mercy.

"Get back, Loren," Soriya shouted over Jessup's death cry. "Get back!"

Jessup's eyes begged for a reprieve, for one more moment to make his case. To be heard finally. But the only sound he made was a groan as his body collapsed along the couch, smoke trailing from his chest.

Loren lowered his gun. "Well, that was unexpected."

CHAPTER EIGHT

"What did you do to him?" The father of three circled the room, wide-eyed and afraid. His gaze flew back and forth between his worried children and the dead man.

Soriya looked over the body, trying to ignore the panic in the man's voice or the lack of gratitude at their intervention. Loren handled things better from his end, trying to calm the father of three.

"Sir…"

"What did she do to him?"

"She didn't do anything to him," Loren said. Realizing the gun was still in his hand, the detective tucked the weapon out of sight. Then he leaned close to Soriya. "You didn't do anything to him, did you?"

"Thanks, Loren." Soriya stood, leaving behind the smoldering corpse and the stained couch, never to be used again. She wondered if she should make an offer. If she ever found an apartment, she would need the furniture.

"Just checking."

"You saw what happened."

"I wish I hadn't."

Careful not to disturb the scene, Soriya quietly examined the remains. "Cold? How? He was sweating one second and cooking the next."

The father swiped at the air. "He had a heart condition and you whaled on him."

"I barely touched him."

"A heart condition?" Loren questioned, his calm tone having no effect. "He had a pacemaker?"

"For years."

Soriya backed away from the body "He burned through it."

"Have you ever seen anything like this before?"

Both knew the last time they had seen a man burn to death, though to a more profound degree. Henry Erikson. The man had refused to relinquish the Medusa coin even as the powerful obol melted between his fingers. Because of her actions. Was that all she was good for? Death and destruction?

"Seen anything...?" The man shook his head, pulling away from them cautiously. "Who the hell are you people?"

"Loren. Homicide," the detective announced. He patted his pocket then sighed. "I left my badge in my other coat."

"Well, there's your killer!" the man shouted, pointing a frantic finger toward Soriya.

"Now, sir..."

"Shawn. Shawn Prentiss."

"I know this is a lot to take in. If you could just..."

Soriya was grateful for Loren's presence. He always handled situations better with people. He had a humanizing effect, the ability to connect with the victims allowing him better insight into the cases. It opened up avenues of questioning. Soriya's bulldozing model for personal interaction tended to send people running for the hills. Or, as in the case of Mr. Shawn Prentiss, reaching for pitchforks and torches. She wasn't sure which she preferred.

Loren stood between Prentiss and the body. The barrier appeared to calm the man. "He came to talk and I wouldn't listen..."

"Who was he?"

"Buchanan Jessup. An employee."

"There's a name." Soriya chuckled. Loren glared at her. "Sorry."

"He works—worked —for me," Shawn continued. "Hearing aid technology. The man was brilliant. I never told him that."

"What was he doing here?"

"Some breakthrough," Shawn said. "I've seen the specs but it wasn't cost effective. Not a viable option for our shareholders. He believed otherwise. Very passionately, it seemed."

"Passion."

"Loren?"

"Gina Fisher." Loren snapped his fingers, recalling the report. "Something about kissing some long unrequited love before her jump."

"I should have listened," Shawn murmured behind them. Two bodies marred the pristine estate. "I should have taken the time but my family…my kids…"

Loren nodded and walked with Shawn to the hallway and his waiting children. "Take care of them."

Before they reached the hall, lights flashed outside. Soriya stepped away from the body. A briefcase lay against the stained couch and she pulled it close, inching for the room's shadows.

A pair of officers stepped inside, weapons at the ready. Loren flagged them down, prodding Shawn and his family ahead for the door. "They can help you outside. Take your statement."

"Sir?"

"Loren. Homicide."

A nod passed between them but confusion remained. They would call it in, hoping for confirmation of the man's identity. Once they discovered Loren was on leave, there would be more questions.

Shawn Prentiss and his family exited their once serene home. Loren rushed back into the living room and the waiting Soriya Greystone.

"This could be anything, right? Some bizarre coincidence that has nothing to do with Erikson?"

Soriya snapped open the briefcase, digging through the files within. Hearing aid technology meant little to her but the object underneath, resting in a pocket with the man's corporate ID, made things clear.

"I wish that was the case, Loren."

"What is it? What did you find?"

A red feather spun between her fingers. "Look familiar?"

Loren winced, the connection clear and undesired. Soriya hoped the feather was a one off, that whatever had escaped—whatever Erikson had summoned—left and would never return. But things never worked out that way in Portents.

"It's the same, isn't it? The red—"

"Like fire," Soriya said. Burning. Like the victims.

"That red, though. Like…" Loren whispered, lost in thought. Then his eyes widened. "Oh, hell."

"What?" Soriya asked. "Red like… Oh."

Both rushed for the front door, staring out at the flashing lights of the patrol cars on approach and beyond. Shadows stretched over the street in the Riverfront district. Shadows and emptiness. No one walked the streets at night in Portents.

Except one.

"Dammit," Loren muttered.

"The woman," Soriya said, realizing where they had seen that shade of red before. "The woman we passed coming here."

CHAPTER NINE

The music blared in her ears. Dissonant noise with a melodic beat. It sang of beauty and hate wrapped under the crashing of synthesized drums, the squeal of electric guitars and the out-of-place clatter of rhythm sticks.

She loved it.

Not only the sound but also the venue. The bar catered to a heavy crowd despite the late hour. A perfect location in the heart of downtown where people wandered in after work and lost track of time as they filled their gullet, drowning away the day's events. Inhibitions were left at the door, the musk of sex and desperation filling the air. The inhabitants forgot about the world for a little while and started living.

The way it was always meant to be.

Society burdened too heavily, wrapping normal everyday folk with rules and obligations. None mattered. Life was the end goal, the only one worth its weight in gold, dollars, sex, or whatever other currency held value at the pearly gates.

The bar allowed the freedom to be whole, to throw off the shackles of family, friends, and loved ones and simply *be* for a moment. One she hoped would last forever.

She camped out at the bar nightly, ever since her arrival in the city. The staff knew her well. She had no name, though attempts were made to come up with a moniker. *Honey* and *baby* were thrown into the mix and met with copious resistance. *Red* appeared to be a clear winner and the name grew on her with each use, not that she spread it around. The label certainly fit with the flowing locks of hair that ran down her back.

Red circled the room, the way she did most evenings. Her ears perked to every conversation in the bar, always on the lookout for someone special—someone with heart. She sipped her drink, fruity and light, her heels tapping along the tile to the music's beat. All movement stopped at the edge of the bar, her lips grinning at the sound she had been waiting all night to hear.

Quiet desperation with a tinge of hope.

"She never understood," the man grumbled to the inattentive bartender. He needled the beer in front of him, taking small sips as more a sense of obligation than satisfaction. His hair grayed along the temples but remained thick and mangy on top. His beard was more a thin stubble from a hard day's work. He looked tired, his eyes windows to a sad soul beneath. *Norman*, she read from his look. *His name is Norman Butters*. "It was always about her, about her life, her dreams. I made all of them possible. I worked a dead end job, washed my electrical engineering degree away to keep her content. And then she tosses me away."

Passion laced his voice. Passion for a woman and lost love. Lost but never forgotten, unable to extinguish. At least at his end.

"Not ambitious enough," he continued. "Not living up to my potential. I could have been. I could have been so much more but she didn't want that. Until she did."

He swallowed his bitterness with a long gulp of his drink. A replacement quickly slid in front of him, and his wallet opened reluctantly to pay for the pleasure.

"So busy ignoring me, she never saw it," Norman said to no one as the bartender walked away in mid-sentence.

Red leaned against the bar beside him, offering him a smile and an ear. "How could anyone ignore you? I bet you could do great things."

He straightened on the stool, surprised at her attention. "I…I could," he stuttered. "I know more about this city than she realizes."

"You should show her."

"I would. If she would give me a chance. If anyone would."

Her lips inched to his ear. "I will."

"What?"

A feather rested between her fingers and she placed it on the bar in front of his beer. "Here's your chance, Norman."

"How?" he asked, staring at the feather. "How did you know my name?"

"Take it, Norman," Red whispered. "You've earned it."

He lifted the long object from the bar, holding it in front of his face, fascinated as it danced between his fingers. She watched the wonder grow in his eyes, turning to a burning blaze.

"I have earned it," Norman said. He stood, confidence filling him.

She smiled. "Do great things, Norman."

"I will," Norman replied. He rushed for the door and the waiting city. "I'll show her. I'll show them all."

CHAPTER TEN

Loren rubbed his eyes, trying to wake up. Another sleepless night. Another day spent staring at the photo of Soriya, unsure what to do and what to say. He needed the rest. His arm hurt like hell, his chest burning from the previous night's activities.

Doctor's appointments kept him distracted in the afternoon. Some *Sports Illustrated* on the waiting room table followed by playing with the otoscope while waiting in the examination room filled up more time than he liked to admit, but it made the day pass fairly smoothly.

When evening settled over the city and rush hour traffic took over the highway, Loren made his way to Heaven's Gate Park. Curses littered his breath. He didn't want to be there, didn't want to continue down the path they were heading. Didn't want the anger to swell again.

The damn photo plagued him.

Myers called while he waited. Another headache, but one of his own making. She was concerned over his appearance at the crime scene the previous night. The Kindly Killer. He didn't belong at work anymore than he did at the park. Where did he belong now? With a busted wing and stitches running up his torso, what good was he?

Her concern was met with his usual snark. She played along but it annoyed them both. In the end, Myers passed along the names of the five bodies found in the woods behind the former home of Walter Shriff, the Kindly Killer. Five more innocents caught up in the insanity of Portents.

They repeated on him even as he sat on the park bench. Running through them kept him sane as his exuberant partner went through the details of their own dilemma.

Soriya's smile bothered him, the excitement she carried when they were together. Didn't she know? Couldn't she see what it was doing to him? Because of that photo?

"Wish fulfillment."

Loren shook his head, finally snapping back to the conversation. "Pardon me?"

Soriya stood from the bench, pacing back and forth. "Jessup wanted to be heard. Fisher reached out to some love of her life."

"Wish fulfillment," Loren repeated. "You're talking genie in a bottle stuff?"

She shook her head. Of course he was wrong. When wasn't he? And now he was going to have that damn song in his head too. *Definitely not my night.*

"Djinn," she clarified. "And I don't think so. I haven't heard of an active sighting of their kind in decades. There are others, but none feel right for this."

Loren didn't want to know what felt right about any of this. He could only imagine what nightmares fit the scenario perfectly. The dangers set upon them he had no business understanding or recognizing in the first place.

"Erikson." Soriya collapsed beside him on the bench. "I meant to get to his house sooner. If I had, maybe I could have prevented this."

The mere mention of his name made Loren's blood boil. Erikson set the ball rolling but he paid the price, the pain like a bad itch running through his upper body. Soriya pushed him away, her lack of trust in him now reciprocated by the image on his coffee table.

"Loren?"

He turned, wondering how long they had sat in silence, how long Soriya had been staring at him. "Hmmm?"

She sighed. "Want to tell me what's going on with you? Do you need to rest?"

"I'm fine."

"Then what?"

He shook his head. "Nothing."

"Seems like something," she said, standing again. She always preferred to loom over him. "I mean other than some crazed woman handing out wishes like candy for some unknown reason, but isn't that always the way around here?"

"It's not a joke."

She stopped, the smirk wiped from her face. Both were surprised by the anger in his words.

"What?"

"It's not funny, Soriya. The crap that follows you around this city. Erikson conjured this damn thing up in his own desperation, not caring about the consequences. Not caring about the lives endangered. People are dying and you're joking about it."

"That's not…" Soriya took a breath. "You know what? Never mind."

"What?"

"Make it about whatever you want—and if you want to be pissed at me, go ahead. I'm right here when you want to man up and talk to me about it." She paused, taking a sharp breath. He waited, refusing to be baited. Her eyes were saddened at the silence. "I know people are dying out there, Loren. I'm doing everything I can to figure it out, not stewing over some slight to your precious ego."

"My ego?"

She nodded. "My leaving you behind at the Library of the Luminaries. I made a choice."

"And I paid for it," he shouted. "Like I always do. Like I always have. Ever since Beth."

"Beth?" Soriya asked, backing away in confusion. "What does she have to do with any of this?"

His eyes hardened. "Like you don't know."

"I don't."

"Then I'll tell you," he snapped. "I know. I—"

The lights went out. Not just the quaint streetlight over their bench, not just the running lights along the entrance to Heaven's Gate Park. Blocks and blocks went dark in an instant. Central Precinct down Main and Evans and the heart of downtown lay in shadow.

"What the hell?"

"A blackout?" Loren muttered. "Now?"

Soriya moved for the exit, guided by the moonlight. "Is that really what you think right now?"

"No," he answered. "No, I don't."

He chased after her, the two fleeing the park in front of the William Rath statue. Traffic slammed to a halt all around them.

Miles of vehicles gridlocked throughout the downtown area. He stepped forward, then stopped, held back by her hand.

"Loren, I…" Her eyes begged for more. A way to fix this.

He shook his head, pushing forward. "Come on. Let's end this."

CHAPTER ELEVEN

They raced across the city's darkened streets. Soriya set the pace, rushing away from Heaven's Gate Park heading east down Main for the expressway. Horns blared, lights flashed from moving vehicles unable to drive more than ten feet at a time.

Loren did his best to keep up with her pounding feet. His breathing was heavy in her ears despite the rising chorus of shouts from the angry commuters and the terror slowly filling the undercurrent of the city. Pain filled his eyes and she slowed. His stare matched his words, rage mixed with blinding agony over his injuries.

She wanted to stop him. They needed to talk, to work through whatever was happening. The split she felt in his presence. But the city needed them first. Always.

Six blocks went by in a blur, sirens mixing with citizen's cries. To no avail. There was no way for the police to circumvent the growing jam of commuters throughout the area.

They stopped in front of a power station. Loren fought to catch his breath, tucking his arm close. His eyes shut to block out the pain. She reached for him then thought better.

"This is it," he said. "If someone did this, it had to be here."

Soriya nodded, her jaw clenched. Ignoring the tension did nothing to help the situation. His inability to look at her, the edge in his voice; it was like it had been back in the beginning. Right after Beth's passing, when Loren was always falling—falling so far and she could do nothing but watch.

He started for the junction and she held him back. "Loren."

Pulling his gun loose from its holster, he looked back to the hesitant Soriya. "Cops will be here eventually, assuming all hell hasn't broken loose in the city—but let's face it, of course all hell has broken loose."

"We should—"

His eyes flared. "If you're going to say talk, you're wrong. Trust me, Soriya. Not that you ever have, not truly. But trust me now. You do not want to have this talk."

"I get it," she said. "I screwed up. I pushed you away out of fear. I tried to protect you. And it was wrong."

He shook his head. This wasn't about her actions during the Erikson case. Not completely. There was more going on, more that she couldn't see, couldn't know until he let her. After so much time together, all the trials they had been through over the years, their partnership remained strong. It ebbed and flowed over time, the same as any, but the work remained the priority, and with it their bond.

Why was Loren throwing everything away so suddenly? What had changed? And why wouldn't he work with her to repair the damage done? They needed each other, that lesson crystallized after Erikson. More than ever, the two of them had to be there for each other. For protection. For the betterment of the city and themselves, personally and professionally. She needed him. Why did he no longer need her with the same passion?

"I'll take the lunatic in there," he said, gun in hand.

"We both should."

"You'll be busy."

Her brow furrowed. "What are you—?" Loren pointed down the block. A single figure, tall and lithe with shocking red hair, ambled along the sidewalk for the open road. "Loren, listen—"

Cold eyes fell on her, his words matching. "This is bigger than us, Soriya."

"It always is," she replied. She moved for him and he pulled back closer to the door to the junction. "It always will be."

"Not always."

"Loren."

He refused to turn. Unwilling to delay any longer, her partner headed for the junction without another word. She had her own task to handle, but remained locked on him, watching him fade behind the closing doors.

Be careful.

CHAPTER TWELVE

When the door slammed shut behind him, Loren's heart stopped for a beat. He meant to take things easy during his recovery. He meant to figure out what the photo with Soriya truly represented in his search for answers. Work, the city, his personal and professional lives. Everything was on the table for introspection while his body knit itself back together from his confrontation with Death.

Instead he was in the thick of it again, struggling to breathe as the city continued its never-ending quest to drown him in its growing quagmire. And to have Soriya with him again so soon after learning about the image? No wonder he couldn't breathe; no wonder he couldn't have a thought without feeling the anger build in his chest.

Loren inched deeper into the junction, which sat in a nondescript building off Main. The only notice of its place in the city was a worn sign drilled along its edifice by the power company, long since needing replacement. If the power was out in this section of the city, the fix was here.

And possibly the problem.

The chance remained, of course, that the power outage was a random incident. If old souls could return after hundreds of years and avatars of Death could hide in rotund coroners, then surely there existed some means for a coincidence to occur within the city limits of Portents.

Loren hoped that was the case.

Nothing looked familiar. The layout of the building branched off in various directions and the darkness didn't help. He traded his flashlight for a gun and now wondered if he would ever pick the right tool for the job. He shuffled off his sling and it fell to the ground, the pain staggering but tempered through gritted teeth. Reaching into his pocket, he pulled out his phone, using the screen to light his way.

Giant mechanisms lined the entryway with platforms and stairs flowing between rows of turbines. Loren inched through the maze of equipment, stopping short of the first junction at the sight of lights from above. He turned off his phone before being spotted.

The figure, a man based on the height and build, frantically paced the metal walkway above. He wore a uniform and a hardhat. Thick gloves covered his hands and insulated boots adorned his feet. *An employee. Someone working to end the blackout.*

Loren found the stairs and took them slow, his arm aching at his side. The platform was narrow. Loren huddled down the aisle, afraid to graze any equipment running the length of the room. The frantic figure rushed by and Loren stopped.

"Hey," he called. "What are you—?"

The man turned back, shining the light in Loren's eyes. "The power's out."

"I know it is," Loren said, inching closer. He squinted through the beam of light. The man was covered in sweat, his movements nervous and twitching. "Can you fix it?"

He huffed. "Of course I can. That's what I've been telling her for years. Every time with the 'You don't know anything, Norman' or 'You're useless, Norman.' But I know so much more than *she* ever gave me credit for."

Loren eyed the man, closing in on the uneasy technician. "I'm not exactly sure who you're talking about, pal. Just tell me how we can fix this."

He rounded the corner of the walkway. A woman, thin and delicate, sat strapped to the railing. Her eyes pleaded, her screams silenced by the gag over her lips. Loren spun, raising his weapon.

The man, Norman, smiled. "We don't fix it."

Norman slammed into Loren's wounded arm. Loren shuffled back, his right wrist connecting with the railing, the gun slipping from his grasp. It clattered against the platform. The surprised detective reached for it but the man rushed him once more.

Nothingness surrounded him as Loren toppled over the railing. His limbs flailed, his hands reaching for the base of the walkway, catching the grating at the last moment by the tips of his fingers.

His world spun and he tried to get his bearings. The floor was too far away, the equipment too close to avoid. And climbing up was going to be an issue with his arm.

Not to mention Norman standing over him with his fallen sidearm.

"Great."

Norman wiped the sweat from his brow, his eyes bloodshot and crazed. He waved the gun between them, screaming as he lorded over them. "We don't fix it until she sees what she threw away!"

CHAPTER THIRTEEN

"Not another step!" Soriya shouted, racing down the alley away from the power station. Loren's anger sat in her every thought, but she tried to tuck it away. Ending the threat was the priority. No one else would die because of her failings. She would make sure of it.

The woman continued to stroll along the shadows, unaffected by the shouts of her pursuer. Nothing bothered her, nothing slowed her gait. The clicking of her heels blocked out much of the world.

Soriya ran faster. Catching sight of a fire escape along the alley, she jumped. Fingers snared the bottom of the hanging ladder and she swung forward, spinning through the air like a top. The scarlet-haired vixen pressed forward, unaware of the dark-skinned warrior until she landed in front of her with a wide smirk.

"That's far enough," Soriya said. The ribbons of Kali whipped down her left side, aching for release. The stone hummed along her hip and her fists clenched. It was time to end this.

Her ruby lips spread. "Nice night for a walk."

Soriya eyed her curiously. There was nothing but joy in her stare, nothing to denote her malicious actions over the people of the city. She wore a skintight dress, red to match her hair and the fire dancing in her dilated pupils. She tried to continue deeper into the night but Soriya cut her off.

"If you don't mind the dark or the total anarchy," Soriya snapped.

"You mean life."

Soriya huffed. "That's your thing, isn't it? Life. You amp someone's passion up to eleven and sit back to enjoy the show."

She shook her head. "I give them a chance to express themselves fully. Something this society frowns upon, it seems."

Gina Fisher and the love of her life, kept apart because they worked together. Buchanan Jessup and his ingenuity, unable to press forward because of an inability to express himself in a capitalistic industry. The blackout tied into this theme, Soriya had no doubt. One thing, however, nagged at her.

"Why not Erikson?" she asked.

"Who?"

Soriya pulled out the feather from Erikson's secret alcove. "The man who brought you here."

"Ah," the woman replied. She ran her hands through her hair, fluffing the thick, scarlet strands casually. "Such an ugly man. Dark and bleak. And demanding. You should have seen his face when I denied him."

"Why leave the feather?"

She grinned. "A parting gift."

A slap in the face. One deserved, but the others? "Stop this. All of it."

"Why?" the woman said with a sigh.

"People are dying," Soriya pressed. "You're killing them."

"I offer life. A rebirth of spirit."

"One that can't last. They burn themselves out."

"After a time," she said. "But before that? They live. Truly live."

Dammit, Soriya thought. There was no talking the woman back, no stopping her. Not without the stone raging against her hip. "If you won't stop it, then I will."

The Greystone sat in her hands. She had seen fear and terror in the eyes of those facing their end. She had heard the pleas and the prayers from the worst of the worst. What Soriya had never seen before was defiance in the form of the smile on the woman's face.

"A Greystone," she said with a laugh. "How quaint."

Soriya screamed, her anger filling the stone until the light exploded from the surface.

ᚺ

The sky raged and lightning screeched along the clear horizon, racing to its final destination. The woman never blinked, never turned, never strayed from her path. She simply stretched out her arms and welcomed the end.

It came in an instant, her body disappearing in the stone's white-hot rage. Only ash remained. Soriya let the stone settle, the light dimming and the hum fading as she placed the weapon back against her hip in the hand-woven pouch.

Satisfied at the end, Soriya turned back to the power station. Loren needed help, his injuries hampering his effectiveness more than he cared to admit. And there was still the split between them—Loren's hidden anger that needed answering.

She stopped at the sound of a murmur building from the pile of ashes. The small mound, the shell of the woman's remains, shifted and shuddered. They spread and built, brick by brick, cell by cell. Fingers formed, then a hand, an arm.

The woman reached from the depths of her broken and shattered form, rebuilding her body. Soriya could only watch it happen, the revelation of the event as prevalent as the woman's curves, her naked figure standing confidently in the alley as if nothing had occurred.

"I really liked that outfit."

Soriya staggered back, the stone humming loudly once more. Out of everything the woman could have been, all the dangers in this world, and every other plane of existence, Soriya never imagined she would bear witness to the presence of the creature before her.

"A phoenix."

CHAPTER FOURTEEN

Sweat dampened his palms. Loren tried to pull himself up to the platform, unable to maintain a strong enough grip. His chest begged for a reprieve. His arm screamed to be back in his sling but he needed more time. The gun pointed at him from the frantic man above didn't help matters.

"I need you to listen to me," Loren said.

"That's all I've ever done is listen," Norman screamed. "'Norman, you're so lazy. Norman, why don't you try more? Norman, I don't love you anymore, if I ever did.' It's time for everyone else to listen to me!"

Every word caused the woman bound and gagged along the metal walkway to jump. Her eyes locked on the gun Norman waved around like a flag.

"Norman." Loren's fingers dug into the mesh grating of the walkway, inching farther to give him a better grip. "She's scared."

He turned, towering over the victim. "Then she knows how I felt every day of our marriage. *Am I good enough? Can I do more for her? Be more for her?* I gave up everything to make you happy and it wasn't enough! It was never enough!"

Loren grimaced, pulling his weary frame higher and higher to the platform. "Norman."

"She was wrong," Norman yelled at his terrified ex-wife. "And everyone is going to see it."

"They won't."

Norman spun around, his eyes sparking against the dim beams of white offered by the flashlight resting along the walkway. Loren lay on the edge next to the railing, breathing hard but facing the gun that leveled against his brow.

"That's not how this ends," he said to the jilted husband. "Please, Norman, I can help you. We can walk out of here together and put this behind us."

"No," he snapped. His stare pierced the dark at his cowering ex-wife. "She has to see."

"Norman," Loren repeated, hoping to be heard. "Look at me, Norman. Not her. Just take a breath and look at me. People are scared out there. The lights are out and people are scared. You hear those sirens? They're not coming for you. They're trying to help people. Mercy Hospital is what, three blocks over?"

"Grid 87-B." His eyes flared and the gun was back on the cowering woman. "I know where *everything* is in this city. Like I always tried to tell you."

Loren fought to his knees, hands always visible. "Norman. Mercy Hospital."

"Yes," he replied. "Three blocks east."

"How many emergencies can they handle before their generators run out? How many lives are in jeopardy because the equipment isn't running?"

"I don't—"

"Where is the C Line, Norman?" Loren pressed, inciting the man's agitation.

"The C Line? What does that—?"

"Norman," Loren said, fighting to stand. "The C Line. How many people are on it right now? How many hundreds are waiting for the grid to come back up? How many families are missing a loved one tonight?"

Norman hesitated, shaking his head. "That's not—"

"Important to you? Yes, they are. They have to be. They don't get to be some statistic, some collateral damage for you. None of us should be that."

The image of Soriya in his apartment flared in his thoughts. The reason behind his anger. The lie of it all. Beth. That was why he did what he did, why he did it so well. Always for Beth. To make sure it never happened to anyone else.

Tears wetted Norman's cheeks. "I wanted her to see how special I am."

"She knows, Norman." Loren reached for the weapon. "We all do. But what really matters is that you know, right?"

"I…"

"Let her go, Norman. Let us go."

Norman raised the gun, the barrel swallowing up that small ray of hope. Then the frantic electrician let the sidearm swing loose from his finger, handing it over to the waiting detective.

"Good man," Loren said. He holstered the pistol and started for the woman strapped to the walkway. Cries filled the air as Loren ripped her gag loose and held her close. The man watched, saddened by his actions. "Okay, Norman. So how do we fix this?"

Norman's hands rested on his chest and he collapsed to his knees.

"Norman?"

"I don't feel so well." He fell over, the walkway clanging beneath his heavy frame.

"Norman!" Loren rushed to his side. He was burning up, sweat pouring down his face. Norman's ex-wife stood behind them, tears of sudden concern and confusion dotting her eyes.

"What's wrong with him?"

He's dying. Loren held his tongue, unwilling to say the words. Unwilling to admit that Norman used up what little time was offered by the red-feathered creature. He couldn't admit defeat, refused to—a shred of hope returning. Norman wasn't like the others. He didn't fulfill his lifelong desire. He didn't reach the pinnacle of his life in one grand gesture.

Norman hesitated.

Loren pulled him back. That had to count for something. It had to be enough to stop the chain reaction set off in his chest, burning him out. It had to be enough to save one miserable life out of the countless millions in the city.

"Come on," Loren whispered. Norman wasn't breathing, his heart stopped from shock. Ripping open his shirt, Loren started chest compressions. "Stay with me, buddy."

It wasn't up to him. Nothing ever was. Not completely and in the darkness of the electrical terminal walkway, Loren prayed for help from the only person that could.

"Come on, Soriya. Help me fix this."

CHAPTER FIFTEEN

The woman stood before her, blazing red hair shining against the pale of her skin. Naked and fierce, the Phoenix did not make a move against Soriya. None was necessary—her display of transformative power was enough to show the young Greystone bearer the odds of success.

Soriya didn't know what to do. When coming up with some plausible explanation for the threat against them, nothing could have prepared her for the nude, picture perfect woman sauntering along the alley's deep darkness as if she owned the city. The Phoenix was a being of pure light, unfiltered good. A fairytale for a place like Portents.

To give witness to her arrival in the physical world should have been a celebration. To life. To love. To all the wonder of the world, of any world. Instead, the Phoenix abused her abilities, driving people to death through their wish-fulfilling actions. To the increased passion amped up within their delicate and fragile souls. People were dying and the radiant creature didn't care.

To say Soriya was astonished was an understatement. *Disappointed* barely scratched the surface. Still, she stood before the being of pure light, unafraid and unwilling to back down, no matter the cost.

"It doesn't have to be this way," Soriya called. "I don't want to do this."

"Good," the Phoenix said. She held no shame in her body as she stepped closer. "Then you're finally seeing the light."

"That's what you're supposed to be. For all of us."

The woman with the fiery red mane snapped her fingers and a feather came to rest in her grip. "Then you will receive my gift?"

"Gift?" Soriya shook her head in disbelief. The Phoenix didn't understand. After everything, how could she not understand? "You're killing people!"

"I am giving them life to its fullest."

"Like touching the sun," Soriya snapped. "You're burning them out. People are dying."

"They always will," the Phoenix said with a wry smirk. "Poor child, you do not yet understand the coming darkness. There is so little time left to live. Let them burn bright."

The coming darkness. The same threat she felt in the background of events plaguing her city at every turn? The same implied by her friend, Gilgamesh, or something more? It didn't matter. Nothing beyond the moment mattered to Soriya Greystone. The threat was clear and remained directly in front of her.

"Look!" she cried over the screams flowing through the downtown area. The chaos raged behind the scenes, unaware of the cause and of the danger at its heart. "Please just look around you. The fear, the terror? You've brought that to the people you are supposedly saving. Not some jackass with delusions of grandeur and with some unrequited passion. You set this off and *we* are paying the price."

"Can you put a price on living your life to the fullest?" the Phoenix asked. "Can you ask the people of this city, of this world, to duck their heads and walk in silence when their every instinct is to scream their passion from the rooftops?"

"No," Soriya replied. The Greystone slipped from her hand-woven pouch into her palm and she held it before her once more. "But I have to, don't I?"

The Phoenix grinned. "What will that do?"

"Enough," Soriya said. Her eyes pleaded for another way, another moment to think of some solution. To convince the great and powerful being of pure light to understand, to truly see what was happening. But time had run out. The anarchy gripping the city had to end. The only way threats ever did when it came to Soriya Greystone. "I'm sorry."

Another lightning strike pounded the earth, shattering the cacophony of sound permeating Portents. The bolt slammed into the Phoenix, who did nothing but accept the blow.

Her ashes came to rest in the alley, sparking from the lightning's intensity. Soriya crept closer, watching them shift along the ground. The Phoenix fought to return, and Soriya knew there would be no more attempts to rip her from the world. Soriya closed her eyes, wishing for another way. Wishing she could find a better path and a light at the end of it.

"I'm so sorry," she whispered.

The mound of ashes congealed to form fingers, and the red-haired beauty's hand quickly took shape.

Soriya closed her eyes. "Not this time."

ᚺ

Another strike and the pile scattered across the alley. Soriya forced every erg of will into the stone, her eyes shut tight and a tear running the length of her cheek.

ᚱ

Wind swirled. A gale force picked up the scattered ashes of the Phoenix and sent them soaring in all directions. Soriya allowed the rune to remain, the winds shuffling and shifting the ashes away from each other. She didn't know how long it took, how long she kept her eyes closed from the act of taking the radiant creature's light from the world.

When she opened them again, only a few specks remained along the ground. Soriya approached them tucking the Greystone away. She crouched low and let them rest against her fingers.

"Soriya?"

She didn't turn at his presence. She brushed the ashes from her fingertips, allowing the breeze to carry them into the air and away from the city.

"It's over." Slowly she stood, weary from the night.

Loren nodded, a sad smile on his face. Behind him, EMTs escorted a man and a woman from the power station. The woman held the man's hand and he squeezed it tight as they entered the waiting ambulance.

"You did it," Loren said, following her gaze.

"So did you."

"What was it?"

"Pure light." Soriya looked up to the sky, sparks flashing along the ashes whipping overhead. They faded against the darkness of the city.

No more.

CHAPTER SIXTEEN

Darkness was winning. The shadows spread for a mile all around the brooding rooftop figure of Soriya Greystone. Inching for the ledge of the high-rises of downtown, the wind whipping around her, she wondered where the light had gone.

The shadows in Portents twisted, distorted from their true intent. Even the Phoenix, a being of pure radiance—of rebirth and rejuvenation—turned to darkness. Everything changed, evolving like the Bypass itself.

But into what?

Was this the point of transformation? A trial before the dawn, or had light truly slipped from the world and the shadows ruled all? Is that what was happening to Loren? His anger and his distance returning to test the resolve of their partnership, their friendship?

No answers came—no great wisdom from beyond or within. Mentor would not appear with a lecture and a lesson to be learned from the night's events. No one would anymore. She stood alone in this. Her city needed her—she couldn't fail.

And she wouldn't.

Soriya clenched her fists as the ribbon of Kali whipped through the breeze like a blanket against the darkness. She refused to wait for the answers to appear, to sit on the sidelines while the screams of the innocent filled the air. To curl up and take the trials as they passed was not an option.

It was time to fight. Until the very end.

The city agreed with her. Lights returned with the flick of a switch, the skyline blazing brighter than the dawn. The terror of the night, the cries for help echoing through the air, dimmed then silenced as a calm settled over Portents.

The light stretched to the horizon. All eyes lifted to watch the beauty of the city shine. From the lowest tenement to the obsidian tower reflecting the city against the brightening sky, Portents returned to life.

Soriya smiled, thankful to have the city at her side—to know it would always remain with her, for her, and never against her. A true ally and one she refused to let down.

Soriya Greystone raced along the edge of the rooftop, leaping deeper into her city.

Ready for anything.

CHAPTER SEVENTEEN

Loren's forehead rested against the thin pane of glass that stood as his window. The coolness contented his sweating brow. It soothed the heat rising from his arm and chest.

Too much activity for the night. Too soon after his assault by the Charon. Too much, too soon, all around.

The scanner continued to run in the background, blaring numbers and addresses during the blackout. The sound was little more than static to Loren, white noise to fill the emptiness of the apartment. A vain attempt to drown out his own spiraling thoughts.

An unopened bottle of beer sat beside the scanner. He stopped at the convenience store on his way home when the old habit called to him, a temptation not felt in years. One he regretted the moment he pulled the bottle loose from the six-pack. All six would find a home down the sink before the morning dawned. Instead, he slipped a stick of gum between his lips, chewing loudly, wishing it was a cigarette.

Peach mango. Unfiltered. *Filthy habit.*

The photo sat in his hands. He barely realized its presence in his grasp, as the image was embedded in his mind, always broadcasting when he closed his eyes. Soriya in the window of his apartment, Soriya present the day his wife left this world.

They never spoke about it. He wanted to—he should have. The weight of the image was too much for him to carry. He needed answers, needed the truth, no matter the heartache caused by someone he had grown to trust over the course of his career.

A friend. A partner. And now…?

He stopped himself. He could have screamed at her, pulled her aside and demanded answers. No more lies, no more omissions.

The story of what happened to his wife, the true and tragic tale that darkened his sky worse than any blackout could.

In answer, the city sparked to life. Lights returned, beaming from downtown and spreading out along the Knoll and beyond. Loren offered a moment of silence, a sad smile, to the act. Thankful yet disturbed at the same time.

Loren wondered what else was missed during the darkness. They had spent the whole night cleaning up the mess left by Erikson, the police doing the same for the Kindly Killer. But what of the consequences of their focus? Of the blackout? What hell had slipped into the shadows waiting to strike?

There would be one, bigger and bolder than the last. All selfish in their desire. Destructive in their nature. They would always be out there—the next threat, the next terror, the next darkness hoping to drag down Portents as collateral.

Loren held the photo to the window. Taking the gum from his lips, he stuck it over the image, pinning it against the glass. He knew the truth of his dismal queries. The true consequence had already taken hold; in his every word, every spark of anger he carried for the woman in the photograph.

The split between him and Soriya. Growing with each glance. Building with each breath.

Their friendship. Their partnership.

No more.

TRUSTFALL

CHAPTER ONE

Ruiz smiled. Bright and bold, the impenetrable grin spread across his face. The dishes were almost complete, and a celebration was in order. How he managed to use as many pans for a single meal astounded him. But that wasn't what caused his grin. It wasn't the chorus of his two youngest in the next room, trying to sing in tune with their favorite boy band for the week.

It definitely was not the boy band itself.

His joy was from everything. His life over the last few weeks, since his leave of absence from the department, had made him lighter on his feet. His spirit soared where once it was pulled down by the endless pursuit of criminals and the inevitable paperwork involved with each case.

There was a twinge of guilt at his contentment, at the growing sense of family and love spreading throughout the Ruiz home since his return. The death of his best friend remained in the background. Edgar Rusch was gone, his end met much too soon.

Edgar always wanted things this way with Ruiz and his family: to put the job aside for a brief moment, to refocus on what truly mattered. He was right. He was always right.

Putting away the chaos of Portents, refusing to acknowledge the world outside their doorstep, helped Ruiz file away the nightmares of the past. From Nathaniel Evans to Henry Erikson, from his scarred right hand to Loren's brush with death, Ruiz needed a break. His family helped.

Until his daughter, Zoe, came home for the weekend.

"Have you been eating at all?" Michelle, Ruiz's wife of twenty years asked. She stood next to the kitchen table, folding two baskets of laundry.

"Of course I have," Zoe said. Her head was buried in a cupboard. She brought out three cans of soup and a box of cookies, which slipped into the growing number of paper bags near the back door.

Zoe started at the University of Portents a month ago. Eighteen years went too quickly for the aging parents, an adjustment for all. Especially Ruiz. Having worked so hard to keep the world outside at arm's length from his family, to see his daughter embrace it scared the hell out of him. And with her decision to live on campus instead of commuting from the comfort and safety of their home, Ruiz fought back the overprotective parent routine as best as he could.

Michelle continued, "If the dining hall isn't enough, we—"

"I eat, Mom."

"We know," Ruiz said, drying the last of the pans and placing it on the counter next to the sink. "The way you downed dinner tonight—"

"Dad."

Ruiz put his hands up, pointing to the growing cart near the back door. "And the bags of groceries?"

Zoe shrugged, dropping a dozen apples into the closest paper bag. "Groceries are expensive."

"I'm well aware. I bought them."

Michelle dropped the shirt she was folding. "You can buy them again."

"I can and I will." Ruiz paced to the end of the room, looking over his departing efforts. He stopped, grumbling under his breath before reaching into a bag for the box of Froot Loops. "But this stays."

"What do you mean?" Zoe snatched the box out of his hands and put it back in the bag. "Since when do you eat kid's cereal?"

Michelle smiled. "Your father likes a little sugar in the morning, Zoe."

Ruiz's laughter joined his wife's. They both enjoyed the shivering form of their uncomfortable daughter. For a long time, under the weight of his secrets and lies—some years old—their relationship appeared destined for failure. Another divorce, like half the population. Like his parents, before the end.

His last case opened his eyes, pushing him to open up to his wife. The truth was difficult, to say the least. There were arguments at first. Worse than all the lies and the secrets. The truth held them together, though. They took it the rest of the way. It was one of the brightest spots of the last few weeks; their time together.

It had been good. Very good.

"Gross, Mom," she chided, unable to look at either of them. "Just gross."

"Try living with them," Teresa said. She walked briskly through the room, her twelve-year-old mind focused on the mission at hand.

"I did, squirt. Like last month."

Teresa slipped a hand into the cookie jar and removed some Fudge Stripes then opened the drawer below for the tape measure. Grinning at her older sister, the middle child bolted for the living room.

"What's with the tape measure?"

Teresa ran faster. "Good seeing you, sis!"

"Mom?" Zoe pressed.

"What?"

"Dad?"

Ruiz turned away. "Didn't see anything."

Zoe groaned in disgust. She started for the living room, stopping at the sound of her mother's sigh.

"Your room is the biggest, Zoe."

Her eyes thinned. She looked like her mother. "Don't even think about it."

Zoe went back to her grocery bags, shifting one's contents to fit in another two-liter of Sprite. Ruiz wondered if he should start taking inventory, although he knew that none could cover what the girls managed to sneak by him. When she started shifting the bags closer to the door, Ruiz held out his hand.

"Dad?"

He threw her a hard glare. "The cereal."

Zoe sighed, pulling out the sugary box of deliciousness. "Fine. But I'm taking the prize out of it."

"Don't you dare. I've been working for it for days."

Michelle's arms slipped around him and pulled him close. "Yes, you have."

Ruiz's cheeks flushed. "Michelle."

"Oh, you were too skinny."

He patted his stomach. "Give me a few weeks. You'll regret telling me that."

"Especially if you keep buying the groceries."

The small voice of their youngest, Angela, cried out from the living room, "Please let Daddy buy the groceries!"

"We need more cookies!" Teresa yelled.

Ruiz shrugged. "The kids have spoken."

"Add laundry detergent to the list, then," Michelle said, stacking the laundry baskets next to the grocery bag army. "I think Zoe wore her whole wardrobe this week."

Zoe grabbed her coat from the closet. "It was a long week."

She hugged her father and pecked him on the cheek. He looked her over. "This going to be a regular thing?"

"I miss you too, Dad."

"Not what I'm saying."

Michelle cocked her head. "Alejo."

"What?"

"We talked about this, Dad."

"We did but we can again. Living at home isn't a punishment."

"It isn't a picnic either," Zoe muttered, inching for the door.

"Hey."

Michelle hugged her daughter, her soft voice countered by the hard stare at her husband. "College only happens once, dear. Hopefully only once. Let her have her time."

"I'm just saying, we have a bed here. It's quiet."

Zoe pointed to the growing screams in the living room at the sound of yet another boy band bonanza. "Sometimes."

"And safe," Ruiz finished.

"Dad."

He held tight to the back of a kitchen table chair. "There have been some robberies in the area. A rise in assaults. Breaking and entering. If you're out, walking around by yourself—"

"Are you checking up on me?"

"I have friends in campus security."

Zoe shook her head, arms crossed against her chest. The same as Michelle. "He's been checking up on me."

"Walking alone at night isn't safe in the city."

"I'm with friends." Zoe glared at him. Ruiz fell silent, waiting until the look softened. "I need to be able to make friends, Dad."

"What about the boys from high school?" Michelle asked. "Jerome goes to the university, doesn't he?"

"Football scholarship," Zoe said in a mousy voice. "He doesn't even know me, Mom. And I am perfectly safe on my own. I'm just not under the watchful eyes of Captain Alejo Ruiz."

"*Zoe*," Ruiz called.

"The school is safe. There's security and meetings and even counselors for people needing one—including my Intro to Psychology teacher, Professor Dobson."

"Dobson?" Ruiz choked. The world paused at the sound of his name. "Erik Dobson?"

"Yeah. Why?"

Ruiz hesitated then shook his head. "Nothing."

He pulled his daughter close and hugged her. Michelle wanted to press him, her eyes needling him for a reply he refused to give. Ruiz kissed Zoe's forehead and moved for the mountain of bags and baskets lining the door.

"I'll help you load up."

"Are you sure—?"

He smiled. "As long as you're safe."

"Always, Dad. Trust me."

Ruiz waited until the girls were asleep to pull out the lockbox under the bed. He opened the metal tin slowly, his personal revolver staring at him. He added it to the small pile of clothes at the edge of the bed. He locked the box and slid it out of sight. When he stood, his wife was in the doorway.

Michelle wore nothing but a towel and an angry glare. "What the hell was that all about?"

"Michelle."

"We talked about this, Alejo," Michelle snapped. She had been holding back since Zoe left, and was unable to contain her frustration any longer. Unwilling to fall into the old trap. The great divide. "Well, I talked and you ignored me."

"I'm trying to keep Zoe safe."

"By spying on her?" Michelle let the towel slip away. He tried to focus on the conversation, cursing their need for an argument right at this moment. She covered herself with a shirt, one of his, ending the distraction. For the most part.

"Having people look out for her is not spying. It's monitoring."

"Big difference."

"Tons." A pair of sneakers fell out of the closet and he collected them from the floor to add to his growing pile.

"What are you doing?"

"Nothing."

"Doesn't look like nothing. Looks like packing."

"It is, Michelle."

"Stop." Michelle reached for his hand, holding him back. "Just stop."

He pulled away in anger. "Something is going on at that school."

"So make a call." She closed their bedroom door, hoping to buffer their rising voices from their sleeping kids. "Call Greg."

"He's still recovering."

"Like that matters. You could—"

"No. Not for this."

"It was him," Michelle said, leaning against her dresser. "That professor Zoe mentioned. Dobson."

Ruiz stopped, his fingers grazing the pistol. "Erik Dobson."

"You know him."

"I do."

Michelle reached out again, fingers lacing between his and squeezing. "You promised me, Alejo. You promised this would stop."

"And I am trying, Michelle. I am."

"Then tell me. Who is he?"

Ruiz sighed and paced the room. He kept his right arm tucked close, the heat rising from his scars. So many scars over the years but they all stemmed from that first night. That night he learned the truth about Portents.

"Do you remember right before Zoe was born?" He kept his back to Michelle, staring out the window. "That night I ended up in the hospital?"

Michelle nodded. "From some hoodlums. They were chasing you."

"I was investigating that murder with Harvey."

"The kid with the feathers," she whispered, moving closer to him. "You had nightmares for weeks after that. Being chased by them."

"One of them."

Her hands slid under his arms, holding him close. "Something about his pale skin."

Ruiz nodded, lost in memory. "And yellow eyes."

Fly away, little bird. Faster, little bird.

"Erik Dobson." Her head rested against his back, her warmth feeding him. "You think he's involved with these crimes?"

"I don't know," he said, wishing he had a better answer. "I'm here, and I'm trying to stay here for you…but she's my daughter, Michelle."

"I know."

She fell away and he felt cold. He turned, hoping to coax her back, but she was at the closet. She dug through the debris that came with their busy lives, pulling out a small black bag.

"What are you doing?" he asked. Michelle lifted his growing pile and tucked them within the bag, zipping it up with finality. Then she held it out to him. "What's this now?"

"This is you moving your ass over to that campus to keep our little girl safe."

CHAPTER TWO

He found Dobson's office first. It was early morning; a few students filtered through the campus, having been forced to accept the dawn as the start of their days. They were all too drowsy to notice the stranger in their midst.

That's what Ruiz was, a stranger. An outsider. He never felt like one more than when he stepped out of his car and tracked down the second-floor office of Professor Erik Dobson.

Crispin Hall stood as a crossroads for the entire university. Staff offices occupied the second and third floors, overflow from their prospective departments as well as fitting those with multiple functions on the campus. Dobson's sat on the eastern corner overlooking the harbor.

Locked.

Too early. Part of him considered picking the lock, rummaging through the man's files for some indication of culpability in the crimes plaguing the school and the surrounding areas. He couldn't risk the exposure and he didn't have any evidence to the contrary.

Yet.

Disgruntled, Ruiz stalked the building's first floor. There was a common dining area for visitors and staff members. On the other side was an auditorium for presentations and fairs. At the ends of the building were shops—a beverage center for on-the-go students with too much money and little control, and a campus store with university paraphernalia: ball caps, T-shirts, notebooks, pens, and more. All bearing the Portents name and seal, and all insanely overpriced.

But it remained his best option to blend in, something Ruiz needed desperately. As the early morning shuffle of the student body shifted into the late morning blitz of hundreds, more and more eyes turned to the pacing Ruiz. All looking for some explanation. He kept his eyes low, his interest firmly on the clothing racks outlining the edge of the shop.

His purpose was twofold: He sought mostly a chance to view Dobson in his element, to follow his movements for the day and see what came from them. His secondary concern was Zoe. She didn't know about his visit—couldn't know, not after their fight the previous evening. He needed to handle this, to keep her safe, and he didn't need her permission to do either.

"Can I help you with something?" a voice called, and his hand almost ripped a sweatshirt clean off the rack in surprise.

Ruiz turned to see a young woman with striking red hair clipped short on the sides. She offered a wary smile, her eyes dark against the overhead lighting. She carried a single folder full of colored flyers and a coffee in her other hand.

"I'm fine, thanks." He scanned the hall for signs of Dobson and Zoe, not wanting to miss either.

"Well," the woman said, approaching from the other side of the rack, "I could take you at your word but you've been here for quite a bit."

"I'm waiting for someone," Ruiz said, trying not to look too closely at the woman. She was his daughter's age, barely eighteen, from the looks of it. Her tight shirt and jeans portrayed her confidence well. Her eyes, however, the thin black surrounding her pupils, seemed older. Much older.

"So is the store," she said.

"I'm sorry?"

She smiled. "Out of place gentlemen tend to scare away customers."

The store had no other patrons since his arrival. He blamed it on the early hour or the fact that most of the campus had already procured their annual allotment of poorly weaved clothing from third world countries. How had he not noticed his own impact? The attention he pulled just by being around?

"That out of place?" he asked, letting go of the sweatshirt rack.

"Definitely. Like a cop on a stakeout. A less-than-smooth cop at that."

Right on the money. He was out of his element, for sure. "Would some sunglasses and a mustache help?"

"Couldn't hurt."

Ruiz nodded, backing away from the store. He pointed to the coffee shop at the other end of the hall. "Maybe I'll—"

She pressed, calling after him. "So, Officer—"

"Not an officer," Ruiz said with flitting eyes of concern. He was in the middle of the hall—too open, too exposed. "Not today. Just a concerned parent."

"Ah, one of those," she replied, expectantly. "First one?"

"Yes."

"A daughter," she guessed.

Ruiz sighed, hands on his hips. "This usually works the other way around, miss?"

"Concerned student," she answered. "You want my advice?"

"Please."

"Don't let her catch you here. It never turns out well and the parent is always in the wrong. Always."

Not this time, Ruiz thought. He gave a slight nod of acceptance and she turned for the exit. Ruiz's brow furrowed, and he called after her. "Hey, I thought you worked here?"

"Never said that." She tossed a wave as she departed. "Happy hunting, Officer."

Ruiz watched her leave, the confidence behind each step. She called him out on every level, knew his story better than he did. She knew the reasons behind his arrival, and the reasons it had to be him to investigate instead of relegating the task to Loren or even campus security. People he could trust to do their job. People who would look out for everyone at the University of Portents and not the lone daughter of an overprotective cop.

He needed to forget about the crimes. He needed to forget about the name he heard from Zoe—Dobson. Erik Dobson.

"You should have told her," a gravelly voice from the past hissed in his ear.

Ruiz's heart stopped, nightmares two decades old returning in an instant. Racing through the night, chased by that voice.

And the two yellow eyes behind it.

Ruiz turned slowly. Erik Dobson smiled, towering over him. His pale skin glowed under the fluorescents and his eyes never blinked, the yellow still present. Staring right through him.

"It's not officer anymore," Dobson said. "It's captain."

CHAPTER THREE

Dobson let his backpack fall against the side of his desk. The door closed behind him; Ruiz pushed it open and stepped inside the corner office on the second floor of Crispin Hall.

It was small—not in size, but in free space. Books lined shelves, the overflow streaming in piles on the floor along the right-hand wall. An L-shaped desk took up the left side, Dobson's computer screen in full view. Spreadsheets and articles covered the desk. Work and nothing but.

Two chairs sat opposite the desk and Ruiz reached for one, but he stopped short. This wasn't a social call. There was no reason to sit and chat with the man he had been hunting all morning. There was no friendship here; the photos dotting the walls reminded him why. Where most set up inspirational images or family photos in their personal space, Dobson went his own unique way, with a subject near and dear to his heart and Ruiz's terror.

Birds.

Photos of birds in large and small frames. Some soared, some nested. A snow owl held a place of prominence behind Ruiz. It took all his willpower to avoid turning around after catching a glimpse of the nocturnal creature's wide yellow eyes.

"Can I get you anything?" Dobson asked, circling the desk. He reached underneath to a mini-fridge next to his filing cabinet. "I have water, water, and more water. Clean living and all that."

"I'm fine," Ruiz replied. "This is you now?"

In the distance the sun rose, offering a full view of the harbor, the water shimmering under the bright morning light. It was serene, peaceful. Not what a drugged-up psychopath like Dobson deserved.

The professor ignored the intent behind the question and sat. "A couple classes a week and a campus counselor."

Ruiz nodded, looking over the books on the shelf. It kept him from focusing on those watching eyes. Always screaming in his memory. *Fly faster, little bird.* "Do they know—?"

"About my past?" Dobson asked, a wry grin forming. "Of course. No getting around things like that."

"Yet here you are."

"Change is inevitable, Captain. I've changed."

Ruiz closed his eyes. He could still see the flapping of wings surrounding him in the tenement. Dobson and his friends were high on a drug sapped from a mythical harpy, using it to soar above their problems and terrorize anyone who stood in their way. One kid crashed hard when the drug's diminishing returns escaped him in mid-flight, sending him in a tailspin to an unfortunate end as street pizza. It was one of Ruiz's last cases before his promotion to detective. One he never filed a report for, letting another take the credit to avoid having to tell the story to his colleagues.

It was also the first time he held back from his wife, marking the start of the great divide with her and the rest of his family. Because of those damn yellow eyes. Because of Erik Dobson.

"There's been a rise in burglaries in the area," Ruiz said. He faced Dobson, hoping for a reaction, a glance, a shift in position. The man never budged. "Assaults as well."

"I'd heard," Dobson replied casually. Ruiz waited, his glare thin. The professor leaned closer to his desk. "Some students have stopped by to discuss the incidents. Troubling, but I don't see why you would... Oh."

"Yeah. 'Oh.'"

Dobson smiled. "That was a long time ago, Captain. That night with you? I fell hard after that. Detox from the drug. Plenty of rehab and counseling. Not to mention a ton of community service.

"I cleaned up," he continued, getting comfortable in his chair. "I went back to school, made something of my life."

"After that night," Ruiz repeated softly.

"I should thank you. Always wanted to, in fact. If you hadn't shown up and stopped us—"

"I didn't," Ruiz snapped. Someone else did—a man he came to know as Mentor. Another victim of Portents and the world tucked beneath the surface. A world difficult to hide from once it had you in its clutches. If Mentor hadn't shown up when he did and stopped Dobson and his friends that night, Ruiz would not be standing here now. He wouldn't be standing at all.

"You tried," Dobson offered. "Like now." He reached for the fridge once more, removing a bottle of water and snapping open the lid. "Are you sure I can't get you some water?"

"No, thanks. I should—"

"Your daughter attends now, doesn't she?"

Heat seared his skin at the mere mention of Zoe. "What did you—?"

Dobson shook his head. "She's in my class. I noticed the name. Bright young lady."

"Always has been."

Dobson took a short sip. Ruiz tried to slow his heart rate as the man savored the water in his grip. Ruiz stood at the door, yellow eyes peering through him. "Are you here as a cop or a father?"

Ruiz didn't understand the question. Dobson's grin widened at the hesitation.

"I know," he said, circling the desk. He sat on the end, in full control of the conversation. "There's little distinction really. Both protectors. But one has a civic duty and the other? Well, it's not surprising given your occupation."

"What's that?"

"A lack of trust."

Ruiz turned for the door, wishing he had never entered. This was getting him nowhere fast. There were no answers coming from this man, this nightmare from the past. Nothing but the memory of him. His bony frame was almost withered from the drugs in his system. And the eyes. *Why did the eyes have to be the same?*

"I trust Zoe just fine."

"So she knows you're here?" Dobson pressed. "She knows about me? Our history?"

Ruiz's head fell low, no answers slipping from his parted lips.

"I didn't think so. All the security and patrols we have here weren't enough for you either. You had to come. Was it my name that brought you? It was, wasn't it?"

Dobson savored the moment as much as his bottled water. Every verbal jab landed as soundly as a punch against the outsider in the room.

"Yes."

The former addict turned professor nodded, watching Ruiz's guilt form like a blanket. "I'm sorry to have wasted your time then."

Ruiz caught the deep look in his eyes. The one that haunted his dreams for months after their time together. Everything screamed at him, swore up and down that this was the wrong path. That Dobson, like many of his kin, had found their way back into the world and did everything they could to put the past to rest. To find a way to live their lives, burying their mistakes away so no one would find them. But then there were those eyes.

Fly away, little bird. Or I'll find you.

"Right," he said and opened the door.

Dobson approached, holding it for the retreating captain. "Is there anything else I can—?"

"No. Thank you for your time."

"Of course," Dobson said with a smile. Ruiz started for the stairs, feeling the man's gaze follow him. "I'll keep my eyes open for you, Captain."

I'm sure you will.

Ruiz's chest heaved, his breath coming in short bursts when he reached his car. He sank into the driver's seat, clutching the steering wheel. His knuckles turned white from the strain of every held back word, every thinly veiled accusation from their conversation.

Curses ripped through the interior of the sedan. They carried on for a few minutes before he finally settled and stared at the building. Wondering. Thinking. About the past and the present.

Why they always came together in one form or another and never as expected.

That question stuck with Ruiz for much of the day. Hours in the car, waiting and watching Crispin Hall and the parking lot— and the small SUV of Erik Dobson across the aisle. Doubt crept in about the legality of his actions, compounded with each hour wasted waiting for something to happen.

As the sun waned, along with Ruiz's patience, Dobson started for his car, turning in for the night. The SUV roared, the muffler on its last legs, and then it was on its way down the long driveway to the campus main entrance.

Ruiz waited before turning the key on the sedan. The engine purred and he cringed, hoping Dobson kept his eyes on the road ahead.

Before he could put the car into drive, a hand tapped the glass of his window and a bright light flooded the interior.

"License and registration," the man behind the flashlight commanded. Ruiz watched the SUV turn at the exit and disappear out of sight.

"Shit." He thought about kicking the car into drive and speeding after his target. Instead, he reached for his registration, rolling down the window in the same movement. "This isn't what it looks like."

Through the blinding glare, Ruiz saw the man smile. "You mean you aren't stalking your old buddy, Dobson, to see if he'll turn into a bird monster again?"

Ruiz squinted against the light. "Who the hell—?"

The flashlight clicked off. Before him stood a short man in a fedora and overcoat. Wrinkles dotted his skin, a massive liver spot on his right cheek, creased under the grin of Julian Harvey.

"You can tell me all about it over a beer," Harvey said. He circled the car, climbing into the passenger seat before Ruiz could answer. Ruiz's former partner and mentor patted the dash and pointed to the road ahead. "Your treat."

CHAPTER FOUR

Two quick knocks on the door, followed by sliding a flyer into the room. Then she moved to the next. She had been doing it for an hour, navigating from dorm to dorm, slipping the announcement into each room she passed and to everyone who ran by in a rush to their next class.

"Party tonight," the young woman with the striking red hair exclaimed. "Sig Tau house."

Hands clapped. Hooting and hollering answered her calls.

"Nice," one replied, flier in hand to spread the word.

"Can't wait," another chimed.

Not everyone would come. Not with so many other events occurring on campus. But the promise of cheap beer and companionship for the night was tempting.

None of it truly mattered to her. She appreciated the rushing of feet, the excitement of the night ahead, but there was doubt weighing on her every move.

The cop gave her that doubt. Waiting outside the campus shop as she finished printing the flyers for distribution. Coincidence or something more? He played it carefully enough, even with her pressing questions. He never looked at her too closely but then he didn't have to, did he?

He knew the truth.

How could he not? He smelled of her, the young ingrate that sent her on this path. Their encounter in the coves started her fall. Working out of that dank, abandoned theater. Lording over her boys and the small trinkets they showered upon her. Having fun above all else. That was her calling, and she did it so well over the years. Hell, over the centuries.

But since then, nothing had gone right. She left the coves behind for greener pastures, brighter paths in the darkness of Portents. Each time she met an immovable obstacle, a path blocked by others.

She found herself hunted on all sides. From cushy jobs in the political arena to the inner circle of the police department, the woman with the short scarlet locks had done everything she could to get back on track with her plans. Her fun with the city and its citizens. All for naught—she was found out and forced to flee in each instance. Now she was stuck, a lowly student at the university.

Her last refuge.

Doors passed by in a blur, and the sound of her knocking fell into the background, like the steps in the hall following her from afar. She came to this dorm for a reason. The university, while pale in comparison to her position of old, remained hers. No cop would take it from her. She would not be hunted any longer.

Especially by Captain Alejo Ruiz.

Her hand fell on the door at the end of the hall. Instead of slipping the flyer under and moving on, the young woman waited for the sound of steps approaching.

"Coming," a voice called. The door opened and Zoe Ruiz answered. "Yes?"

"Party tonight at the Sig Tau house."

The flyer fell to Zoe's side. "I can't. I have to—"

"Come to a party tonight."

Zoe grinned, cheeks flush. "Listen…"

"Kit."

"Is that short for something?"

"Yes," Kit answered.

"Okay," Zoe said, drawing out the word, hoping for more of a response. "Kit."

"And you're Zoe, right?" she asked, pointing to the name on the door.

"Gotta love freshman customs."

Kit leaned on the frame of the door, keeping it open. "Let me guess. You have studying to do. Reading to get through. And an early night? Just like yesterday and probably tomorrow."

"Something like that."

"Or—big emphasis on that by the way—you could *not* study for one night and see campus life the way it's meant to be seen."

Zoe hesitated, the books that littered her desk calling to her harder than Kit's cooing at the door. She read the hesitation clearly, gesturing down the hall. The reply came quick, rushing at her gentle push. Always hoping to please her.

"Is she coming?"

"I'm trying to convince her," Kit said softly. Zoe peered down the hall to see the tall, broad shoulders of a black man. Instantly recognized, Zoe fell back in her room, hand to her lips.

"Was that—?"

Kit grinned, blocking her view. Her fingers danced along the frame in rhythm with the boy's departing steps. Temptation always worked better in short bursts. "Football players are so impatient," she whispered. "Jerome asked for you specifically, Zoe. You went to high school together, right?"

"Yeah, but—"

"Must have been close, the way he talks about you."

"Really?"

Kit reached out, lifting Zoe's hand with the crumpled up flyer. "One night, Zoe. What do you say?"

The question was unnecessary—the answer was clear. Still she waited for the quiet nod and the breathless excitement that escaped after the door closed. Of course Zoe Ruiz would be there.

Kit needed her there. She was not going to lose this life. Not without a fight.

CHAPTER FIVE

The Town Hall Pub smelled of decay and defeat. Ruiz felt at home for the first time all day and he hated every second of it. The day was a waste, a disappointment of awkward conversations and little in the way of progress.

What was he doing? He came in a vain effort to play the protector for his daughter once more. The way it had been when she was scraping her knees with each fall as a toddler. Daddy's little girl. Always and forever.

Except now things were more complicated, all centered on a face from the past. Erik Dobson. Nothing pointed to him, but nothing had to either. Not for Ruiz. He knew the man, seen the crazed look in his eyes all those years ago. He recognized the danger present, one that could never be swallowed and forgotten no matter how much time had passed.

Yet did that justify his suspicions? Was anything here other than a spike in crime, something easily explained as a matter of circumstance? Ruiz couldn't see it, not with the guilt he held for not talking to Zoe first.

And more guilt at sitting next to Julian Harvey rather than working.

"What happened to the minivan?" the eighty-two-year-old asked between sips of Milwaukee's Best. Harvey looked the part of a man unable to walk away from the job. He carried his stubbornness, the true strength that had kept him going all these years, in every glare and every smile. His presence didn't sit well with Ruiz, but then again nothing sat well today.

"Drove it through the front of a house."

Harvey lowered the beer from his lip, dangling between his fingers like the question demanding to be asked. He held it back—was forced to anyway, by Ruiz.

"How's retirement, Harvey?"

Harvey looked forward at the mirror across the bar. Ruiz kept his head low, needling his bottle of Bud Light. "Busy. How's yours?"

"I'm not." Ruiz stopped at the man's grin. "Pratchett."

Harvey tipped his bottle. "Nephew's good for something at least."

"It's just a leave of absence." Ruiz took a long swig, feeling the liquid burn his throat. A beer was the last thing he needed, yet it hit the spot.

"For now."

Ruiz bit his tongue, refusing to engage. He took another sip then nodded to the bartender for a replacement. Harvey drank casually, letting the silence settle between them.

"I'm sorry I haven't called lately," Ruiz muttered. They used to chat monthly after Harvey's retirement. That went on for almost five years. Then monthly turned to quarterly turned to annually over time. It's the way things always went when life took over.

Harvey waved the apology away. "Bodies dropping every few minutes in the city? Not surprised."

"You do stay well informed."

"That egomaniac of a captain helps," Harvey sneered.

"Mathers," Ruiz huffed. Suddenly the beer turned sour, just like the conversation. He had made an effort to avoid work talk since his leave of absence started.

"Never happen in my day," Harvey said, finishing his drink. "We kept our mouths shut."

"I remember."

Harvey grinned, sharing the memory of their first case together: dealing with Dobson and his crew, their drug habit at the hands of the harpy. It was something Ruiz still had trouble understanding, much less being able to describe it when pressed by Michelle.

It was the night Ruiz learned about the city. When he found out how much he truly didn't know about Portents or Julian Harvey. He still felt that way about both.

"You came for Dobson."

"You knew he was here."

Harvey nodded. "Kept tabs on him after our run-in. Figured you did the same."

"No." *I tried to forget.* He set his beer down, pushing it away. The moment was gone. "So he is up to something."

"Not sure," Harvey replied. "But something is definitely going on here."

"The increase in crime."

Harvey shook his head, fixing his position to the center of the stool. "That can happen anywhere. A scorching summer. A damn full moon. No, what's different here is the organization of it all. Everything is too coordinated. These aren't some drunk ass punks."

"Could be Dobson."

"Could be," Harvey said without looking at him. He was holding it back, the answer Ruiz had been hunting for all day.

"Why are you here, Harvey? Why do you care about any of this?"

"I've been mapping out the crimes reported," he said, ever the detective. "There's a pattern. Slight…but there, if you know what you're looking for."

He reached into his pocket and slid a piece of paper to the waiting hand of Ruiz. "What's this?"

"An address."

"I know it's a damn address," Ruiz spat. "I can read. For what?"

"Frat house."

Ruiz rubbed at his eyes. "I thought this wasn't a bunch of drunk ass punks."

"Exactly. Thought I would check it out and—"

Ruiz stood and grabbed his coat, slipping the address into his pocket. "Go home, Harvey."

"What?"

"You're not a cop anymore."

"At the moment, neither are you."

Ruiz stopped. He didn't need another argument on top of the rest of his day. His hand fell on Harvey's shoulder. "Enjoy your retirement, Harvey. You earned it."

Harvey started to stand but Ruiz stopped him. A couple of bucks fell on the bar, Ruiz's request for another beer silently made with the bartender. Satisfied with Harvey's position at the bar, Ruiz moved for the door.

"Be careful, kid," Harvey called. "You know how this city can be."

Ruiz watched the smirk fade on the old man's face as he turned back to the mirror. He nodded, his keys jingling between his fingers, ready to get the hell out of the bar.

"Yeah," he whispered, staring out at the night sky over the cityscape. Nothing ever felt right in Portents. Not since Dobson. Not since Harvey. And now both were back in his life on the same day.

"I know exactly how this city can be."

CHAPTER SIX

"You've got to be kidding me."

In all circumstances, in every possible scenario played out in his thoughts during the drive down the waterfront to the frat house, this one never percolated for Ruiz. He imagined skulking through bushes or paying off one of the drunken idiots for a peek inside the house. He imagined bongs and bottles scattered across the floor, despite what Harvey believed to be the case of the Sig Tau fraternity. But he never considered this.

A party. A Goddamn party. Tonight, of all nights.

Leaving seemed to be the most logical next step. To come back at a less crowded time, to ask questions with the new day, after a good night of sleep at a nearby motel. He needed to figure out the goal behind the crimes, the increased violence and assaults in the area—and Dobson's place in it. Those eyes haunted Ruiz. There was no getting around them or the feeling that the professor was involved. He had to be. Hell, even Harvey played a role in this, but what that meant eluded the tired and overwhelmed captain.

Instead, the door to the car opened and Ruiz stepped into the night air. No jacket, just a long sleeve cotton shirt and jeans. As low key as he could get these days. The nights began to reflect the shift to autumn, a cool breeze running from the docks less than a mile away.

Ruiz closed the door and grumbled, "Yeah, this will go well."

He kept his head down, not that it did much for him. His salt and pepper hair—mostly salt nowadays—gave him little concealment. Not that the oversized kid working as the party's bouncer noticed with the amount of young ladies roaming the house. He didn't glance in Ruiz's direction, instead taking the cop's cover charge of five bucks then holding out a red plastic cup.

When Ruiz continued into the house without it, the kid shot him a quizzical look.

"Cup?"

"Pass," Ruiz muttered without looking back as he shuffled through the crowd.

A blast of music almost sent him back outside. The force of the speakers set up in the corner was loud enough to send crumbling bits of plaster down from the walls.

Dozens of people mingled, screaming to speak to each other while gulping down cheap beer. Others made out under the black lights while waiting for the bathroom that would be occupied the rest of the night. *Can't say they don't know how to multi-task at least.*

Decorations hung from every fixture, drooped along the railing to the second floor and down to the basement. All made from beer cans. How they managed to empty so many with the semester only one month old was a question for scholars and not an anxious cop in their midst. The amount of effort to decorate appeared to be extensive—much more so than any attempt to do schoolwork, no doubt.

Ruiz scanned the room, eyes still adjusting to the blinking lights. They irritated him to no end. The drunken calamity around him didn't help, either. How kids could be this stupid amazed him.

"Hey man," a kid called to him right on cue. "Hold this for me. I gotta take a leak."

The kid dropped the cup and Ruiz scrambled to catch it on instinct. The foamy liquid splattered up his sleeve. His curses were buried under the sound of the kid's pants unzipping.

"This isn't the bathroom."

The kid turned his head—and thankfully only his head. "It's not?"

Too late.

Ruiz backed away, tucking the plastic cup behind the couch. Young ladies pointed at the display in the corner with abject horror, others with copious laughter. A story to tell their roommates later. One young man rushed over, trying to curb the damage. Ruiz stopped him with a hand.

"Call a cab for him. Now."

The kid, definitely not twenty-one, pupils dilated and unable to focus on his words, looked over Ruiz. *Call one for yourself too*, he wanted to say. In truth, he wanted to end the fracas with a quick call to the closest precinct, but he drew enough attention just by being there.

He needed to see what was actually going on. Harvey swore this wasn't a bunch of drunk ass idiots, though Ruiz saw plenty of evidence to counter that argument. He found an opening between the living room and what could have been an expansive dining room, except for the beer pong tables set up in the center.

Catching his breath, Ruiz took the moment to look around. Drunken conversations—the drama of youth meant little to him. What he focused on was everything else. The movements of people in the house. Slow, to be sure, but deliberate. It took a few minutes but it started to clear.

There were no fraternity members at the party. No one showed off their letters, no one walked around recruiting the next wave of morons to participate in God knows how many hazing incidents never reported to security. The only pair of frat brothers visible was near the back, adjacent to the kitchen. They wore the same red and blue insignia on their chests, leaning in close with a pair of young ladies. Ruiz recognized the red hair of the woman from the campus store that morning. Coincidence or something more, Ruiz couldn't be sure, nor did he care when he realized who stood next to her.

"Zoe!"

His voice was lost to the rampaging decibels. It did not stop him. The crowd couldn't either, and he pushed through for the back of the house. The two brothers moved closer to Zoe, inching her toward the open door to the backyard.

"Zoe!" he yelled once more.

She stopped at the doorway, horror in her eyes at the sight of her father pushing through the crowd. The red-haired woman and her friends continued for the back door calling for Zoe to join them. When she refused they slipped into the darkness of the night and she cut off her father.

"Dad? What the hell?"

"Language," he said without thinking, immediately regretting it.

"Seriously?" Zoe turned back to her friends to see no one in the doorway anymore. "Great. I can't believe you did this."

Zoe blitzed through him, her eyes fighting back tears. Ruiz reached out for her, catching her arm. "Zoe, wait. Hold on."

"No, Dad," she snapped, shrugging off his hand.

"Why are you up in arms?" he asked, following her through the crowd for the front door. Onlookers paused their conversations, the drama before them too juicy to ignore. "You're the one at a frat house underage."

"Am I drinking?" Her hands were empty. No cup.

"Not yet."

Her eyes rolled. "Thanks for the confidence."

"Like I don't know how this turns out, Zoe. I was almost a damn urinal two minutes ago."

She stopped before the oversized doorman. "When did you stop trusting me? Did you ever trust me?"

"Zoe, that's not—"

"Whatever."

"Let me explain."

"You mean make up another excuse, don't you?" Zoe said, looking every bit like her mother. The anger. The concern. And the sadness. "You never explain anything, Dad."

"That's not fair."

"Then I guess we're even on that front." Zoe pushed through the crowd. Ruiz moved to follow but the kid at the door shuffled off his stool, blocking his path.

"Zoe!"

The kid glowered at Ruiz. "Walk it off, pal."

"Out of my way," Ruiz said. The kid refused to budge, grinning. Ruiz leaned close, eyes thinning. "Three seconds."

"What?"

"Three seconds, then I break your wrist and fracture your foot," Ruiz said slowly, watching the grin fade from the kid's face. "Two. One."

The bouncer backed off, returning to his stool.

"Thank you." Ruiz shoved his way outside. He searched the crowd, unable to find his daughter, wondering how much time he lost thanks to the kid's power play at the door. "Zoe!"

He rounded the corner, hoping to catch sight of her on the road heading back to the university. Instead he was met with the redhead from the campus shop.

"She's gone."

"I met you earlier," Ruiz said, scanning the grounds. There was no sign of Zoe anywhere.

"Kit," she said, extending a hand.

Ruiz pushed it away. "Don't really care."

"Nice try. Like you're not here for me."

Ruiz stopped. "What the hell are you talking about, lady?"

Kit smiled, backing away. "I'm not talking at all. And neither will you."

"What does that—?"

A black bag covered his head, the light sucked away in an instant. Pounding fists connected on both sides and he fought to escape, to gain a quick moment to recover. It never came—he was surrounded by his attackers.

Ruiz fell under their assault, and the darkness took over completely.

CHAPTER SEVEN

Cold wind blew over Ruiz as the black bag lifted from his head. The sound of rushing water filled his ears, and he saw the river stretching out along the shoreline. Waves beat against the edge of the cave entrance. Dark walls surrounded him on all sides.

Ruiz tried to stand, his hands bound behind a chair. Footsteps echoed behind him, muttering voices conveying quick messages lost against the wind and water.

The young woman with the scarlet locks and black eyes circled him, the hood in her hands. She stopped to glance out into the night.

"Welcome to my home away from home."

Ruiz strained against his bindings without success. "Cozy."

Kit huffed, tossing the hood aside. "It's abysmal. But it's all that's left to me, thanks to—"

A shadow fell over the room, rushing toward Kit. Ruiz recognized him from the neighborhood—one of the few kids from the cove that stuck it out in the city. Jerome something or other, from the football team. Ruiz had been to a few of their games over the last four years, very few considering his schedule, but he discerned Zoe's interest in the young man went beyond his talents to catch a pigskin.

Jerome whispered into Kit's ear, the woman's eyes never giving away the story. Afterward, Jerome rushed off. Kit stepped close, her fingers grazing Ruiz's swollen cheek.

"Get as comfortable as you can, Captain," she whispered. "This will be over soon."

The sound of her heels echoed in the distance as she walked away. Ruiz took a deep breath, pushing against the ropes along his wrists and ankles. He screamed as he struggled for some slack. None came.

"Great."

His sides ached, a result of the assault from kids less than half his age. He could feel the bruises forming up and down his torso. The wind chilled him and silenced the heat rising up his right arm. He closed his eyes and waited.

"Need a hand?"

"Christ!" Ruiz screamed at the sudden voice.

A hand fell on the rope. Then Ruiz saw the yellow eyes of Erik Dobson and quieted himself.

"A little louder, Captain," Dobson said. "Get us both caught."

"What the hell are you doing here, Dobson?"

Dobson worked the ropes, navigating quickly through the knots. "Scoring some drugs."

"Are you serious?" Ruiz asked, his eyes flaring.

The ropes fell away and Dobson pulled the bruised officer to his feet.

"No," Dobson said. "I thought the moment required some levity."

"You thought wrong." Ruiz pulled away.

"Fine. After you left my office, doubting every word I said—don't deny it—I decided to look into the crimes you were ready to pin on me. To prove my innocence. Need more proof?"

Ruiz hesitated. There were other explanations. Dobson had to be involved…yet everything screamed otherwise.

He heard steps behind them growing closer.

He swallowed his unfounded suspicions. "No. Just the exit."

"Good," Dobson said. "This way."

Dobson led him to the left, down a series of corridors and connecting caves. Kit and her goons had taken the right-hand route, deeper into the large structure carved into the hills south of the docks. At the end of the corridor, with the exit in sight, Ruiz stopped.

"Ruiz, we need to—"

"Fly the coop?"

Dobson grinned. "I wasn't going to make the joke."

"You go ahead."

"Are you the one kidding now?"

Ruiz sighed. "I wish I was."

Before Ruiz could call for help, he needed to know the manpower involved. Sig Tau's presence seemed limited, the pattern too obvious if they were the only players involved. And there was the question of Kit. She acted as if he had come for her, targeted her specifically, yet Ruiz knew nothing about her upon his arrival.

"Go." Ruiz pointed to the exit. Dobson's life was still at risk, something he didn't need. He felt guilty enough. The confused professor paused, then nodded. He slipped into an abandoned field outside of the cave's mouth. Ruiz watched him depart before racing back through the structure.

He passed his broken restraints, the chair fallen on its side. The waves rushed harder against the shore, water carried along the night wind spraying him. Ruiz kept running, deeper into the caves. Eventually the darkness gave way to flood lamps set up along the floor.

Crates filled the largest of the caves. A number of them remained open, trinkets and cash in full view—the profits from their thefts. Ruiz reached for a closed lid when a voice stopped him.

"Slipped your bonds yet stayed?" Kit called. "Curious."

"This is all you, isn't it?"

"Who did you think?" she said, sauntering closer. Ruiz kept the crate between them, quietly cursing his ignorance. Their run-in at the campus shop was coincidence and nothing more but she recognized it as something else. She believed her operation was in danger. The party, Zoe's presence, was planned in retribution. Instead of protecting his daughter, he had placed her in the center of things.

"With help," Ruiz spat. "Your boy toys at Sig Tau?"

"And a dozen other fraternities."

"Dealing drugs and robbing kids blind."

"Beer isn't cheap. Not in the quantities necessary to keep my boys happy."

"For what? What does this get you exactly?"

Kit ran her fingers over the crates. "For now? Little. But I'm trying to make this place a home, the last one left to me. It takes a village to keep the queen content."

"Your village deserted you."

She smiled. "They work for my pleasure. Just like they will hunt down the man that helped release you. He'll be found and punished. Like your daughter."

"Don't even think about it," Ruiz said, wishing he had his gun. Something to work with. The growing confidence behind her black eyes unnerved him.

"Any repercussions fall on you." Kit circled the crate between them. "I warned her to stay out of my affairs. My fun. I didn't mean for her to send a poorly prepared proxy."

"Who?"

Kit bared her teeth, small fangs growing on the sides. Her nostrils flared. "You smell of her touch. The stone's touch."

The stone. "Soriya?"

"We didn't share names though she knew mine." The young woman with the scarlet hair changed before his eyes. When she rounded the crate's corner she was no longer a woman at all, but a man, six inches taller than the petite redhead. Black eyes remained, as did the fangs. Another change happened as smoothly—this time the man became a young girl with pigtails. As she stepped in front of Ruiz, she was no longer any of them.

Before Ruiz stood a fox.

"What the hell?"

The fox snarled and pounced at the man. Ruiz fell, the weight of the beast crushing his chest. The creature snapped its wide jaws at him, its breath hot.

"I won't give this up," she hissed. "I have been hunted and chased by you and your growing shadow over the city. You surround everything now, slowly tying the noose around us all. This is my last chance, my final stand, and I will not give it up."

"Get the hell off me!" he tried to shout, constricted by the weight of her paws.

"I have lived for centuries. Sat in luxury, surrounded by devotees. And to be reduced to this?" The fox snapped again and Ruiz's head fell hard against the cave floor to avoid her fangs. "But I will survive. You can have your war out there. When the dust settles, I will still be here."

"Doubtful."

Black eyes widened and the salivating power behind her jaws went slack. Ruiz peered down to see a blade of silver jutting through her neck, blood pooling over his shirt then spreading along the cave floor. Kit fought to speak before collapsing to the side of her captive. She didn't move again.

Julian Harvey stood in front of Ruiz, his face triumphant. He extended his free hand. Blood dripped from the silver blade in his other. Ruiz hesitated, the look of satisfaction on Harvey's face startling him.

"Thanks for the help, kid," Harvey said, grinning at his kill. "I couldn't have done it without you."

CHAPTER EIGHT

Four hours of sleep and a change of clothes ushered in a new day for Ruiz. And, he hoped, the end of a nightmare.

Having just knocked, Ruiz stood outside the door to the second floor corner office, his hands shaking. The metal slab eased open, exposing yellow eyes within.

"Captain," Dobson yelled, nearly falling off his chair. He rushed to the end of his desk, waving the exhausted man into the cramped space. "I was hoping you would stop by. After you went back I was concerned."

"I noticed." Ruiz grinned, rubbing his neck. He could still feel the heat of the fox's breath. Only her blood felt hotter, still coating his skin even after an hour-long shower. "I didn't think the campus had that much security on call."

They surrounded the scene minutes after it ended. From every angle, down every street surrounding the frat house and others of its ilk, in a six-block radius. Arrests were made; members of each house pulled in for questioning as more crates were discovered. Stolen goods, drugs, cash. The band of thieves circulating the campus was broken in a single night.

Ruiz kept Harvey out of the reports, content to take the credit and the blame for the night's events. When asked about the dead fox at his feet and the knife beside her, Ruiz barely recalled the lie of it all, telling them he found the blade resting on an unopened crate. How a fox found its way into the city in the first place, let alone the caves, remained a mystery never to be explained. Animal control handled her disposal.

Medical personnel checked out Ruiz, bandaging his torso and the growing rainbow along his skin. He ignored their recommendation for a checkup at the hospital. Too much time had been spent in the white anti-septic wings lately.

A long night, but it was over—thanks to Erik Dobson.

"I can be very persuasive," the professor said.

"I remember." Dobson's grin faded and Ruiz waved the comment away. "Sorry."

"Don't be. We all carry our pasts."

Ruiz shook his head. "Not at the expense of our future. You've done well for yourself, Dobson."

"Erik."

"Erik." Ruiz laughed, reaching out with his left hand.

"What's this?"

"A thank you."

Dobson took the hand and shook. His yellow eyes were soft under the morning light. "Not necessary. I was simply returning the favor."

Ruiz nodded, quickly excusing himself from the office and the man from his past. He wanted to go home, to forget about the last twenty-four hours. The guilt over his decisions, his need to protect his family, had caused nothing but distance with his daughter—distance he had yet to resolve. If he could at this point.

He tried to call Zoe, but each attempt went unanswered. He'd screwed up. He didn't trust her enough to see the truth. She needed to be here. Away from him. Away from his control and his safety net. To find her own path in the dark.

"Going to keep an eye on him?"

Harvey waited at the top of the stairs, appearing well rested and fresh. A finely pressed plaid shirt and khaki pants. A clean shaven face tucked under his signature fedora. As if he hadn't murdered someone, or *something*, hours earlier.

"Isn't that what you do now?" Ruiz asked. He sidestepped the old man, heading briskly down the flight of stairs.

"It's only natural," Harvey said, following close. "He put you through hell that night."

"A long time ago. He's changed. We all have."

Harvey held up his hands. "Now I know you're steamed about—"

"Steamed?" Ruiz barked. He took a deep breath, pulling Harvey away from the growing crowd on the first floor of Crispin Hall. "You used me as bait."

Harvey smiled. "No one forced you to charge in there, Ruiz."

The truth: This was his call—all of it. It didn't make it any easier to swallow.

"What was she?"

"Kitsune," Harvey said, straightening his collar. "Trickster god or some such. Ran into your little vigilante friend a couple years back in the coves. I've been tracking her since."

"Hunting her down," Ruiz corrected. She was afraid. At the end, not just with the blade in her throat, but before. She had feared the shadows growing around her.

"Things are more dangerous than ever, Ruiz."

"Dammit, Harvey. You're eighty-two."

"And not dead yet."

Ruiz shook his head. "You will be if you keep this up."

"I've seen too much to walk away." His eyes were cold—watching everyone around them, sizing them up. Ruiz wondered what he saw that couldn't be seen by everyone else. And why that made him so uneasy. "I can't bury my head in the sand and watch Portents get swallowed up by these things."

"That's not your job."

"No," he snapped. "It was yours. And you walked away. But there's no walking away from what's coming, Ruiz."

"Is that a threat?"

"An invitation," Harvey said. He held out his hand.

Ruiz batted it aside. "Not a chance in hell."

Harvey hesitated then let the hand fall. "We'll see."

Across the wide hall Ruiz noticed Zoe rushing through a growing crowd. He turned away from Harvey, putting the man behind him like the previous night. "Goodbye, Harvey."

"Take care of yourself, kid."

Ruiz heard the words of his former partner, the man who taught him about the city—the *true* city—and wished they wouldn't haunt him the rest of the day. Or longer. But they would. Harvey had changed. More than the simple passing of time. There was something darker in him.

Harvey used him. Trussed him up and served him on a platter for the Kitsune to snatch up. What if he hadn't shown up when he did? Would he have cared if he had found Ruiz dead as long as the Kitsune followed swiftly? Ruiz feared the answer.

When did trust become an issue for him? When did a man like Dobson earn more trust than a fellow officer—a man he worked with for years and kept in touch with for decades following their tour of duty together?

More than that, he hated not knowing what was happening in his city. He did walk away, putting his family first for a change. Part of him knew that the bill was coming for that decision. Soon.

"Zoe," he called, stopping her short of the exit.

"Dad," she whispered, her head falling to her chest.

"Now I know you're still upset with me—"

"Upset doesn't even touch how I feel." Her eyes still held tears from the night before, red and puffy. She looked tired. *Had she slept?*

"I know."

"I can't believe you would show up like that out of the blue. Like this, right now, and just—"

"I'm sorry."

She stopped, brow furrowed. "Wait. What?"

"You heard me," Ruiz replied. The pair shuffled to a quieter corner of the hall, the crowds rushing for their next class.

"I've never heard it before. Not from you."

"I was wrong, okay? Not about how you shouldn't have been at that frat house or the crimes going on around campus or—"

"Dad," Zoe said. "You're ruining the moment."

Ruiz sighed. "I should have trusted you. I do trust you, Zoe. Sometimes, when you're a parent—"

"Or a cop."

"It's hard to let things go."

"So what now?"

Ruiz hesitated, looking across the hall. Harvey stood at the door, watching them. Always watching. He held out his hand and Zoe took it, the two of them heading in the other direction.

"You trust me to always be there for you and I'll trust you to never ever leave your dorm room again."

"*Dad,*" she said, drawing out the word in a whine.

He laughed. "Breakfast then. On me."

"And an explanation for why you smell like a sewer?"

Her eyes caught his and he nodded, unwilling to lose the moment, to lose her and the time they had left. No more great divides.

"It was a long night."

They walked west, away from the rising sun, and he told her the truth of the night—while holding back the truth of the longer ones to come.

THE APARTMENT

CHAPTER ONE

The mirror squeaked, water droplets running toward the frame. Small drips collected at her fingertips and fell to the tile below. The towel was wrapped delicately around her hair, tied in a knot against the back of her neck.

Chrissy Williams reached for her oversized T-shirt then paused. A thin smirk passed over her face. The shirt fell into the small pool beside the deep tub and another towel circled her waist, tucked efficiently along her breasts, cleavage on full display.

Her bare feet skirted along the dimly lit hallway. She took her time, savoring the trip. Wallpaper stretched the length of the corridor, a vertical stripe pattern of green and tan illuminated by the moonlight.

The living room took up the right half of the apartment. The sliding door on the far side led to a balcony with a view of downtown Portents and the obsidian tower at its heart. Picture perfect except for the snoring figure sprawled on the couch.

Chrissy rolled her eyes, watching drool run from her friend's lips to the armrest. She hoped for more privacy, but nothing was going to stand in her way. She shook off the drunk's presence, returning to the end of the hall, her stark silhouette hugging the frame.

Josef put down his book, his eyes wide at the sight of his half-naked girlfriend of three years. He licked his lips and her grin grew, gauging his reaction from head to toe.

"Is Cheryl really couching it tonight?" Chrissy asked, offering a fake pout.

"Did you see her pounding shots like they were candy?"

Chrissy laughed. They all had done their share of imbibing today. It had been a welcome celebration from moving the collective crap the couple had accumulated in their twenty-six years of life. Friends on both sides brought food and drinks: greasy pizza and barbecue wings, red wine and shots of Jäger. None of it was as satisfying as the envious looks from everyone in the room, especially from the drunk down the hall.

"They did taste like candy," Chrissy admitted, sauntering into the room.

"*You* taste like candy," Josef replied. He reached for her, pulling her close. Small pecks lined her arm, his fingers dancing along the towel.

"Smooth," Chrissy said, feeling the chill of each touch. "I like it."

Josef stopped and smiled. "Not as much as the shower though."

"Oh. My. God. The water pressure is amazing."

"For the entire thirty-five minutes?"

"Miss me?"

Josef pointed to the nightstand on the other side of the bed. "Your mother did."

Chrissy sighed, circling the bed. She tucked the towel in once more, then worked on removing the one around her hair. Satisfied it had done its job, she patted her blond locks and tossed the thick blue towel into the corner. She picked up her phone, swiping the screen for a list of notifications.

Three missed calls and a text. "She was just here."

"Don't need to tell me," Josef said.

Chrissy huffed, dropping the phone on the table without replying to the messages. "And did you see that top she was wearing? Does she think a divorce somehow resets the clock by three decades?"

"Again, don't need to tell me. I can still feel her lipstick on my cheek."

"Every male at the party shares that sentiment. Except—"

"Your dad." Josef nodded. "Lucky bastard."

Chrissy saw him as heartbroken and alone, content with his stoicism and solitude. Unless it related to his daughter. With her, he was fire and brimstone. God forbid he didn't have an opinion on everything when it came to his pride and joy.

"He asked where your bed was," Chrissy said. "Welcome to the twenty-first century, Dad."

Josef leaned close, warm breath along her neck. "And you told him—?"

"The couch." Chrissy smiled. "Have fun with Cheryl."

"Thanks." He inched closer, hands joining his lips on her cooling skin. "Seriously, though. Regrets?"

"None. Great guy. Great place." The curtains moved in the autumn breeze. Portents swirled under a dark cloud and the soft patter of rain tapped along the glass. "Definitely a great place."

"No way should it have been available."

His kisses lingered, his body swallowing her. Her breath caught, the words a whisper. "Not at that price. We can actually afford it."

"It's perfect," Josef said, nibbling her ear. "Like you."

Chrissy pulled away and stood. "You beat me to it."

"Make it up to me."

"Gladly."

The towel fell to the floor and Josef embraced her. She kissed him hard, forcing him against the mattress. He struggled under her to remove his shirt. She grabbed his wrists and forced him down, straddling his waist.

A growl erupted behind them and Chrissy stopped kissing Josef, worry replacing passion. "You hear that?"

"I heard lots of things," Josef said. His hands ran down her tanned skin, hesitating along each curve. "All good things, by the way."

"Cheryl?"

"Is sleeping," he cooed, pulling her down.

"I thought—"

"Old building," he whispered. "Thin walls."

She hesitated, his kisses running along her neck. "I guess."

He grinned. "Come here."

Her eyes closed, the sweetness of his lips soothing her. His body was a furnace, warming her cool skin. Looking over her lover, she was surprised by the sight of her breath in the air, out of place with the fifty-degree weather of early autumn evenings.

Like the fear on Josef's face. "Chrissy…"

"What?" She followed his gaze, turning for the door. "What is—?"

The walls shifted in the shadows, like a wave rippling through the wallpaper dotting every inch of space. The waves lessened and took form. Hands reached from the depths of the walls—reaching for them.

In the room's center, they converged on a single figure. He emerged from the shadows, glowing in a soft ethereal hue. His foot shambled along the creaking floor, the sound echoing in their minds as fear blanketed them. The figure sneered; the right side of his face melted like wax from a candle.

Chrissy fell beside her boyfriend, covering her naked body with her hands. She joined Josef in his scream.

"Let's not end the fun already." The ghostly visage stood at the foot of the bed with a vast grin. "We were enjoying the show."

CHAPTER TWO

Six weeks—that was all it took. Six weeks of motels and living out of the single duffel bag she owned, of restaurant fare and an empty water bottle for unlimited refills. Her pocketbook could handle the load; the IDs and accounts left by Mentor were more than enough to cover the cost as it always had, but her stomach told another tale.

Luckily, fate stepped in.

Soriya Greystone paced through the living area of the eleventh floor apartment at the Golden Palisades complex. A false grin rested on her lips, matching her slow gait. Her nails were painted, her pants pressed. Her hair was tied back. She kept the pink ribbon and the stone in a small purse that matched the blouse and pantsuit combination she purchased on her way over.

And planned to return on the way back to her current living arrangements.

Appearances were a necessity, unfortunately. No one wanted to rent a space to someone wearing torn jeans and a blouse with blood stains along the sleeves. Truly a sad state of affairs, considering her entire wardrobe met those standards.

Golden Palisades spoke of a better, more dignified way to live. The complex took up the block along Sardella and Terrace, a stone's throw from Saint Sebastian's Church in the heart of downtown Portents. Not a Walker original, like the church, though the Palisades still bore the early twentieth-century construction that marked the area.

Decorative arches and extensive latticework adorned all sides. Balconies were added decades after, opening up the space with wider sliding glass doors instead of old crank-style windows. Fifteen floors holding a dozen apartments on each level made it one of the prime spaces of real estate on the market. And one of the most expensive.

Until now.

Soriya stopped to admire the view, her smile turning genuine for a moment. Sunlight beamed through the glass, reflecting a bright brilliance of Portents rarely seen from below. The obsidian tower at the heart of downtown glowed with renewal at the arrival of the midday sun.

The young man behind her caught the smile reflected in the glass and cleared his throat. "Two bedrooms. Nine hundred square feet. Deep tub."

Soriya turned, curious.

The young super, or Glenn as he preferred with a puff of his flabby chest, shrugged. "I've heard the ladies enjoy the tub. And the view, of course."

Superficial. Every showcased detail. No one needed living space beyond their means. Nine hundred square feet? She owned *a bag*. What the hell would she do with the other 850 square feet? The tub sounded fantastic, though. Maybe she was more normal than she realized.

"It's perfect," Soriya said, her voice higher than normal. Perky tended to reflect better with people, although she found it tiresome. "But come on, there's no way that's the rent. Unless you charge by the week. Do you charge by the week? Is that a thing?"

Glenn turned away, his cheeks flush. The paperwork sat on the kitchen island. He thumbed through it.

"No," he said. "No, that's the rent. Monthly and everything. The manager…he's been offering a special lately."

Outside, residents walked by, glancing at the potential tenant to join their ranks. Mutters trailed their stares, conversations with loved ones and friends. Dozens in a matter of minutes. Glenn played with the paperclip on the edge of the lease.

Life in the city. Yet instead of filling her with pride at joining the community, why was dread the first emotion to crop up?

"Nice guy, the manager?" she asked, shaking away the thoughts.

The young man needling the lease rolled his eyes then caught himself. "He's…he just doesn't like empty units."

"Keeps you busy, at least."

"You have no…"

He stopped at the arrival of a woman in the doorway. Soriya offered a wave, one that was left unreturned. The new middle-aged visitor had crossed arms and a stern look.

The young man lowered his voice as he approached her. "I know. I am working on it. I will be there soon."

"You told me—"

"New neighbor, hopefully," he interrupted her, pointing to the waiting Soriya. The potential renter's awkward smile did not merit a like-minded response. "The boys will like her, I think."

The woman huffed and turned for her door across the hall. It opened quickly and slammed with a booming echo. Glenn shuddered at the sound, closing his eyes tight to wipe it from the record.

"The boys?" Soriya asked.

"Couple of kids," he said, shutting the door to avoid more interruptions. "Good kids. It's a good building too. Friendly faces."

Nodding, Soriya paced the room once more. Creaks came from above. "How about the people upstairs? Heavy walkers?"

"12-A?" Glenn choked, eyes bulging. Once flush, his cheeks now ran deep red, bordering on a purple hue. "That one… Well, it's empty at the moment. Wasn't right for the last couple, I guess. Last few actually." He laughed, shrugging. "Picky people, right?"

"I thought I heard—"

"Probably from the hall," he answered. He held tight to the lease paperwork, his nervous smile spread wide. "Sound travels funny in these old walls. Especially at night."

Soriya nodded, knowing exactly what he meant. "If upstairs is free, maybe I should take a look. I'm sure the view is even better."

"Oh!" he shouted before pulling in a deep breath. "I…I would love to show it to you but…it's being renovated. The last tenants may not have stayed long but the mess they left…"

"I see."

The young man's sweat ran in thick globs from his thinning hair down his neck. His concern was for more than losing a potential renter. It was at her discovery of the apartment on the twelfth floor—and the reason Soriya Greystone had arrived in the first place.

It started with cold spots and frost on the windows at the peak of summer. Closing doors and slamming cupboards in the kitchen. Small, unexplained shifts in the periphery, like the walls were moving. Disturbances frequent enough to cause unease among the apartment's tenants, so much so that they abandoned the place. But that was only the beginning. Resident after resident had been driven from the unit.

Then three people went missing. A young couple and their friend vanished without a trace from apartment 12-A after throwing a welcome bash. Soriya learned about the incident through a family friend, and this was only because she found herself seated at the adjacent table one night—a rare benefit from her eating out for every meal over the six weeks.

Plenty of reason existed for the disappearance. None felt true to Soriya. None could be, not with what she knew at stake. The fluctuations in the Bypass continued to increase, even with her presence in the city ramped to full time. Fluctuations opened doors, ones that needed to stay closed.

For everyone's sake.

"Listen…"

Glenn stopped her, his hand dabbing the sweat deeper in his scalp. "Hey, if you need time to think about it, there is no rush and we—"

Her gaze inched up to the apartment above. There was no leaving. Not yet. She smiled to the nervous young man.

"With a view like this? Where do I sign?"

CHAPTER THREE

Davis Sirnow was alone.

His parents tried to be there for him, to be involved and take an interest. At first, all parents do. Like most they reached a tipping point, a moment where their own lives took priority.

Davis' father, Richard, worked in accounting—a top-level associate at a local firm, though the way he spoke made it seem he was lower than his business card stated. The crap flowed downstream yet ended at his desk, which he promptly brought home to share with his family. Or not share, as the silence at meals became more commonplace.

His wife, Heather, was an investment banker. More numbers. More facts. All leading to a very analytically minded eldest son, Davis. One that became cold and jaded due to his stolen youth.

His younger brother, Kevin, was the opposite. He reveled in his youth. Nine years old and at home with the world of superheroes and the fantastic. He soared around the eleventh-floor apartment at the Golden Palisades complex wearing a Superman cape more often than not. Action figures were his best friends and the stories within their play were a seeming endless display of possibilities.

It made Davis sick.

Watching his brother lose himself in fantasy, forget about the problems plaguing the world around them, filled Davis with anger. His own childhood was lost with his parents' innocence. Why should Kevin get the opportunity at one?

And who made Davis his brother's keeper? His parents left them alone for hours daily, making the elder sibling strangled with the chore of handling his brother. Their parents used work as an excuse, although the truth was obvious to Davis: They didn't like having kids or what their darling sons had done to them over time.

Davis sat in front of the television, his cold pizza on a paper plate—no cleanup necessary—resting on the couch armrest. A woman wailed on screen, running away from a masked murderer with an over-the-top machete and a penchant to move excruciatingly slow after his intended target. Just another movie marathon, one that held no interest for the young man. Its purpose was twofold: to kill time, and—even more important—to keep Davis from having to interact with his brother.

Kevin didn't mind most of the time. He existed in his own world. After a slice of pizza and a can of Crush, Kevin zipped around the apartment, arms outstretched in flight. Superman flew beside him, Batman caught in his other hand. Chasing criminals. Saving people.

No one was coming to save Davis from his own misery, though.

"Are you really going to sit there all night?" Kevin finally asked, as the latest film—the term applied loosely—ended. It was the only time words passed between them over the course of the never-ending night.

Davis appreciated the silence. He would have appreciated it more if he didn't have to see the kid scooting around in his superhero duds or have to share a room with the four-color magazines filling every corner of open space.

"I think I might," Davis said as the opening credits on the next movie began.

Kevin jumped in front of the screen. "Mom said you have to play with me."

"She says a lot of things," Davis said, looking around his brother to the screen. They needed a bigger television to avoid this problem. "Suggestions mostly."

"Are not."

Davis sighed and turned off the movie. "Definitely are. Besides, how much longer are you going to play with these things? Superheroes are for babies."

The pizza plopped on the plate and Davis skirted from the couch. Kevin backed away, unsure of his brother's intentions. They never could get a read on each other. No connection, not even after nine years of sharing the same limited space offered by their parents.

Davis snatched Superman from his younger brother. Kevin tried to grab it, pushed away with little effort. "Hey! What are you...?"

Davis ignored his obvious question, heading for the door and the silence of the hallway. He stopped at the landing, staring down the winding stairwell. Superman dangled between his fingers. The twelve-year-old waited for his brother to arrive, panic in his eyes.

"Davis, don't!"

"Superheroes aren't real, Kevin."

The Superman dropped, and both boys watched the action figure crash and shatter outside the lobby.

Davis smiled. "See? Can't even fly."

"You jerk! I'm telling."

"You usually do." Davis rolled his eyes. "Fine. Want to play?"

"You mean it?" Kevin held up the lone Batman figure.

"No way."

Kevin's eyes fell, disheartened. "Then what?"

Davis waved him to the stairs leading up to the twelfth floor. "A little exploration. In apartment 12-A."

Kevin shook his head. "No."

"Kev..."

"It's... I don't think we should."

Davis circled around his brother, his hands falling on his shoulders. Slowly he coaxed him up the steps, leaving their apartment door slightly open for the few minutes they would be away. At first Kevin resisted, but was easily overcome by his older brother.

"You don't believe the stories about that place, do you?"

Their parents shared them enough, typically while talking about the money the landlord was losing with the empty apartment above. Money was what it all boiled down to in their eyes. Not to the young man of nine listening to the other details filtering through. To him it was about noises in the emptiness, about the walls shifting like a roiling wave along the wallpaper in every façade of every unit in the complex.

Then came the screams—after a welcome party for the new tenants. Davis' father had yelled at them to quiet down. He had been trying to catch up on work, forgetting his promise to take Kevin, and by extension Davis, to the movies. By that night the tenants were gone, their screams the only reminder of their presence in the building.

"Mom says—"

Davis continued to prod his brother along. "What Mom doesn't know can't hurt her. Or are you scared?"

"I'm not."

"Not how it seems," Davis said. "But that's fine. I'll just go back to my movie and—"

Davis stopped at the bottom step, watching his brother's chin fall to his chest. "All right. I'll go."

"I knew you were the brave one," Davis said. He ran up the stairs to the twelfth floor, Kevin following along in defeat.

They stopped in front of the door, the large 12-A in its center.

"It's just an empty apartment, Kev. What's the worst that could happen?"

CHAPTER FOUR

"Three hundred sixty-seven…"

The tennis ball bounced against the ceiling then back into Soriya Greystone's waiting palm. She squeezed, watching the shadowy circle grow darker along the otherwise white ceiling. A sigh escaped her, interrupting the slow ticking of the clock.

"Three hundred sixty-eight…"

How do people live like this?

Sure, work was a distraction. For some, the only thing that mattered in life. But even still, hours were spent in the domicile every day. And what about the weekends? What the hell did people do with their time?

She finished reading her sixth book on the week, ran for her daily ten miles, and sorted her closet for optimum space—she didn't own much. Night couldn't come fast enough.

"Three hundred sixty-nine…"

Two weeks at the apartment and not a single connection. Not a hello on the stairs or a *how ya doing* from the kids across the hall. Everything seemed strange to her, foreign. Soriya wondered if it would always be that way or if she wasn't trying hard enough. Hell, was she trying at all?

They were nervous. She could tell that right away looking at each of them. Something in the building made them nervous. Maybe it was the way everyone stared at the apartment off the twelfth floor landing before rushing down the steps. Either way, their fear was palpable—like something was coming for them that they could not see or understand.

Soriya understood it well yet two weeks passed and not a blip from the Greystone. She circled the apartment every day but nothing jumped out. Nothing—except the feeling surrounding her. Something was waiting, just below the surface. But what?

Soriya squeezed the tennis ball and started to toss it once more before stopping short. A grunt escaped her lips and the ball flew across the wide living area for the kitchen across the way. It bounced off the sliding glass door to the balcony and rolled into the corner out of sight.

The young woman spun off the couch and stood. Her bare feet skidded along the carpet that needed to be vacuumed. First she had to buy a vacuum. *Where do you buy a vacuum?*

Another mystery, like the city outside. Soriya pressed against the glass, clicking the handle lock. The wind rushed in, blowing thick black strands out of her face. She closed her eyes. The temperatures continued to dip, autumn in full swing. Snow was right around the corner. But the view, that picturesque view, would remain to enjoy.

Saint Sebastian's Church sat to the east, its single bell's peal still powerful enough to clock in the new hour for most of downtown. Train whistles blew to the south out of Tolliver's Grove. The city was a living, breathing work of art at her fingertips.

Footfalls in the hall pulled her away from the city. Her city. The potential to connect, even for a brief moment, was too tempting for the new resident to the Palisades. Soriya opened the door as a pair rushed away from the twelfth floor landing.

"Are they working in there?" the older gentleman asked. The woman at his side, his wife by all appearances including the rock on her finger, followed close, her eyes at the upstairs apartment.

"Who knows? Place gives me the damn creeps."

Both fell silent at the arrival of Soriya in her doorway. She waved, and the couple reciprocated before continuing to race down the stairs.

"And hello to you too," Soriya muttered to the fleeing pair. She stopped at the landing, watching them rush, the sounds of their whispers fading with each floor. Then she peered up into the darkness of the twelfth floor.

Apartment 12-A.

Two weeks and nothing. No sign of anything strange occurring, though three people had gone missing from its confines. Soriya reached to the pouch at her side and released the stone within. It sat against her palm, a lifeless rock. She knew better—about the Greystone and the apartment above.

The real reason for her living in the building was not to connect, not to thrive, but to protect and serve as she always had. Everyone else above her own needs.

A scream reminded her of the importance of those values. Those lessons taught by the wise Mentor.

The scream was from someone young—a high-pitched wail that carried down the steps from the apartment off the landing.

"Apartment 12-A."

CHAPTER FIVE

The great thing about fear was its cumulative effect. Shock and awe worked well enough but failed to linger in the victim's eyes. But fear? Slow growing, building from within, possibly from the empty haunted apartment on the twelfth floor of the Golden Palisades? A fear like that would linger for a long time in Kevin Sirnow.

At least, his brother hoped as much.

Davis held the door to the hallway closet open only a crack. His smile filled the gap and then some. The rare attribute on his face pained his cheeks from inactivity over the years.

"Davis?" Kevin called, wandering through the empty living space. The rising moon offered streams of light through the open windows. And plenty of shadows. "This isn't funny. Where are you?"

Upon entering the forsaken apartment, Davis had broken away from his brother. He rushed ahead into the dark. That moment was all Davis needed to slip out of sight, leaving his brother to wander. Watching his fear take over with every step comforted Davis.

"Davis?"

"BOO!" He jumped out at the approaching Kevin, who screamed before falling back and slamming his head against the wall.

Kevin's scream shifted from fear to anger as he unloaded a punch on Davis' arm. "You jerk!"

Davis laughed, nursing his arm. Kevin held tight to his Batman action figure, leading them toward the door. "Oh, don't be such a baby, Kev. There's nothing to be scared of."

Kevin refused to glance at his older brother, continuing for the door.

"Oh, come on, Kev," Davis said.

Another voice joined them: "Yeah, Kev. Come on. Nothing scary here at all."

Batman fell from his brother's shaking hands, clanging along the tiled floor.

"Kevin?" Davis asked, his voice cracking. The fun of scaring his brother disappeared as a chill wind swirled through the apartment. "Who said that?"

Kevin didn't answer. Worse, couldn't answer. His eyes widened in terror, looking at his older brother.

"Me." A hand fell on Davis' shoulder. Then through it.

Davis tilted his head to see the glowing digits pass through his flesh. He followed them up the wispy arm to the ethereal eyes of the figure looming over them. Its left eye beamed with glee; the right appeared wider because there was no eyelid, though it was barely noticeable as the burned flesh down that half of his face took the boys' attention.

"HOLY SHIT," Davis sputtered back. His younger brother snatched his arm and dragged him down the corridor for a door that suddenly seemed miles away.

The spectral image in the apartment shook his head, his arms outstretched. "I thought we were playing! Weren't we having enough fun, kids?"

"What the hell?" Davis muttered.

Kevin was crying, and dribbles of liquid spilled down his pants.

Davis had done this, had caused this. *What the hell is wrong with me?*

Worse, what was wrong with apartment 12-A?

The walls shifted down the long stretch of hall. The wallpaper rippled, bleeding into itself like a wave. There were no such things as ghosts, as specters, as whatever the hell that thing was supposed to be. There couldn't be—could there?

"We have to run," Davis said, and his brother nodded his confirmation. "We have to—"

Davis fell, tripping on something from below. Looking back, he saw the object of his downfall. So did Kevin, who fought another scream.

It was a hand.

Reaching from the wall, the appendage pulled at the wallpaper, struggling to release itself. It was not alone. Dozens pulled at the walls around them, reaching and growing, moaning for another inch toward the boys.

Kevin yanked his brother to his feet. They fell into the closest wall and a face greeted them, transparent but its smile clear.

"*We* were having fun," the eyeless face said.

"Loads," another added to the chorus behind them.

"Run," Davis whispered, shoving his brother from the collapsing walls.

Kevin couldn't move, was unable to look away from the faces and hands reaching for them on all sides.

"Kevin, close your eyes. Hold my hand and run. Now."

Davis led them for the door. The moans from the walls chased after the pair, lost under his screams. He squeezed his brother's hand, pulling him along. He needed to save him, needed to forget his own idiocy and love his damn brother. If they could only reach the door, things would change. They had to change. *He* had to change.

"Hold it."

Davis skidded to a halt, slamming into the brick wall of a body before falling to the floor. His brother joined him, eyes still closed. Slowly, they opened and both boys stared up at the looming presence of a woman who hadn't been there seconds earlier.

"Not another one. It can't be another one." Davis shook his head in disbelief, leaping for the door behind the woman. She stopped him, gripping his collar and pulling him back.

"I said, hold it."

Her features, while heavily shadowed thanks to her dark complexion, made her appear old. Old, yet very much present in the apartment.

"You're real?" Kevin gasped, mirroring his older brother's thoughts.

The woman smirked, a hand on her hip. "I like to think so."

"Let us go, lady," Davis said. "Before they get us."

"Who?"

All three turned down the long passageway. The moans had silenced; the hands and faces reaching for them were absent. The emptiness returned as if nothing had happened.

"How?" Davis tried to ask. "They were—"

"Who was there?"

Kevin shuffled his feet. "The ghosts."

"Where?"

"Everywhere, lady," Davis yelled over her. "So let's get the hell out of here, please?"

She hesitated, then stepped aside. "Move it."

"Glad to," Davis replied with a scoff. He reached for the doorknob and twisted hard. Suddenly pizza and a crappy movie didn't sound so bad. Hell, playing with Kevin's action figures would have been a treat compared to the last few minutes.

The knob refused to turn.

"Um, lady?"

"What is it?"

"The knob. It's stuck."

She shifted next to him, pushing him away from the door for a better view. "I just used it. What are you…?"

The pair watched as the new arrival fought with the door. When pulling the handle failed, she kicked the oak, hoping to knock off the knob and free the door. Nothing worked.

"That can't be good," she muttered.

All looked to the growing shadows. Davis cursed his actions louder and louder in his mind.

"Now what?"

CHAPTER SIX

Soriya Greystone slammed her shoulder into the edge of the frame to snap the locking mechanism and release the large oak holding them in place. Nothing happened. The door wouldn't open.

Why the hell won't the door open?

"Dammit." Two weeks she had played tenant, waiting for this moment. Too late. Always too late. Now, the unit found new victims. Two boys, their lives pulled into the maelstrom.

She never should have left the place unattended. The second she signed the lease, she should have resettled in the mysteriously vacant apartment on the twelfth floor of the Golden Palisades and waited for the nightmare to start.

One last kick left her and she huffed, turning away from the stubborn door. "It's not opening."

The older boy's eyes flared and he rushed to take her place. "It has to."

She waited, letting him struggle and curse at the tarnished handle. "It's not. Let it go."

"Davis," the younger one called, unable to look from the darkness settling through the hallway. "What are we going to do?"

Davis let the door loose and moved for his brother. "I don't know, Kev."

Soriya shook her head. Where the hell were their parents? What were they thinking coming in here? Curiosity. She would have done the same had the circumstances been reversed. If she ever had the chance at a normal life, away from the danger and the drama that came with the true city of Portents.

Her hip vibrated; small flickers of light escaped the pouch tied to her belt. The stone reacted to the room around them. Stepping around the boys who did their best to tuck away from the walls, Soriya strode deeper into the apartment.

"Come on."

"Lady, are you nuts?"

Soriya didn't bother looking at the older sibling. She was busy catching the small shifts along her periphery, the rippling effect the two boys had witnessed in earnest before her arrival. It was subdued, muted since she joined the party. Not gone, however. Just waiting.

"Davis, maybe we should…"

"Not even be here," Soriya snapped, trying to lower their voices. "Let alone give me attitude about being stuck in here."

The kid inched closer, his fist clenched. "Davis," his younger brother whispered, holding him back.

"Don't, Kevin."

"But—"

"We'll be fine," Davis said, backing away to the door. "We don't need her help."

Kevin stepped between the two opposing forces. "Yes. We do."

"We don't know her."

"She's trying to stop this. She's—"

"Don't even say it." Davis shook his head. "No cape. No tights. Just attitude."

"She still is."

Soriya waved them deeper into the apartment. "Are you coming or not?"

She waited a moment as the younger of the two reached for his brother's hand. Davis sighed then joined them as they inched down the long hall.

"What's going on?" Davis asked in a low voice. "Can you tell us that much?"

"A door opened. I'm trying to close it."

"If this door gets us outta here, shouldn't we take it?"

"She doesn't mean a physical door," Kevin said, causing both to stop and turn. "Right?"

"Smart kid." Soriya smiled. They cleared the living room in a wide arc, circling the room to allow the stone at her hip time to lead them to the next room. The walls shimmered in the moonlight but remained silent. Soriya waved the pair on to their next destination. "Call it a rip, a tear, whatever you like. It's giving some very bad people a second chance."

"Why is it never the nice ghosts?"

Soriya wondered the same thing. For many years, the same thought helped her carry on when things were darkest. The idea that there was a way to return, a way to see those loved and lost again. Her parents. Mentor. Vlad. So many lost friends. All gone. Yet not totally, carried through eternity by the glowing orb at the center of her destiny. The Bypass.

Soriya shook her head. "The good ones don't need to come back. Not after seeing the other side."

They stopped at the edge of the back bedroom. Soriya listened to the hum increase in tone and intensity. She pulled the stone from the hand-woven pouch and held it out, the light brightening better than a flashlight.

"Anyone ever tell you how cheerful you are, lady?" Davis said with a sneer. "Thought you people were supposed to be funny?"

"You people?"

Davis shrugged. "You know. Banter. Quips. That crap."

"What is he talking about?" Soriya asked his brother.

Kevin reached down to a shadow on the floor and lifted the object at rest. She didn't recognize the character, but understood the implication offered by the cape, the costume, and the mask. "You're a hero, aren't you?"

Soriya blinked. "I'm…what I have to be."

She didn't need their hopes raised. Not without seeing a way out of the apartment, out of the danger that surrounded them. They entered the bedroom cautiously, circling the perimeter, maintaining a healthy distance from the walls. The light grew as they approached the left-hand wall.

"Here."

Davis appeared confused. "How can you——?"

Her fingers reached out. The boys tried to stop her, afraid of the hands and faces from their earlier encounter. The tips of her lengthy digits dabbed the wall. It splashed like a puddle at her touch, sending a ripple down the length in all directions.

"Whoa," Davis said in a quiet voice.

"It's a fluctuation in the Bypass." Soriya stared at the shifting wall. "A door into forever. It's causing rifts outside the chamber that holds it here. The rifts pop up, uncontrolled and neglected until someone finds them."

"Casper the less-than-friendly ghost," Davis answered.

Soriya grinned. For a moment she thought Loren was next to her. "Among others, I think."

Letting the stone act as her guide, Soriya peered deeper into the rift. Hidden from perception, the door opened before her. The Bypass made manifest outside the confines of the chamber concealed beneath the city streets. Every past and future side by side. All possibilities. All truth. And all right in front of her.

With it came a clear view of the world beyond the veil. Twin specks of light gazed back at her, watching the watcher. They held off, lost in the haze of forever but they were getting closer. As they neared, they took shape and color.

Eyes. Two of them, both of deep crimson.

"Evans." She pulled the stone away from the wall and her window into the world of the Bypass.

Kevin inched closer, clutching tight to his action figure. "Where are they? Why did they stop?"

"Me, I think," Soriya said. "They sense my presence, that there's something different about me."

"So do I." Kevin rapped Davis on the arm. "What?"

Soriya held out the stone, the light glowing on its surface. "This, kid. They sense this."

"A rock."

Kevin shook his head. "A stone."

Davis cocked his eyebrow. "What's the difference?"

"Hopefully enough to save your life so you can grow up and make more people miserable." Soriya moved closer to the rippling wall. "I just need—"

A chill enveloped the room, whipping around like a stiff breeze that encircled them. Soriya was pushed away from the boys as the presence took form behind them.

"I don't think so," the wispy figure sneered. His hands clasped the boys by the neck, its fingers pale but formed unlike the rest of him. Soriya, shocked by the sudden presence, realized the ghostly visage was growing stronger and would continue to with the gateway to the Bypass open.

"Help," Kevin cried, legs flailing as the figure lifted him from the ground.

"Get off!" Davis shouted, reaching for his brother.

The ghost grinned. "Greystone."

He knew her. He would, having been lost in the Bypass, probably from years of seeing her presence in the chamber. But this was something more. There was hate in his declaration, anger and seething rage at her moniker.

"I know you."

Recognition took longer than she cared to admit. The scarred and burnt flesh adorning the right side of his face didn't help. Nor did his ethereal form. It was his smile that clinched it, the grin he carried the moment they met until she carted him off to the police, the night she formally introduced herself to Detective Greg Loren.

"You should smile more. People don't smile anymore. No respect. It's rude. I dislike rudeness."

"The Kindly Killer." Walter Shriff. He murdered eight people four years earlier. A greeter at a big chain store that couldn't abide by the growing apathy people carried for their fellow man. So angry that it pushed him to the point of murdering those that didn't follow his particular code of civility. Rudeness, indeed.

"A horrible epithet. I'll do better next time."

"There won't be one." She raised the stone to the wall.

"That's right, uggo," Kevin said through gritted teeth. "She's a superhero."

"Stop saying that, Kev. It's embarrassing."

"Thanks for the confidence, kid."

Shriff tightened his hold on the boys. "Open the door, Greystone. Open it or they die."

She flinched, the stone pulsing in her hand. There was no telling how long it would take to close the door. A second? Three? How long would it take Shriff to kill the two innocents in the room?

Kevin's eyes pleaded. "You can't—"

"Yes, she can, Kevin," Davis yelled, trying to grab his brother without success. "She has to."

"Yes, she does," Shriff grinned. "Don't you, hero?"

"I'm no hero, Kevin," Soriya said, catching his disappointment. Then she lowered the stone. "All right, creep. You win."

CHAPTER SEVEN

Complications. Whenever she entered a room, she brought them in spades. From a simple exercise in closing a door that should never have opened, now two lives were in jeopardy. At least three had been lost before this night.

That was three too many for Soriya Greystone.

"Hurry. I feel like celebrating," Walter Shriff, the Kindly Killer sneered. His hands faded in color but kept their hold on the brothers' necks. The boys' eyes were wide, screaming pained looks from the strength of his grip. Both held more than that, though, for the dark-skinned heroine—disappointment.

Hands reached from the walls around the bedroom. The bubble connected to the Bypass was bursting, threatening to spill whatever rested near its edge back into the world. Starting with a murderer ready to add two more bodies to an already extensive tally.

Soriya hesitated at the gateway. The hair on her arms stood up. The door widened before her, the pair of crimson eyes within growing, almost willing their passage back into the city.

Not him. Never again.

"The kids go free first," Soriya said.

Shriff squeezed tighter, raising Davis and Kevin in front of him in a display of power. "Negotiations are closed, Greystone."

Placing the stone near the shifting wall of light, she shook her head. "Then so does the door."

Kevin choked, struggling for air. His fingers clawed at his captor's grip to no avail. Shriff's eyes thinned. "Don't. Even. Try. It."

"Kevin!" Davis yelled, kicking the air. His feet sailed through the translucent form of the Kindly Killer, unable to connect with anything solid. "Let him go, you ghostly douchebag!"

Shriff pulled Davis closer. "What do they teach kids these days?"

"Put them down! Now!"

Shriff refused, squeezing eagerly. Kevin's skin darkened, his eyes bulging from the struggle. Davis cried out but his words were lost in Soriya's thoughts. She lowered the stone and stepped away from the door.

"All right!" she shouted. "I'll do it! I will!"

She waited for a reaction, his grin confirming his intentions. The grip around Kevin's throat lessened and the boy sucked air in heaps to replenish his missing supply. Davis found the floor, his disgusted expression permanent.

"You can't..." Kevin wheezed.

"No choice, kid."

The young boy pleaded. "You're supposed to save us."

"She's not a hero, Kevin," Davis said, his eyes on the floor.

"No," Soriya answered. "No, I'm not. And neither are you two. Got it?"

Davis peered at her, confused. Her deep brown eyes flitted between the brothers and their captor.

"What?" Davis muttered, following the gaze to the Kindly Killer's solid feet.

"I'm only the first, Greystone. There are so many of us waiting. You won't believe the nightmares ready to greet you. And you've earned each one of them," Shriff said. "Now open it."

"You want it open?" Soriya asked, turning her back to him. "Fine."

The Greystone lit up along its surface, the heat from the rune rushing along her arms. The light burst from the surface of the wall and encompassed the room. Soriya fought to close her eyes but curiosity won out. It always did. There in the light were the twin crimson specks, widening with each glance, a sick and triumphant laughter in each glowing orb.

Hands reached from the other walls. Arms stretched forth, followed by feet and legs in all directions. Bodies pushed through the opening rift from beyond. How many killers stood among them? How many had she had a hand in putting down? *The nightmares waiting to return.*

Her thoughts dimmed to the cries from behind. Peering over her shoulder, Shriff glowed brighter than the stone. An expression of ecstasy slipped over his features, color returning to his limbs and the scars running down the right side of his face.

"My God," he exclaimed. "It feels… It feels!"

All watched his body return. He was once a whispering wind, but had now acquired flesh from the tips of his fingers still wrapped around the two brothers' necks all the way to his feet.

Soriya grinned. "Now."

Kevin and Davis raised their legs in unison then slammed down with all their strength on the closest foot of the Kindly Killer.

Shriff screamed, falling back. His hands fell from the boys' necks. Davis pulled Kevin close, hugging his younger sibling as if for the first time. Both turned from the surprised and pained face of Shriff to their savior.

"Run!" Soriya yelled over the pouring light behind her. Davis nodded, dragging Kevin out of the room and the stretching hands of innumerable souls for the hallway and the exit beyond.

Shriff found his balance, fists clenched at his sides. "That wasn't very kind of you."

"At least I'm smiling now, you bastard."

He stopped, the light fading from the stone. Cries of freedom silenced all around the apartment, limbs caught in the rippling walls. "What…what are you doing?"

Soriya cocked her head and raised the stone once more. "You wanted to feel something? You wanted back in the world? Hope you enjoyed it."

"NO!" Shriff raced toward the woman, reaching for the stone.

Lightning raged outside the downtown complex, sparking the night sky before screeching through the window. It caught Shriff in the back, his eyes pleading for another moment before they were gone with the rest of him. Ash on the floor.

Soriya crouched, taking a deep breath and closing her eyes. When she opened them again, Kevin and Davis stood in the doorway.

"Whoa," Kevin whispered.

Davis nodded. "Holy shit, lady."

"Watch your mouth," Soriya said. She stood and threw them a thin smile. "And it's Soriya, not lady."

She turned back to the rippling wall, light creeping in brighter. The door was still in place but not for much longer. If it fell, there would be nothing for her to do, no way to keep the rip contained and the souls in place within the Bypass chamber.

And those damn eyes…

"What are you doing?"

Soriya raised the stone, throwing every bit of energy into the weapon and leveling it on the wall. "What does it look like? I'm saving the day."

Soriya poured her will through the stone, the fluctuation shifting and fading. The color of the infinite filled her vision, the beauty of forever calling to her, welcoming her with open arms. Where she would always be greeted without question, connected to all that had come before and would come after. A place she would always belong. Where her parents resided. Where Mentor rested.

A perfect place.

Shaking her head, Soriya snapped her eyes shut. The stone took control, beaming brighter as the light from within the Bypass dimmed.

Screams echoed within the apartment, the death throes of the defeated. Shriff joined the chorus, adding to her satisfaction. The crimson eyes followed suit, from confident to terrified.

Then gone.
The door closed and light vanished from the room.

CHAPTER EIGHT

The grocery bag threatened to spill over in Soriya Greystone's hand. A loaf of wheat bread lay mashed in the middle, indicating the bagger would likely be stuck in training for the rest of his career. She could have asked for two bags. Instead, she let it all ride in one oversized haul. Not that she bought much—enough to last a day or two before a repeat trip, giving her something to do during the day, someplace to be, somewhere to connect.

Routine. That was what life was to most, wasn't it?

Soriya stopped at the corner of her apartment complex. The sun crested against the skyline, struggling for another minute to shine as the darkness streamed in from the east. Evan's Tower cast its shadow across the neighborhood, a black spear ticking down the seconds to night. Day versus night, shadows versus light. Two sides of the same coin. Constantly struggling for balance.

The fluctuations remained but diminished. Something was still coming but she had staved off one cataclysm. Another wouldn't be an issue, at least not for a while. She would find it and handle it, the same as before, without abandoning her new home.

Home. She started calling the apartment that in her mind the night after closing the door to the Bypass. She ordered appliances and furniture—minimal but essential. She shopped; she couldn't believe the amount of shopping required to maintain a place. How she had managed to miss this vital information during her time with Mentor astounded her.

Everything around her fell into a comfort zone: the shops, the people, the sounds and the smells of the neighborhood—her home, her place in the city. She considered herself *with* the city instead of apart from it. Connected, for the first time in her life.

Each step was slow and deliberate, savoring her surroundings. Kids played on the basketball court across the street. Couples screamed at each other, unwilling to close the windows for some privacy. The good and the bad.

Evening approached too quickly for her now. The work ahead would always be there, pushing her out into the night. Portents endured.

First there would be dinner. Some fresh salmon to fry up and lettuce to chop for a side salad. All by her hand. Protein bars and trail mix were the extent of her culinary abilities for so long. Now she owned pots and pans. Hell, she even considered purchasing a television.

Like a normal person. Soriya smiled at that sensation.

The cool metal of the door handle slipped into her grasp and she pulled hard. Before entering, she noticed a group approaching. She ducked out of the way, still holding the door, but gave them enough room.

"Thank you," Davis said, passing her with a smirk. One she reciprocated. Kevin followed close, a red and blue clad action figure in his grasp.

"You're welcome, Davis."

"Soriya."

His cheeks flushed at the glare from his mother and father. Both pulled him close, the older gentleman patting his eldest son proudly along his back.

"Something you want to tell us, Davis?" his mother asked loud enough for Soriya to hear.

"Leave him be," Davis' father replied. They stopped along the wide walkway, laughing. "Now where were we? Ah, yes, the tiebreaker for our movie pick. We have action for *moi*—the only true choice this evening, in my humble opinion."

"So noted," his mother grumbled.

"A delightful comedic romp for mother dearest. Blech."

"Hush," she said, slapping his arm.

"Or, and no surprise here, the superhero flick of the week from Kev. The choice stands before you, young Davis. What will it be?"

Davis cocked his head to his brother without hesitation. "I think we should see what Kevin wants to see."

His father stopped his celebratory victory dance in mid sashay. "Wait. What?"

"Are you sure, dear?" his mother said, equally surprised.

Davis spun on his heels, leading them away from the building for the off-street parking structure down the block. "Show's in thirty. Let's move it, people."

"You check his temp?" Davis' dad asked.

"No. But I will."

Kevin sidled up to his brother. "Thanks."

Davis put his arm around Kevin, giving him a slight squeeze. "Thank me if it's good. Now come on. Popcorn's on me."

Soriya smiled, watching the family disappear around the corner of the building. Together. Embracing life, one day at a time, without the worries of the future. Or the growing shadows of Portents.

Another tenant slipped through the open door and nodded to the young woman. She offered her own silent greeting then stepped inside, leaving the noise of the community behind.

But never gone.

She was part of them now. Part of the city. She heard every sound, caught every whiff of the humanity that surrounded her. Normalcy might elude her, now and forever, but that didn't mean she had to be alone.

And she wouldn't be. Not anymore.

BLACKMAIL

CHAPTER ONE

Samantha Myers needed a drink. Not one of those fruity drinks with a slice from some exotic fruit sitting on the lip. She dreamed of a slab of corned beef nestled between two hulking slices of rye bread and the darkest pint glass imaginable kind of drink—possibly in the shape of a boot.

It was Tuesday.

Not even an *I can't believe what a nightmare that Monday was* type of Tuesday. Paperwork had that effect on her. Dominating her schedule were reports from over a dozen closed cases from the last three weeks. Internal reviews blanketed the upcoming calendar month, as well as preliminary hearings and a court appearance or ten.

Reports were part of the job. Same with the rest. Most cases clearing her desk landed in the straightforward *I shot him because he stepped on my toe* pile. Open-and-shut *no excuses to your mother and say goodbye to your freedom for twenty to life* pile. Her favorite.

Of course, there were others. Like the kid with the porcupine shoots and the demonic ritual in Rose Riley Forest with the actual demon making an appearance. Those cases took a little more to explain—or fathom at all.

Loren went the other route. A lack of explanation to their superiors, or in his case, blatant lies on an official report. He never viewed them that way, though. To the unkempt detective slumped over his desk, the omission of fact in the final report saved the people of Portents the headache of knowing what the hell was actually going on around them.

Ironically, Myers hated the lie. It irked her, not being able to understand every little nuance that came with each case. The true city. She didn't understand much of Portents, including the man seated across from her in the cramped second floor office.

"Put it down."

Loren continued to type with a single finger—aggravating. How the man managed to work through one report let alone the stack on his desk astonished her, but it answered the question of his inability to find two minutes to shave his damn face daily. Myers closed the dossier and pushed it out of his reach.

"Myers," Loren said with a sigh.

"Come on." She pulled his coat from the hanger and tossed it to him. He caught it with his left hand, the move instinctive. His arm, while finally healed from his recent brush with death, was not used to the action and she caught the wince in his eyes. He hid it well, but it remained a lasting scar.

"I'm working," Loren muttered. He dropped the coat beside the desk and snagged the corner of the half finished dossier, sliding the folder back into place next to his keyboard.

"Our shift is over," Myers said. "There are beers with our names on them."

His typing grew louder, the single finger slamming against each key.

Myers sighed. "Fine. My name on them. You can have your snooty water with lemon. I'll even let you lecture me about the vile nature of alcohol.

A smiled cracked the surface. "Wish I could."

"You can." Myers slipped her coat on then leaned against the frame of their open door. "Major Crimes is celebrating. Huge bust in Lowtown. Might be in the millions. Who keeps that much cash on hand?"

"Drug dealers?"

"So it would seem."

"Tell them congrats for me."

Myers groaned. "You tell them. Let's go."

"Next time." She waited and Loren stopped working once more. "What?"

"Super secret work again?"

"Myers."

"Right," she said coldly. She pushed from the frame and stepped into the hall. "Next time."

She had seen it often since his return. The small asides, the quick tucking away of witness statements and crime scene photos. Things easily explained yet kept from her intentionally. She let it lie, giving him the time and space he needed, but after weeks of working together it remained.

Not that Myers didn't have her share hidden from sight. His reticence surprised her, though—especially with her work to win his trust during the Charon case—but he continued to keep things close and private.

She could have hacked his files, broken into his desk, and taken what she was after. Instead, she continued to test the waters, to try to bridge the gap naturally. Unfortunately, Loren mystified her on too many levels. And other parties were not as patient as she was.

She really needed that drink.

At the end of the hall, the elevator doors opened to two groups waiting to depart for the after-work party. Few bars remained open for the night shift crowd but there was always one willing to entertain the Central Precinct's best and brightest every night. The way Myers was feeling, a cab ride home looked promising.

Something caught her eye. A small envelope sat in her designated mail slot, a rarity despite her being a member of the team for months. As she reached for the letter a voice called, "You coming, Myers?"

The envelope slipped between her fingers and she turned to see Officer Juan Alvaro flagging her down. He wore a button-down, the sleeves rolled up. A large tattoo adorned his left arm, mostly obscured by his sleeve. Myers had never noticed it before. Or how nicely Alvaro cleaned up at the end of the day. His wife was a lucky lady.

"In a second." She lifted the letter. "Might be my check for a million bucks."

Alvaro laughed, tossing her a nod before departing for the parking garage.

She shared the laugh. Part of her was glad to have the company, glad the night crew's acceptance of her had gone smoothly. The other part, however, tended to voice its concerns louder. The worry that came with trying to prove herself time and time again. The part afraid the truth would eventually sneak out—that they would know the real Samantha Myers.

Confirmation came with the letter in her hands. She tore open the envelope and caught the thin sheet of notebook paper but a photo floated to the tile beneath her feet. Two words marked the single sheet of loose-leaf.

I KNOW.

Myers crooked her head. "So no check. But what the hell is this about?"

Crouching low, she retrieved the image from the floor. Myers held it in the corner, keeping her prints to a minimum.

The figure at the heart of the photo was a young man. Broad-shouldered, lean and muscular. Handsome without having to work at it. A natural beauty she remembered quite clearly. Like the young girl running beside him in the photo.

Samantha Myers at eight years old.

"Dad…"

CHAPTER TWO

They parked the Cadillac a block over and walked the rest of the way. Samantha Myers wore an elegant dress, hair clips adorning the front of her neatly layered black locks. She walked tall, her shoes flat and comfortable. Perfect for the task ahead.

Twelve years old yet she carried herself as a young lady in her early twenties. Bright smile and sharp looks at everyone they passed through the wrought iron gates of the estate. Cars lined the lengthy driveway, with more parked on the grass on either side. Myers held tight to her shoulder bag with one hand.

And her father's hand with the other.

Kenneth Myers was a god in her eyes. He could do no wrong. Since her mother ran out on them when she was just an infant, he had stood as the driving force in her life, always there for her, always pushing her to be better. Every lesson, every edict, was followed to the letter. She refused to let him down.

They stopped at the circle surrounding the entrance to the estate. The party within was boisterous, the music filling the air for miles. Lights blared in strobe colors as patrons raced in and out of the mansion at the center of the six-acre plot in Westchester County.

"Ready?" her father asked, squeezing her hand.

"I'm not sure." Myers pulled away, pressing against her dress to iron out imaginary wrinkles. Fear was never an answer but it was there. Everything they had spoken about over the last few weeks had built to this moment.

Kenneth knelt in front of her, hands falling lightly along her shoulders. Green eyes, sharp as emeralds, beamed at her. His strength rippled down his body into her.

"Deep breath," he said, leading by example. "In, then out. Again. What do we have?"

She smirked. "Control."

"Over…?"

"Myself," she said, remembering the lesson. "My heart rate. My confidence. My body."

"And by extension?"

"My world."

He nodded with a smile. Standing, he shifted aside, allowing her the full breadth of the home's entrance. "What do you see?"

She opened her eyes, removing all distracting thoughts. Cars pulled in slowly, dropping off passengers before heading to the impromptu lot growing at the estate's eastern side. The crowd was balanced between men and women, but some women were surprisingly young in comparison to their companions. The men fit a certain profile: white and heavyset.

A man argued with his wife at the edge of the steps. He wore an oversized coat, not his own, over a shirt and tie combo that had seen better days. The woman was as uncomfortable, with heels too large and a strapless dress she had to constantly pull up. Their argument paused with each passerby then continued.

"The couple arguing. Over money." The woman was furious, and the man sighed so loud Myers may have been standing right next to them instead of fifty yards away. The woman pulled at his hands and Myers saw his fingernails. Stained. His teeth matched. "No. He's smoking again. She didn't know."

"Are they the ones?"

"No." They had potential but they dressed up for the affair and clutched their tickets for all to see. This meant something to them—more than the formality it bore for the majority of the crowd. Social gatherings were more hassle than enjoyment for most.

The crowd parted at the approach of another vehicle. Something foreign. Ostentatious undersold the extent of its presence. A giant phallic symbol with a license plate on both ends.

"Him."

The man put the car in park. He stared at the young woman in the passenger seat then opened the door, eager to circle around and introduce her to the staring crowd. He was young, not quite fitting the mold.

He bashed his head against the doorframe, trying to escape from its clutches. Rubbing his forehead, he raced around the car and let his passenger out. She didn't bother to thank him.

A valet stepped over and the man dropped the keys in his hand without a glance. He was too busy staring at his date. She took out a small mirror, fixing her makeup. The crowd, once transfixed, moved away from them for the door.

"Why him?" Kenneth asked, trying to hide a grin.

"His date," Myers said. "The way he looks at her. Like he's never seen her before. He paid for her."

Her father nodded. "A distraction. Very good." He held out his hand. "Shall we?"

Kenneth set the pace, never rushing and never sauntering, always flowing toward the entrance. Neither looked at the target, yet both kept him in sight.

The woman continued to fix her makeup, the meter running on their date. He didn't mind; he remained enthusiastic at her presence, remained determined to have her at his side. He was so focused that he never noticed Kenneth brush along his backside.

The duo took the steps in stride, Kenneth sneaking the tickets from the pilfered wallet before dropping it in the bushes surrounding the railing. Myers fought a laugh, and her father shared in the excitement as they reached the door.

A burly man stood in wait, bored yet determined. "Invitations?"

Kenneth passed them along. "Lovely evening, isn't it?"

The employee failed to respond. He scanned the ticket for authenticity then did the same to the pair awaiting entry. "Is this…?"

"My daughter," he said, eyes never leaving the man at the door. "And family friend. If you please?"

Myers loved to watch him work, loved the control he took in every interaction, steering the conversation in his favor at all turns. Putting people on the defensive gave him an opening. It gave him leverage, especially with simple veiled threats mixed with good manners.

"Of course," the doorman said, briefly glancing through her bag before giving them access to the foyer. "Enjoy the party."

Myers stopped short in the home. She expected opulence, grandeur. It came with the family whose name adorned the mantel, one that owned several real estate enterprises throughout the state.

No amount of imagination matched what she found inside: chandeliers more expensive than entire homes, crystal in every vase, in every candle holder. Colors beamed in every direction, caught by every piece of furniture, spreading around them like a rainbow.

"Eyes sharp," her father whispered, prodding her forward. She closed her gaping mouth and followed him deeper into the home.

The ballroom ahead was their destination, filled with wealth and the people influencing every major decision in the state. They danced away the evening or spoke in low tones in dark corners. Myers watched them all, wondering what changes would come from this gathering.

"This way," Kenneth called, motioning for the stairs to the right. She nodded to a number of onlookers, mostly curious due to her age than anything else. At twelve she held little in the way of beauty—not the beauty the party members enjoyed, anyway.

They turned the corner at the top of the stairs to see a landing overlooking the festivities. Opposite the view, a number of doors lined the wall. Bedrooms and offices were tucked behind each one, half of which no doubt never saw any movement except for their daily cleaning by the staff.

Kenneth walked her to the edge, smiling at the oblivious crowd below. Myers joined him, watching the flashing lights swirl over the dancers. A sharp click snapped at her back.

"Dad." Her head tilted for the opening door behind them.

He reached into his pocket for his phone. "Smile."

"Hey," a man shouted upon seeing the pair at the landing. Kenneth continued to snap photos. Myers did her best to act oblivious as the muscle-bound security guard headed their way. "You can't be here."

A small boy followed the guard, the door closing and locking behind him. The boy, not much younger than Myers, stared at her, causing her cheeks to flush.

"I know, I know," Kenneth said, standing and holding his phone. "Just a quick photo."

"Doesn't matter," the guard said, showing them the stairs.

"Look," Kenneth muttered, passively resisting the pull back to the party. "I'm not much of a hand at it. This one is the budding photographer in the family."

Before the guard could continue, the young boy stepped forward. "It's all right, Cedric."

"Alex?"

Kenneth stepped up, seizing the name. "Alex? Alex Sumner? Wow. I remember when you were a wee thing. Time slips by. Right, angel?"

She took her cue immediately, beaming at the young boy. "Right, Daddy."

Alex stumbled for words before Cedric prodded him for the stairs. The upset guard peered back. "Enjoy your photo."

Her father understood the implication. "We'll be quick. Promise."

The moment they turned the corner at the stairs, Kenneth pulled his daughter close with a hug. "Good instincts."

"I thought so."

"Thirty seconds. Let's go."

Kenneth reached for her shoulder bag and unzipped the false bottom. He passed over a black mask that she promptly slipped over her head. Once he did the same, the two raced for the locked door. He removed from his pocket a small package wrapped in red ribbon and held it out for her.

A lock pick set.

"Ready?"

"For me?"

"It is your birthday, Sammy."

It was. Twelve years old. Practically an adult now and treated like one by her father. Her perfect father and his perfect smile, filling her with confidence. She took the lock pick, releasing the red ribbon to the floor.

"Twenty seconds."

"I'll take care of it," she said, setting to work on the door.

"I know you will."

She felt the instrument slide into place, the second half of the pick working on the latch. Exterior doors held much of the security for a residence. Interior locks were simple, even with the time constraints placed on her.

Control. Control your mind and your body and you control the world. Her father's lessons served as her eternal guidepost.

The lock clicked and Kenneth opened the door, pushing her inside. "Go, go…"

Inside sat a gaunt figure behind an impressive desk. Stacks of cash sprawled across the cherry tabletop. The man, surprised for only an instant, defiantly glared at the new arrivals.

"What is the meaning of this?"

Kenneth closed the door to the office, pointing to the open safe behind the seated figure. "Leave it open."

The man ignored the words, reaching for the safe. A loud click rang out. Kenneth held a pistol with a silencer attached to the barrel.

"Do it, Nicholas."

Pulling away from the safe, Nicholas Sumner raised his hands. A gold watch shone from his wrist, its cost displaying his status to all. He studied the pair carefully, trying to peel away their masks with nothing more than a thought. Then his eyes thinned.

"I know you."

"Dad?" She held open the handbag and he nodded.

"Fill it, honey," he said. "Fifteen seconds."

"Myers." The name echoed in the room. Nicholas snapped his fingers, their silence confirmation of his guess. "It is you, isn't it? You think for a second you can get away with this?"

"I believe I will. Yes."

Myers closed her eyes. The air snapped once then twice and Nicholas Sumner's dead body slid from the chair to the floor in a heap. Blood coated the gold shine of his watch, its face cracked from the fall. The young woman of twelve clutched a stack of hundred-dollar bills between her fingers, unable to move.

"Honey?"

She opened her eyes to her father stuffing bound bills into his pockets.

"The bag."

"But Dad…"

Kenneth ripped up his mask. He smiled at her. "Clock's against us, Sammy. Deep breaths."

Myers nodded, shoving the mound of currency into her bag before slapping it shut. He led her out of the office and down the hall for the mansion's western wing. Footsteps rushed up the steps, their small window lost as the curious guard returned to escort them downstairs.

They slipped into a bedroom opposite the landing, heading for the window. Kenneth opened it and helped his daughter to the ledge. This end of the estate was nothing more than a forest separating the Sumners from their neighbors.

Father and daughter took a sharp breath before jumping from the second story window.

The grass was long, padding them as they rolled with their fall. Kenneth laughed, ripping the mask from his face. He grabbed his daughter's hand and the two gleefully raced for the tree line. The Cadillac waited for them on the far side.

Myers' heart pounded, the night air revitalizing her as much as her father's widening grin. He pulled the bag from her shoulder, feeling the heft of their haul and ran faster for their freedom.

"Happy birthday, sweetheart."

CHAPTER THREE

Myers paced the length of her living room. The apartment was a work in progress and always would be. A sixth floor loft in downtown Portents, two miles from the Pier.

Her bed sat on one end of the room with a kitchenette on the other. A delicately used television took up a small table in the corner, while her keys and badge rested on the state of the art DVR beneath the 19-inch screen. Months of living in the city should have allowed something in the way of decorations for the detective, but the only stylistic choices she made were the flowers surrounding the French doors leading to the small balcony.

It took weeks to settle on the place. The cost alone should have taken it off her list but once she had seen the view, watched her first sunrise from the balcony, there was no getting around the fact that it had to be hers. The place left the shadows and the obsidian tower behind her and gave her nothing but an array of light to lull her to rest with the end of each shift.

The plants were a reminder as well. Her father kept lilacs, lilies, and an assortment of others at each of their homes. Where most mornings the sweet scents filled her with joyful memories, today was different. Memories became much more real with the arrival of the photograph resting on the small coffee table.

Her father's image stared at her. She fell on the couch before wearing a hole in the thin, stained carpet. She ran her hands through her hair, pulling the black strands into a ponytail. When that mindless distraction ended she sought another, this time settling on rolling her lock pick between her fingers.

Comfort in the coming storm.

The call should have come hours ago. It had to be soon, or she would go insane from the thoughts over the photo wracking her brain. *What did it mean? What did they want?*

When the phone rang, Myers jumped and the lock pick fell in a clatter on the coffee table before rolling to the floor. She looked to the phone resting next to the photo only to see a black screen. The ringing continued from her *other* phone—the one she hoped would never ring again.

Yet it always did.

Taking a deep breath, Myers flipped open the burner phone. "Why do I get the feeling this isn't a social call?"

"Who is it?" The voice was robotic, synthesized through a computer program to avoid recognition. The same as every call. There was no way for Myers to know if it was always the same person on the other end, other than the penchant to always piss her off.

Myers sighed. "Of course you know."

"Not from you, though," the voice said. "Don't you trust me yet, Detective?"

"I don't know you." An audible click snapped on the other end. Irritation at her behavior. "Trust has never been your thing."

"Or yours."

More truth. The voice knew her well—too well, considering the amount of secrets they held between them. The count stacked in favor of the monotone and genderless individual on the other end, frustrating Myers further.

"I'll find out who this is."

"I can—"

"I said I'll take care of it."

A pause and a breath. Contemplation at her resolve, or did her mysterious benefactor understand more about the threat at hand? The question sat at the tip of her tongue, ready to fire until the voice continued with a commanding tone.

"See that you do."

Before she could offer her retort, including some of her favorite four-letter words, the line clicked. Myers stared at the phone for a brief moment, letting the screen fade to black.

"Always a damn pleasure."

She tossed the phone, watching it sail across the room before landing on the unmade bed, bouncing beside her pillow. Myers ran her hands over her face, tugging hard to pry her eyes open.

"Shit."

The call unnerved her, unspooled her resolve, one notoriously well maintained. The photo enraged her, made her ready to strike out. Now, her mysterious keeper was involved with a threat of their own. Just what she needed.

Her personal phone rang and she let it dance along the coffee table, hoping for a telemarketer. Maybe one that would tie up the line for an hour or two with their sales pitch. Hell, maybe a timeshare *was* a smart investment. At the fourth ring, she picked up the phone.

"Myers."

"8100 Archer Court. Midnight. $500,000."

Myers waited for the laugh track to begin. "Are you out of your mind? Where would I possibly—?"

"Channel four," said the man on the other end of the line.

"What?"

"The television," he replied. "Now."

"I don't have one," she said, silently reaching for the remote.

"Not one from the last decade but I'm sure it's there for more than decoration. Quit stalling."

Damn. He knew where she lived, how she lived. Yet he had decided to drop the letter off at her work. Why? Was it an easier drop off point or used *because* of its difficulty?

Channel four took over the screen, the volume low but clear. The news anchor cheerfully displayed every tooth available in a grin as he delivered the latest update.

"…Making this one of the largest arrests ever accredited to the Major Crimes department. Estimates range…"

Her head fell into her palm and she turned off the television. Of course the bust was leaked to the press. That high profile of a move was bound to draw attention. Not that the press had to search out such activity from the Central Precinct. They had a captain on their payroll feeding them information.

"Shit," she muttered.

An exhale filled her ear. The man was clearly smiling on the other end. "8100 Archer Court. Midnight. Come alone."

The phone went dead. Myers let it drop, tired of people hanging up without a proper goodbye. Threats were one thing, but what happened to common courtesy?

$500,000. Suddenly things became clear to the troubled detective. Myers stood and stepped to the open doors to her balcony. She closed her eyes, letting the midday sun wash over her, cleanse her from the events of the morning and those yet to come. Her hands fell on the banister.

$500,000.

"Money. It always comes down to money."

CHAPTER FOUR

Much changed over a short period. Myers, her sixteenth birthday behind her, sat across the table from her father. The microwavable meal they shared bordered on extravagant.

Her father was haggard, his eyes bloodshot. Nothing like the man from a few years earlier. A poor string of jobs, all ending in failure, left the once successful criminal without prospects. Where control was key to their survival, now flight became their ultimate response. They had lived in four apartments in the last two years.

School barely registered for Myers. Friends were a luxury never achieved with the constant shifting of homes. She studied hard; it was the only thing to do on a daily basis with her father out on the streets trying to hammer out enough work to pay the rent. With several college credits under her belt already, Myers looked forward to branching out with her studies. It was her one controllable act in the world.

There were no plants here. Myers had grown accustomed to the multiple flowers decorating each entrance to their former homes, but no luxuries were afforded now. No comfort either. Everything was different—lifeless.

Even the simple act of cleanliness faded for her once proud father. He wore a simple white T-shirt, stained from age. His whiskers bordered on a full-blown beard, gray seeping into the corners. He picked at the macaroni and cheese side on the plastic dinner plate, the noodles glued together. The effort of pulling them apart being too much for him, he merely poked the overcooked meal before sliding it away.

Myers tried to make the best of the situation. She smiled. She carried herself the same as always with her father, the great and powerful force in her life. Everything he did was for her, making sure she had nothing but the best in life.

Any talk of work faded. She was pushed away from the life they once shared so completely. She never attended jobs now, never heard about them. That part of their world was closed, kept for him alone, the burden of their failing enterprise.

She knew about it, of course. How could she not? Every whisper, every muttered phone call—everything echoed in the small domicile. Words did not matter as much as the shift in his appearance, the sadness in his eyes.

She despised the constant worry that surrounded him. He was always fidgeting, shifting in his chair, pacing the room to flick open the blinds for another look at the crowded street.

When he dropped his fork on the table, Myers sat up. She noticed the fear spreading across his face. His eyes shifted to the alley on the left side of the building, then turned to the street outside.

"Dad?"

A finger rushed to his lips. The sound of traffic, usually so prevalent outside, was a whisper. No cars? During rush hour? And the stomping of feet? Where were all the people?

Her father stood suddenly, collecting the two plastic bowls with their meals. He tossed them in the garbage along with the silverware. He dumped their drinks and tossed the glasses away as well. Myers looked at the panic on his face, trying to slow him down to no avail.

"The closet," he whispered, pointing down the entry hall. "Now."

Myers refused to move from the table. "What are you—?"

His eyes flared, pleading. "Sam. *Now.*"

She nodded, racing into the hall. She pulled open the cubby drawer for linens and retrieved the two black backpacks inside. After tossing them into the open closet, she followed. Her father held the door open, tears welling in his eyes.

"Dad?" Myers pulled at his hand. "What's going on?"

He smiled and ran his fingers along her cheek. "You look just like her, you know?"

Her vision clouded. Her eyes stung with tears. *Why am I crying?*

"Remember what I taught you?"

"All of it."

He wiped her tears away and kissed her cheek. "I love you."

"Wait," she cried. He shook his head, a finger to his lips once more. The closet door closed, the lock outside clicking into place. "Where are you going?"

Through the slats, Myers watched her father head for the front door. His hand rested on the knob, drawing deep breaths. Control. Always for control.

Then he stepped out on the stoop.

Flashing lights blared. Screams rang out at his arrival. Police. Lots of police.

Myers slammed on the closet door, fighting to break the lock.

Kenneth Myers peered back, his sad eyes filling her view. He turned to the officers lining the block. He reached for the small of his back and the pistol he'd carried everywhere for the last two years.

"No," Myers muttered, slamming harder. "No, no, no…"

Shouts telling him to stop echoed through the air, but all was lost the moment he removed the pistol and took aim. A shot rang out from above—a sniper on the roof. She didn't see where it hit. Didn't see the blood or the pain on her father's face.

She only saw him fall.

"No!"

Police surrounded her father and a pair slipped into the apartment with weapons drawn.

"You hear that?" one asked. The other nodded and they began a sweep.

Myers covered her mouth, skirting to the back of the closet. Fumbling through the dark, she tried to find the switch.

"Shit," she whispered. "Where is it? Where—?"

"Over here," a cop yelled. "I heard something."

Steps approached. Faster. Her sweat mixed with the tears along her cheeks. "Come on, come on…"

Her fingers ran along the wall in the back, desperately searching. One finally caught the small switch, unlocking a crawl space opening. Myers jumped inside, pulling the two backpacks along with her. She closed it behind her gently.

Then she waited.

The closet door opened. The officer peered inside before turning around with a shrug. "Let's clear out. Target is down."

It wasn't until the apartment was vacant that Myers let out the breath caught in her lungs. She sat in the small crawl space, their getaway, the one they created at each of their homes, afraid of the next move. *Why didn't he come with me? Why did he give up?*

"Dad…"

She followed the shaft, each step agonizingly slow to avoid drawing attention. The vent bumped and bruised with each shift, but she continued along its length until coming to an impasse. She turned a quick right and met another opening.

Pushing it open, she stepped into the apartment two doors over. A contingency plan. *Control.* Her father's lessons. Myers clutched the backpacks, dropping both in the closet of the second apartment before joining them. She sat in the growing darkness, unsure of her next move. Unsure of everything except the lessons her father left her. The only thing left in her world with his passing.

Samantha Myers cried herself to sleep that night.

CHAPTER FIVE

The sun beamed bright above the park. Animals skittered across the grounds, slipping between skateboarders and runners in a merry chase for dominance. Kids shouted around the playground as their parents waited for the eventual change from joy to tears.

Samantha Myers waited for the opposite turn.

Six months had passed, but not in the blur of time's ever depressing wheel. No, each day, each hour, each minute was an agony of memory. Six months of uncertainty, of pain, and the loss of everything that mattered to her.

Except the lessons.

Myers kept out of sight, avoiding all contact with her father's friends and her own. School was in the rearview, not that she needed it. After so many advanced courses during her freshman and sophomore years, she had more than enough knowledge in her utility belt. With the last six months dodging the law, previous contacts and the unruly stranger or three, she had plenty of real-world experience as well.

Her go bag held plenty of cash to tide her over. She kept some separate from the hits taken in recent years over jobs lost or botched. Her father did the same, always looking for a safety net. Always in control of their fate.

Only *he* wasn't.

Myers slammed her hands to her knees, leaning forward. The dry heaves always came on whenever she thought of her father. Of the shot that rang outside their front door. Of his body falling, never moving. Never reaching for her. Never calling for her. Never being there for her again.

Motels didn't ask questions if the client appeared old enough and had money. Myers jumped from one flea-infested room to the next, always moving, always planning.

Money only lasted so long and she needed solutions.

There were few phone numbers listed in the burner kept in the go bag. Contacts from previous jobs. Allies. Hell, even some enemies. Myers only needed one number, and thankfully it was still accurate.

When he answered, her heart stopped. There were moments in life, choices made never to be taken back. She could have turned herself into the police, claimed innocence to her father's deeds and started over in foster care. Two years and she would be considered an adult. But she would never stop looking over her shoulder.

Just like now.

She sat on the bench an hour before the man's arrival, a standard for her father. *Be early. Control the meet.* She made her request expecting resistance, although the promise of cash silenced any before the conversation even began. Anything else—playing on the man's connection with her father, any supposed loyalty to past deeds—would immediately end the call and leave her without a hope.

Her early arrival came with its own peril—in her mind, anyway. The odds of recognition were downright impossible. The nervousness, the unease, remained. It followed her to the bench. It followed her every gaze, and every one that came back to her. From every passerby to the squirrels chittering in the trees above.

She was grateful when the man arrived.

Stephen Fitch was not a slim man. Man stretched the definition as well, his acne covering both cheeks and flaring in the midday sun. When he sat, Myers considered vomiting, his odor so overpowering. Like deodorant was asking for too much.

Without a glance in his direction Myers whispered, "Is that—?"

"The money?" Fitch asked, stopping her. He wore thick sunglasses, peering right at her.

Myers took a breath. The envelope tucked under his arm was within reach. It looked packed, filled with the information she required, but she didn't know for sure. She wasn't sure of anything, including whether or not Fitch had played ball with her or if he attempted to stiff her.

All she had were the lessons of her dead father. Myers took a deep breath, controlling the conversation. Trying to control a world spinning away from her.

"Under your seat."

Fitch leaned, his hand inching under the seat.

Myers shook her head. "Nuh-uh."

Fitch stopped, catching the fire in her eyes. He also felt the switchblade poking his flabby midsection. Nodding, he sat up, resting the envelope on his lap. After the switchblade returned to her pocket, he passed over the contents.

"Social security card. License. Passport. And duplicates. Just in case."

"And the other thing?"

"Done."

She glared at him. "Say it."

Fitch grinned, wringing his hands. "All records of your former life have been wiped digitally, which is all that really matters in this century. Samantha Myers, for all intents and purposes, is dead."

Myers opened the envelope, slipping her hand inside. She pulled out the license drawn up by the man at her side. The face was hers but the ID came from another state. A new life. A new history.

"Long live Samantha Myers." She closed the envelope, satisfied.

Fitch continued, taking pride in his work. "Untraceable. I went the extra mile with birth certificates, school records, diploma too, so no worries about that one. Even a job history—you loved that paper route when you were thirteen. No one will question it. Now…?"

Myers stood. "Enjoy it."

Fitch rummaged for the envelope strapped beneath the bench. She heard it flip open and the sweet sound of currency run along the tips of his fingers. She turned north, pushing from her mind the reminder of the majority of her funds disappearing in a single transaction. Fitch stopped her.

"You could have changed it, you know," he called. "The name? You could have been anyone. Why keep it? Why take the chance?"

She turned back, lowering her sunglasses, green eyes glaring down upon the man. "It's the name my father gave me."

Myers left without another word. She made her choice. Her name was all she had left of him. That and his lessons, which would stay with her for the rest of her days.

Only she would do it *her way*.

CHAPTER SIX

Myers tapped an impatient tune along the steering wheel. Her gloves muted the sound—a necessity considering the stolen vehicle. *Stolen* was a harsh word to describe it—more like *borrowed from the salvage yard on Douglas with intent to return*. The black Malibu had seen better days, but ran without a tremendous amount of trouble.

She parked down the street from the Central Precinct and Heaven's Gate Park on the far side of the Rath. The back of the building was not as ornate as the front square and the fifteen-foot statue of the city's founder, William Rath. The parking garage fed into the thoroughfare along Evans with a side exit at Main. The third option, and her focus for the evening, ran along the left side of the building at the corner of Evans and Highland.

The press made it impossible to keep the bounty collected at Central for long. Too many eyes were on the place, too many people flowing in and out of the building. Having a giant target with a dollar sign at its heart was a surefire way to make sure the cash would never be entered into evidence.

Captain Rufus Mathers couldn't risk anything happening to their haul.

That meant moving the funds to a more secure site. Hopefully, soon enough to save her ass in the next couple hours.

Thankfully, it did.

Myers knew procedure, as well as the spectacle Mathers put out to the press more than any other superior she had ever worked for during her career. The press gathered along Main and the exits from the parking structure off the Rath. Spotlights highlighted the caravan of vehicles leaving for the open highway. Police cruisers capped the front and back with two armored wagons in the middle.

Too obvious, though the firepower involved seemed otherwise. The four vehicles slipped into the night, Myers ducking low to avoid being seen from her position. Satisfied at their departure, most of the press packed their equipment up for the night. Some of the more desperate outlets attempted to follow the caravan.

Myers listened to the engine roar to life, the key heavy in her hand. She gripped the wheel tighter, listening to the stretch of her black gloves.

A single sedan exited the little-known entrance off Highland. Nondescript and definitely not official—just like her vehicle of choice for the evening. She let the sedan join the thinning traffic rushing away from downtown for the suburbs.

She recognized the plainclothes officer in the driver's seat. Sloane was young and nervous, hands at 10:00 and 2:00 and eyes on the road the entire time. Afraid to lose focus for a second. Part of the pressure came from his cargo. The majority, though, bore down from the man in the passenger seat.

Rufus Mathers.

Of course he's involved.

Myers grinned, shifting into drive to follow. A distance of an entire block gave her a clear view of the car and allowed other traffic to filter between them without her seeming like an obvious tail. Not that Mathers would check his mirrors, the act too much like police work.

North along Highland with a right on Young made it clear they were headed for the Third Precinct, standard for these situations. More internal personnel with a better set up to handle evidence as an entire floor served as a locker. Retrofitted from a former bank branch, the locker was a complete misnomer—*vault* was more accurate. Once the money entered the Third, the cash would stay there.

She had one shot to take it. She turned left, leaving the sedan behind, and made a quick right to run parallel with their travel. Fewer lights, and a comfortable speed above the limit, allowed Myers to skirt ahead a number of blocks along the route.

To the underpass at Phillips and Granite.

Trains no longer used the bridge, but the tracks remained in place as budget-conscious council members fought to take care of other priorities over the years. It had become a poorly lit and neglected area—the perfect choke point.

Devoid of all traffic and pedestrians, the Malibu coasted down Phillips with a clear view of the intersection. Her eyes tracked the sedan rushing along Granite for the Third Precinct. She took a deep breath then pulled a mask over her face, one she had carried for far too many years.

One block out, Myers slammed on the accelerator. The car jolted forward. The engine knocked back and forth as if nothing held it in place under the hood. The sedan rocketed along the final block for Granite, her intended target oblivious. The driver, hands still locked on the wheel, his nervous eyes wide on the road ahead, failed to notice the sedan barreling down on them until it was too late.

Myers collided at fifty-two miles per hour against the rear driver's side of the car. Sloane panicked behind the wheel, the car continuing its drive even while spiraling out of control until it crashed into the left-hand wall of the underpass. Smoke billowed from the engine, the hood crumpled up against the cracked windshield.

Neither officer within moved. Myers stepped out of her Malibu and rushed across the street, two canisters in her hands. Opening the driver's side door, she dropped the first into place. Smoke filled the cabin as she hit the release for the trunk.

"What are—?" Mathers sputtered, coughing in fits. The man behind the wheel was still breathing but unconscious.

Myers circled the vehicle, opening the trunk. A duffel bag sat within. She unzipped the bag to confirm its contents and, satisfied with the currency inside, she closed the bag and hefted it over her shoulder. She threw the second canister along the road, smoke spraying out in all directions.

"Drop it," Mathers shouted behind her, his gun drawn. He winced from the smoke. His glasses had been knocked off in the collision.

Myers lifted her hands and dropped the bag. When Mathers moved for the bag she spun around, knocking his gun away with a kick. He tried to recover but Myers gave him no time, pulling his arm back then putting pressure with her other arm on his throat. Mathers fought for breath, lumbering for a brief moment before collapsing on the ground.

Patting his back lightly, Myers couldn't help but smile once more before lifting the duffel bag into place. Using the second smoke canister for cover, Myers rushed down the block, deeper into downtown Portents and her fast-approaching meeting.

CHAPTER SEVEN

Myers left the subway station of Bentham, rushing up Dewey for Archer Court. At the end of a cul-de-sac of businesses sat 8100 Archer Court. *For Lease* signs marked the entrance and front windows of the office building. The adjacent buildings loomed over the single-floor structure.

Myers paused outside. No cars lined the block, an easy target for theft. Light beamed from the moon above, showering through the skylight adorning the rooftop. No signs of life were visible within the building.

Myers tucked the duffel tighter to her shoulder and started for the entrance. The door, left ajar for her arrival, opened smoothly. She stepped inside, tapping lightly against the butt of her sidearm.

Shards of light illuminated the open space, once filled with computer terminals and offices now vacant. Temporary walls split the sections, creating a maze of rooms out of the single space. Myers inched inside, heading straight, her knuckles white against the strap of the money-filled ransom.

"Hold it."

Her shoulders slumped. *Damn. Too fast, too soon.* She felt the gun against her back before recognizing the threat. He batted her hand aside and relieved her of her firearm.

"And here I was hoping for a full tour," Myers said.

"Drop the bag," the man replied, his voice deep and booming in the open space. Something about it sparked a memory, but it passed quickly when the bag crashed to the ground.

Myers shrugged, hands open and visible. "Then again, you see one hovel you've seen them all, right?"

He scooped the bag up with one hand, keeping his Glock trained on her. She tried to shift to catch a better peek of him. Tall, broad shouldered, and muscular with a growing tire around his midsection—obviously from age more than anything else. He appeared close to sixty, but focused—quite focused to catch her glimpse before shoving her forward.

"Move."

She refused. "I did my part. Now let's—"

He shoved her ahead, the hammer on his Glock cocking loudly.

"Hey," Myers shouted, stumbling ahead.

"I said, move."

She had seen enough with the stray glances stolen with each step. The graying hair. The defensive stares and the cold eyes.

"I know you," she said.

A chuckle escaped his lips, but he stayed silent at the accusation. His prodding continued until they broke free from the hall into the open space at the far end of the building. The skylight filled the ceiling, raining down the moon's brilliance over the cobweb-infested structure.

Steps appeared from the shadows of the far corner emergency exit. Soft heels clacked against tile, announcing the young man's presence. He wore a suit, cheap and off the rack. The jacket sat too large on his shoulders, the pants wrinkled and the shoes scuffed. Gold chains hung around his neck.

"You do indeed know him," the man said with a grin. The jacket slipped off, showing his armpits stained from sweat, his shirt old and matching the wrinkled pants. "But who remembers the help these days?"

She remembered well enough. It didn't click until she saw his young companion, though. She would have known him despite the cheap suit and the wrinkled shirt. The tipoff was his watch. He still wore the watch, gold and extravagant. The watch that could pay off the national debt in most small countries.

Even with the crack in its face.

"Thanks for joining us, Detective." He clapped his hands as he circled her, chuckling quietly. "I still have trouble saying that. *Detective.* How does that happen?"

Cedric, his diligent bodyguard, backed away at his direction, gun at the ready.

"Alex, right? Alex Sumner?"

He grinned, tapping his temple with the barrel of a small 9mm pistol. Enough to do the job.

"Attention to detail helps, I suppose," Alex said. "It did with your former career too, didn't it?"

"Your father—"

"Is dead!"

The gun leveled with her forehead. Myers refused to close her eyes, watching his rage grow. *Keep pushing him. Idiot.*

"Because of you. You just vanished that night. Like the fucking wind. I was a damn kid. Can you imagine finding him like that? And you just walked away, started a whole new life?"

"It wasn't like that, Alex," Myers said, hands open. Calm. "I had no idea—"

"Ignorance is not the card to play here, Detective. No one gets to run away from their past. Not me. And sure as shit not you."

She understood that better than anyone, the burner phone in her pocket a constant reminder. "I never have."

"Not how it looks on this end."

Myers smirked. "Alex Sumner. Busted for possession four years ago. Assault and battery the year before that. Living off his father's name and a rapidly fading trust fund since dropping out of college."

"You don't know a damn thing about me," Alex snapped, white-knuckling the gun.

"And you don't know me," Myers countered. "Take your money and leave whatever you think you have on me on your way out. That was the deal."

Silence filled the room. Tense glances passed between the two armed men. Then Alex started to laugh, loud and jubilant.

Myers gritted her teeth. "Didn't realize I was doing stand-up."

He quieted, tucking the gun away. "You're a ghost, lady. Not a damn thing I could find tying you to the girl I met once upon a time."

"Then what the hell—?"

Alex reached into his pocket and pulled out a photo. "Your father was another story."

"He's dead."

Alex tossed her the snapshot. It fell to the ground and she slowly retrieved the image. An old man sat on a porch in the midday sun. Golf clubs rested behind him. Sand dominated the yard instead of grass. The old man was smiling, content at the lazy afternoon.

That same damn smile.

"He looks very much alive to me," Alex said. He pulled the gun back out, massaging the barrel. "For the moment anyway."

CHAPTER EIGHT

The photo sat in her hands, crumpled in the corners from her grip. Unable to look away, Myers pulled every detail from the single still of her father's current life: the contentment on his face—his pure satisfaction at the world. Nothing bothered him. Nothing tormented him.

"How?" she choked.

"How?" Alex circled around her, basking in her heartache. "Oh, you mean, how did he survive that day? Outside your house? The whole thing was a setup. He made enemies with the wrong bastards and had to disappear. Witness protection. Unreal, right? He left you. He could have easily made the deal *with* you…but instead? *Poof.* Just like that. Cold, even for a murdering psychopath like your old man."

His joy made him sloppy. Cedric, however, held a gun on her—the smart one of the pair.

"While you've been fending for yourself, struggling to make it, he's been golfing and kicking back at the beach enjoying his retirement."

Heat pierced her cheeks, running down in thick waves along her arms and legs. She felt anger at the enjoyment on her father's face. Anger at her situation being found out by such a miserable little cuss of a man. Out of her control—the one thing she always prided herself on.

"That's it," Alex whispered. "That's the look I wanted to see."

She turned to face him in time for the flash of his camera phone to temporarily blind her. A second picture followed the first in rapid succession, before he slipped the phone into his pocket.

"What are you doing?"

He held the pistol in front of him, wiping the metallic shine clean. "It took years to find you. He was the easy one. A bribe here, a bribe there and bam. But you? Years of private investigators and news alerts and who knows how many other damn things we tried." He shook his head, cocking the hammer. "I had to. You get that, right? The money is a nice bonus and I greatly appreciate it. But that's not what this is about. Never was. It had to be you first so I could show him the photo. Show him you, broken by the truth. Right before the end."

He leveled his gun with her temple, the moon glinting off the barrel. And something else.

Myers smirked. "Sounds like you have it all worked out."

"Didn't you hear me?" he asked, confused by her grin. "Do you not see what is about to happen?"

"Oh, I see it very clearly," she said. "Attention to detail, remember?"

She wasn't looking into his eyes or into the mouth of the small-barreled pistol. Only the red light beaming through the skylight and landing center mass on Alex Sumner.

"What the—?"

Glass shattered from the shot. Alex fell away, the impact sudden and harsh. His body collapsed in the room's shadow.

Cedric rushed for his charge. Myers cut him off, slamming into the senior citizen behemoth with a loud cry. The assault knocked both off their feet. They struggled for the gun. Myers forced it away, pummeling him with her right fist while slamming the firearm against the ground with her left. The weapon jolted loose and skidded across the floor.

Cedric rebounded, knocking her aside. Myers scurried for the gun unable to reach it. Pulled back by the bodyguard, she kicked at him, catching his midsection and throwing him off her for a brief moment. Leaping from her position, Myers grabbed the gun.

"Don't even—"

She turned to the rushing Cedric and fired three shots, each connecting with his chest. The aging bodyguard's eyes went wide before he fell.

Myers felt her breath catch in her throat. She fought for air, rolling away from the dead man at her side. She stood and almost lost her balance. Spots dotted her vision when she bent low to retrieve the dropped photo of her father. The Glock hung along her side as she shambled over to the bleeding yet scurrying Alex Sumner.

"You…" He coughed, blood spreading along his lips. The shot from above did more than enough damage to finish the job but Alex fought for more time.

She loomed over him, blocking the moon. The image sat in her hands and she smiled. "I miss him. Every day. I should thank you for this."

"You knew."

"I did."

"How?"

She raised the Glock, finger tensed on the trigger. "You're not the first person to blackmail me."

Two shots and it was over. Alex Sumner met the same fate as his father, forever cursed for having crossed paths with the Myers family.

Before she could make a move, before a single thought of her next action took hold, the burner phone in her breast pocket rang. She waited, hoping it was imagined. She flipped the phone open and sighed.

"I had this handled."

"You're welcome," the voice said, wind crackling through the synthesized processor.

Myers slipped the image of her father into her pocket. "You swore he was safe from this crap. A couple bribes and this piece of filth almost—"

"He didn't. And bribes can be tracked."

"They better."

"Is that a threat, Detective?"

The red beam from the riflescope swept across her chest—its message clear. "No," Myers muttered. "No, it isn't."

"Dispatch is aware of your location."

"I called it in," she said, having made the call before arriving.

"The police will be here soon. The bodies—"

"Won't be here," Myers confirmed.

"I could—"

"No," she snapped, then took a long breath. "You've done enough."

Her father's lessons echoed in her mind, forever ingrained in everything she did, in every action taken. No matter the consequences.

Control.

"I'll take care of it."

CONNECTIONS

CHAPTER ONE

Rain poured from the cloud-filled sky but refused to stall their dance along the rooftops. Her assailant's weapon slashed the air, cutting the drops of water falling around them and narrowly missing Soriya with each step of their battle.

The Greystone bearer leaped across the gap between buildings, rolling with it before snapping back to her feet to face her opponent. The spear-wielding murderer wore a mask with black circles for eyes and white paint along the cheeks. Japanese characters marked the center of each, though Soriya could not read them through the rain and the woman's quick movements. Calling her a woman, however, was not quite accurate.

An onna-bugeisha.

Soriya knew the legends. A female martial artist from feudal Japan. When the men went to war, the women protected the homeland. They kept their homes and loved ones safe from potential threats. They were warriors in their own right, dangerous and deadly.

Very deadly.

Carrying a staff longer than her lithe frame with a sharpened blade at the end, the warrior forced Soriya back with each strike. Each blow skirted the skin, locking Soriya in place and forcing her to the ledge of the roof. Soriya leaped to avoid falling, exactly as the onna-bugeisha hoped. The staff caught between her legs and pulled her to the ground hard. A sharp kick sent her over the edge of the roof, fingers scrabbling to catch the brick.

Soriya dangled in the night air, pooled water threatening to send her to the ground five stories down. This was not how she intended her night to go. That had been par for the course lately.

It started as it always did, with violence spreading like a contagion through the city of Portents. It flew between citizens, building in potency, swelling in anger, until exploding on the streets. That was typically when Soriya Greystone found out about it—after someone died.

In this case, four someones: local gangbangers. Nasty guys with nastier attitudes toward women, law enforcement, and life in general. They were not the type of crew you tried to take down without twenty of your best friends in tow. Even then, it was iffy at best what the outcome would be.

When they turned up dead, no one shed a tear—not even a loved one or friend. They knew the score, but more importantly, they understood the message sent to the rest of the neighborhood. One that rang clear from the four headless bodies found in the middle of an intersection in the heart of Lowtown one night.

The bodies were lined up, each facing a different direction at the intersection. Their heads were placed in their cupped hands, eyes open wide and staring up at their broken and bleeding frames. Behind them, centered under the blinking streetlight, sat a weapon: a long staff with a sharp blade at the end. The blade was old, yet in remarkable condition, the steel shining in the moonlight.

A calling card.

Racial tensions were blamed. The growing Asian community turned into the perfect target. Seen as weak, they were crowded into tenement housing and bilked for protection money from every would-be crook in the borough. The police did what they could—their words exactly—but it was never enough; it could never be enough, not without more resources and a giant spotlight over the beleaguered section of the city.

The four deaths made the news. The viciousness of the murders, the ritual behind them, gave the major stations their feature for the week. Soriya heard about it while cooking—a new talent, and one that needed some work. If one wanted something charred or blackened to the point of being unrecognizable, she was the one to call.

Kicking ass suited her better.

She questioned the community, confronting would-be suspects on all sides with the hope of finding the owner of the ko-naginata spear found at the scene. It wasn't her usual process, not without Loren by her side. He was easier on the eyes, less prone to violence. His questions were well thought out, pushing when necessary, but more often than not the answers arrived willingly. It surprised her how much she picked up from their time together.

The culprits turned out to be four senior citizens of Asian descent, each standing less than five feet tall. Their way of life was threatened and they took action from the worst possible source. One they unleashed on the unsuspecting Soriya Greystone.

For their *protection*, they said.

Now Portents needed protection. And so did Soriya.

The onna-buegeisha kicked at Soriya's strained grip on the edge of the rooftop. The Greystone bearer scurried away from the assault, and the warrior followed closely. The ribbons of Kali slipped down her arm and raced for the edge of a billboard at the corner of the building. Using it for leverage, Soriya grinned at the onna-bugeisha and let go of the brick. She swung through the air, looping back at the Japanese defender, feet first.

She met only air. The warrior leaped aside and recovered quickly as Soriya found her own footing on the soaked roof. The blade of the spear welcomed Soriya back to the fight, taking a slice of skin from her right arm. She cried out, dropping to the ground and sweeping her legs to bring down the onna-bugeisha. The warrior jumped back, giving Soriya some breathing room. She clutched the bleeding wound and raced to the edge of the next rooftop, bounding over the billboard that read, *PREPARED FOR WHAT COMES NEXT? VISIT LIFE PLANS TODAY!*

Prepared for what comes next? How about surviving the next ten seconds? Soriya thought as the ribbons of Kali sprang from her left arm to wrap around the fire escape on the adjacent building. Her body arced forward, using the momentum to propel across the gap.

The onna-bugeisha was waiting on the other side. The ribbon released just in time to avoid being slashed in two by her ko-naginata. Soriya ducked under the strike, rolling to the far side of the roof. She spun on her knees to face her opponent, the Greystone released from her hip and aimed at the ancient creature.

Too late.

The warrior rushed her. Soriya barely made it to her feet before being bowled over by her attacker. The two launched from the rooftop, Soriya struggling to keep the weapon at bay while freeing the ribbon to save her life.

At the last second the ribbon caught a gargoyle atop a neighboring office building, and their free-fall jilted hard to one side. It spun them through the air, Soriya seeing their destination for only an instant before the pair smashed through the storefront window of the Lucky Kitchen restaurant.

Their momentum carried them into the dining area. Patrons scattered in terror at their arrival. As people raced for the exits, Soriya held tight to the woman and her spear to give them the time they needed. The onna-bugeisha screamed, kicking her away. Soriya slammed against the wall, sliding to the floor. The Greystone slipped out of her grasp and she tried to reach for it. She was met with another kick, sending her reeling to the ground.

The onna-bugeisha murmured a chant, almost a prayer, as she raised her weapon in triumph.

Then the Japanese warrior fell, the clattering of a frying pan colliding against her skull. Soriya blinked, unable to think, then dove for the fallen Greystone. The onna-bugeisha's mask slipped away and she saw the warrior for what she was: a mangled beast of decayed flesh.

Not truly living.

Soriya smiled as light formed along the surface of the stone.

A single bolt of lightning danced through the sky, through the shattered window. It struck the creature in the chest and she disappeared with only a pile of ashes left as a memory of her time in Portents.

Soriya took a deep breath then plugged her nose, finding the scorched stench of flesh pungent. Standing, she brushed off her torn jeans and dabbed at the open wound on her right arm.

"Took you long enough," she said with a smile to her savior.

Gilgamesh held his frying pan proudly. "It's getting so a man can't finish a meal in this city anymore."

CHAPTER TWO

"You sure know how to clear a room," Gilgamesh said with his patented grin. He carried two steaming plates from the counter over to the only occupied table left in the restaurant.

"It's a gift," Soriya replied, impatiently seated in the dining room. Scorch marks marred the carpet where the onna-buegeisha made her exit. Shattered glass spread across the floor from their impromptu entrance.

Placing the dish before her, Gilgamesh sat across the table, picking at the entree with zeal. Soriya paused, eyeing both him and the dish. A brown rice, multi-colored peppers mixed with a creamy sauce and what appeared to be chicken on top. She picked at it and Gilgamesh cleared his throat. He pointed to the fork beside her plate and she nodded, lifting the utensil, and popped a bite into her mouth.

Eyes wide in surprise, Soriya turned to the patrons peering through the slit between the dining area and kitchen. She nodded her approval and then turned back to her companion.

"I'm surprised anyone stayed," she said before taking another bite. She was soaked to the bone; the hot meal felt heavenly going down.

"They've seen worse," Gilgamesh admitted in a low voice. He smiled at the crew around them, quietly working to clean up the mess and stealing glances at the young woman. Their eyes spoke to their history, saddened yet toughened by their experiences. Suffering lived in them, a deep and thriving pain no one would ever understand.

The fork clanged against the dish. Soriya's heavy heart focused on the broken chairs, the overturned tables, and the debris from her arrival. Her first reaction was to joke about it, but the damage caught in her wake was very real to these people. People that had nothing else but this place they managed to scrape together.

"I'm sorry," Soriya called, hoping they understood her sincerity. Confused looks turned to Gilgamesh, who nodded expectantly. Soriya pressed the issue. "Dammit, I didn't—"

"It's okay," Gil said. She tried to refute his claim but he wiped it away with a smile. "They've come into some good fortune of late."

Soriya followed his gaze to the bag tucked neatly under their table. The flap was open; she saw the bag was packed with stacks of hundred dollar bills. His appearance at the restaurant came into focus for the first time. She picked at her plate once more. "Hence the free meal?"

"No such thing. I offered you up for dish duty."

"You did not," she exclaimed with a laugh. "Did you?"

"After dinner."

The staff watched her intently and she bowed her head. "It's the least I can do. Thank you."

They ate in silence. It had been months since Soriya had seen the man, the once proud avatar of Death. Her first encounter with him paled in comparison to their recent reunion. They had fought over the soul of the city and now they were sharing a meal.

Old soldiers.

Gilgamesh finished quickly and wiped his chin. His glances strayed from her, his constant shifting displaying his discomfort. There was heartache in his eyes. Her questions grew unbearable in the silence of their meal and Soriya dropped her fork against the plate.

"Care to tell me?"

"Tell you—?"

She glared at him. "How did you do it?"

"Do what?"

She sighed. "Know where I would be? Helped these people even before they knew why? Do I really have to ask?"

"Soriya."

"No," she said, louder than she hoped. The staff turned to them and Soriya inched her chair closer to him. "No way. You're going to play the coincidence card?"

He shrugged. "Just lucky that way."

"I'm sure." She leaned back, arms crossing her chest. "So how is it? The city? Being back?"

"Good," he answered, holding out the word longer than required. He cocked his head to the side, wincing. "Well, it's been…a little bit of an adjustment."

"A little one?" she laughed. "From avatar of Death to average Joe? Never would have guessed."

He stared out the broken window toward the night sky. The rain slowed, the clouds rushing away from downtown heading east. He looked distant, lost in memory. When he turned back, he smiled. "The company helps."

"Gil, is everything—?"

"Aces, Soriya. Honest." He stood, lifting the plate. He reached for hers and she pushed it toward him. He took them to the waiting staff, and Soriya heard words of thanks passed in an unfamiliar language. Gilgamesh returned with his coat in hand and the black bowler cap on his head.

"About tonight…"

"There is nothing more to it, I'm afraid."

She fought for more, reaching for him, but he pulled away. His lips pursed, locking down any answers to her growing concern, unwilling to share any more than what had been given. The fight had been lost from the start.

"Just a little luck from a normal, everyday guy. Nothing exciting to be found in me. Now, if you'll excuse me…"

"You're leaving?"

He tipped his cap. "The night is young."

Soriya followed him to the door. "Where are you headed? I could join you."

"You could." He tilted his head to the kitchen. "Then again…"

"Right. Dishes." She waved to the growing group of spectators. "You could help, you know."

The doorway was empty. Gilgamesh was gone.

Soriya stepped outside, catching his shadow slipping down the road, heading east out of Lowtown for the Knoll and downtown Portents beyond. She shook her head, then rolled up her sleeves.

CHAPTER THREE

Stupid, Gil. Really stupid.

Gilgamesh shambled down the road, his coat tight around him. The rain had been quickly replaced by the winds, roiling along the streets in large gusts. He pushed through them, rushing along the sidewalk, his head turned from the few drivers ignorant enough to travel the roads of Lowtown at night.

He shouldn't have gone to the restaurant. He had visited twice before, always gracious at the courtesy extended by the recently transplanted family that owned and operated the establishment. They struggled to keep the place, as the opening months had been leaner than expected. Gil, thankful for the warm meal and the company, offered to help.

Knowing what lay ahead.

And she knew the truth now as well. Soriya Greystone. The name sent more chills down his spine than the rustling wind crossing the avenues. They circled each other, intersecting at the strangest of times. A choice he made time and again.

He promised to be around for her after the Erikson affair. When he was needed, *if* he was needed. Tonight wasn't the case. Soriya required no assistance with the onna-bugeisha. Hell, nothing could probably cause her to reach out for help. Especially from Gilgamesh.

No one had needed him since he left his last job.

A smirk spread. *Job?* Centuries as an avatar of Death, as a reaper of souls, and it boiled down to a line item on his unwritten résumé? Where could he go from there? Better still, did he have any right to go anywhere?

He had lived his life, extended it far beyond the realm of possibilities. The world used to be his playground, his position as Death ever present but flexible in most cases. Now he was human.

Now he was bored.

Sure, freedom from Death gave him a new lease on life, a second chance to be among the world. Yet there seemed to be less and less to see, to do. Interactions strained credulity, the past always nipping at his heels.

Not so before. Not with the majesty he witnessed before humanity overtook the world, before cities dominated the globe. Natural beauty faded, the great forests slowly shrinking under the heel of man.

How could the present compare to what he had seen over the centuries?

Gilgamesh pushed through the wind, shaking off his solemn thoughts. He needed to put the night's events behind him—Soriya, the restaurant—before the questions started, his own included, into how he knew to be there.

He missed it though—the excitement, the need. The thrill of a battle and the blood from a fight. Part of him wished he could tell her and more. To be part of her world completely. To join her struggle with the growing shadows of Portents.

Gilgamesh regretted the thought immediately.

A hand reached out and snatched his coat. A sharp tug ripped him from the street into an alley, his hat falling to the ground and rolling away. Gilgamesh slipped into the darkness of the narrow passage between storefronts.

"Death," a voice groaned.

Gilgamesh straightened, watching the figure at the mouth of the alley approach. A second followed. Both wore ornate masks and carried spears. The decorative spears peaked in the shape of a massive eye but it was the jackal masks that made Gil sigh.

"Why do I bother sometimes?"

"Death…"

"You said that already," Gil replied, raising his fists.

"You smell of it," the second jackal croaked.

"Now that's just rude, sir." Gilgamesh stopped. "Sir? Is that right?"

"Take him," the first said.

A spear shot out and Gilgamesh caught it, pulling the second in close before slamming him back with an elbow. Gilgamesh snapped the spear in half, dropping it to the ground.

"Don't take him," Gilgamesh shouted. "He's not takeable."

Two more men entered the alley from the adjacent street, surrounding him. Gilgamesh's chin fell to his chest.

"Not buying it, huh?"

He stepped over the fallen jackal, knocking the spear away from the first. His fist shot out, crashing into the ornate mask. Cartilage crumpled under his blow and the man fell in a heap beside his brother.

The second pair was on top of Gilgamesh before he turned to face them. They subdued him, grappling his arms behind his back before kicking out his knees. Gilgamesh tried to free himself, finding each pull met with a staggering blow.

"You served death," one whispered. "Now you will serve us."

Blood trickled from Gilgamesh's lips. "Never a beautiful woman in the mix, is there?"

The jackals stood at attention, the sound of clacking heels filling the alleyway. Gil peered curiously, hoping to gauge their reactions, stopping at the sight of the new arrival to their impromptu party.

The shadows helped accentuate deep curves. The decorative chest plate barely covered her breasts. Shapely hips sauntered along the alley, inching closer to her captive.

"Oh, sweet, Gilgamesh," the woman cooed, stepping into the light. "All you had to do was ask."

He tried to look away, tried to pretend her shape didn't fill him with a deep longing and that only the resentment from past recriminations remained. Only one woman gave him that feeling and he hated her for it.

Ishtar.

"Oh, hell."

Her fingernails cut his cheeks as she squeezed them. "Not yet. But we'll see where the night goes."

CHAPTER FOUR

She shouldn't have let him go. If Soriya Greystone had been thinking about the circumstances of their chance encounter, she would have seen the truth. She had, to an extent, even pushed him for an explanation. A necessity in her eyes.

Too many secrets already existed in the city's shadows.

Soriya made apologies to the gracious staff of the restaurant, their generosity undeserved. Their shattered establishment needed to be rectified. Gilgamesh, however, came first. If he was hiding something, and she had no doubt in that regard, she needed to know why.

That's what friends were for, weren't they?

She could count on few people, but after their shared ordeal with Erikson and the Medusa coin, she believed they landed in a better place than when the affair began. They were linked, circling each other for the better part of Soriya's lifetime. If she could help, then she hoped he would afford her the opportunity.

She raced down the streets of Portents, looking for some sign of her friend. He turned right when he departed. She stuck to the thoroughfares. She understood Gilgamesh's desire to connect to the city. She carried the same feeling since taking leave of the Bypass chamber, since trying to find her place among the people she spent her life protecting.

Gilgamesh did the same. He attempted to fit in, to blend with the throng of people living in every vein, every major artery of the maze-like beast known as Portents. The main roads afforded some form of interaction, or the best chance at one, as most stayed inside after the sun went down.

It was always safer that way in Portents.

Her search ended three blocks over. When she raced into the night for her friend, she believed it would be a simple case of asking a question and hoping for an answer. There would be some snark involved. It seemed to be a thing with the people she met, the relationships that grew into something more. Friendship, partnership, and the like. How they bonded, how they expressed themselves and related to problems. A few laughs, a little deflection, and the eventual truth.

An easy end to a difficult night.

Then she saw the bowler hat—Gilgamesh's hat. The cap lay in the mouth of the alley off Richmond. She picked it up, dusting off the black brim. His fascination with the Charlie Chaplin style was part of his charm. He would never leave it behind, not intentionally.

Soriya followed the trail deeper into the shadows. The fire escape above creaked with the breeze whistling along the alley.

"Gil?"

Overturned garbage cans and tossed refuse was spread everywhere—but not from the weather. Specks of blood dotted the concrete, glowing in the moonlight. Fresh and dripping, the blood streamed along the concrete.

Soriya crouched to examine the area. Something caught her attention in the corner. A broken pipe of some kind. When she lifted the object, she realized the truth. A staff. One with a unique ornament adorning the peak.

The Eye of Horus.

She recognized the decoration immediately. And what it meant for Gilgamesh.

Trouble.

CHAPTER FIVE

She went alone—an idiotic move, and one she made far too often. When she found the broken staff with the Eye of Horus, her initial thought was of Loren.

Most of the time, her thoughts turned to Loren.

The police were an invaluable resource. One she abused too often for too long, having recently seen the light on their usefulness. She had previously kept Loren and the others in the dark in an attempt to keep them safe. An excuse, one of many she came up with when deflecting answers to simple questions.

With Loren on board, tracking down a likely target with the Eye of Horus would have been simplicity. But Loren had changed. Instead of trying to repair the damage her decisions made in their dealing with Erikson, he widened the divide they caused. Anger sat in every word, in every look. Their last case together, an attempt to reach out and heal from her perspective, failed miserably.

Maybe it was the pain. He hid it well enough but she noticed a strain in his movements. Rest would help but he was too stubborn to listen to reason. Much like herself. Both needed to work through the pain. She wished she could be there for him.

Unfortunately, he needed to deal with it on his own for now.

Gilgamesh was the priority.

The eye remained key. Based in Egyptian lore, the Eye of Horus was believed to have healing and protective powers. The all-seeing eye stood as the focus of a number of myths including that of Osiris, who ate the eye and was restored to life.

Gross.

Lore aside, Soriya knew the perfect starting point for her search. She had her rooftop jaunt with the onna-bugeisha to thank for the welcome assist.

Life Paths.

The office sign covered the top half of the building just east of Lowtown at the start of the Knoll. A seemingly innocuous local business trying to make it in a bustling city, their business logo displayed for everyone to see—the Eye of Horus.

Soriya approached the office front door. Regular hours were long since over, the lights turned off and doors locked. She took the handle, the Greystone pulsing beside her, and snapped the lock with one thrust. The door fell open and she stepped inside, letting it blow in the stiff breeze.

The lobby and waiting room offered an array of magazines and pamphlets to entertain patrons. Computer towers hummed from beneath desks. Offices lined both sides of the long halls stretching from the entrance.

Soriya did some digging before making the approach. Life Paths, on paper, was a life-planning firm. Most people tended to figure out their own career, growing from the dreams of childhood to adulthood. Destiny or fate, some might believe. Others, however, tended to wander, unsure where they might be useful, and often looked for assistance in such matters.

Life Paths, however, went a different route altogether. Life planning was only one direction of the firm. Life Paths went further, digging into the *afterlife* planning market.

Talk about a niche market.

Off the lobby, tucked quietly to the left sat a number of brochures and displays. Each contained images of different animals, some more exotic than others. The brochure first featured incense packages, an offering for one's ascension after the end. They came with their own time frame, some extending out weeks and months—even years.

Sacrifices were the next best option. Each made for a better place in the heaven of your choice, with no mention of the other option downstairs. Soriya dropped the brochure to the ground at the mention of human sacrifice options available upon request.

A scent in the air stirred her from the room and back into the hall. Ancient. Soriya followed it, swiftly checking each room she passed. It wasn't until she reached a conference room that she stopped.

The eye loomed over her, stationed at the back of the elongated room. No other identifying marks decorated the walls, no business name, nothing except the wide, all-seeing eye watching her every move.

Soriya inspected the bronzed icon closely. Her hands ran the length of the display. At the center was a small lift along the image. Barely perceived unless in direct contact.

A switch.

Flipping it up, the wall shifted. The smell pounded against her, her hand immediately covering her nose and mouth. Death infected the air, spilling from the opening in the conference room.

A stairwell led deeper into the complex. Modern plasterboard gave way to stone, small torches adorning the walls. All lit to show the depth of the spiral staircase leading to the impressively hidden structure tucked under the veneer of a simple office building.

Soriya caught her breath, fighting the acrid stench of death and decay. She shook it away and took her first step inside.

"Down the rabbit hole."

CHAPTER SIX

Screams echoed around her, rising from the lower chambers. The spiral staircase descended into the growing chasm. No end appeared in sight, the dim light offered by the torches throwing shadows on everything.

Soriya crept, inching farther into the deep blackness. Each step brought her closer to the truth of what it was, hidden beneath the teeming city of Portents. It was not a cavern or a mine; the structure tucked under the Life Plans office was something else entirely.

It was a temple.

Images of Anubis ran the length of the staircase, the god's eyes tracking her steps. With the head of a jackal and the body of a man, Anubis acted as a guide to the dead. While many viewed him as a protector, he continued to reach into the living world to extend his influence. Influence possibly linked to the screams booming throughout the widening temple.

"Gilgamesh."

Her friend was suffering. *Why?* It was a good question but not the right one, something he always mentioned when together. She picked up the pace, circling into the structure until coming to a rest at the base of the stairs. The correct question was there, tucked in the cries for help surrounding her every step.

How much longer can he hold out?

She refused to wait for the answer. The days of her being too late were behind her. She wouldn't let her friend down.

The temple spread out in a series of narrow tunnels, running along the perimeter of the complex. Soriya followed one then turned into the next. Torches sporadically placed along the walls allowed for enough light. Sunken ceilings shook with each movement. The walls were tight, not allowing for more than two abreast.

Soriya wondered about the structure's stability, dust falling around her from above. She pressed forward, winding around corners, deeper into the complex. With each turn she realized the building layout's complexity. An underground maze hidden in the city. All tucked under the subway tunnels and sewer lines crisscrossing the length of Portents.

An incredible achievement, including the intricacy of the artwork-laden stone throughout. Not only that of Anubis, though much of the complex seemed geared to the lord of the underworld and his followers. Deeper in the structure, more modern glyphs replaced Anubis, depicting events closer to home.

Soriya stopped at a crossroads, noticing the red eyes of Nathaniel Evans staring at her. They rose over the skyline of Portents, surrounding the obsidian tower at the center. She pressed on, shaking away the stare of the man that almost razed Portents to the ground.

The Medusa coin followed, enlarged to encapsulate an entire wall in the maze-like tunnels. Snakes towered over Soriya, reaching for her from their place on the wall. Medusa's wide eyes glowed in the torchlight.

Soriya ran faster, the screams egging her on.

Large hounds caused her to jump back into an adjacent corridor. Another set of glyphs, this time depicting the mangy beasts she faced almost a year ago. The Heads of Cerberus. Only the image depicted many more than the three she faced. Dozens lined the wall but she pushed past them, refusing to give the glyphs credence, though the words of the fallen followed her.

You think there are only three? More will come.

More images pursued her in the dark tunnels. Twists and turns whirred by, her sense of direction lost. She should have mapped it out, laid down clues to avoid getting lost along the winding path, but the images disturbed her more than she cared to admit.

Mentor was among them, his fallen form before the glowing orb of the Bypass. And more: a cloaked figure wearing a white mask, one she hadn't seen since her days as a child in the shadow of a grand library. Hints of greater riddles she could hardly begin to fathom. Nor wanted to, not with the screams growing more intense.

Soriya rounded another corner only to meet a larger chamber. She ducked, hugging the inner wall. Shadows crossed the space, spears in hand. The Eye of Horus adorned the peak of each weapon. Their tall and lean forms wore decorative outfits. Jewelry glistened on their skin. Headdresses masked their faces, shaped like the head of a jackal.

Followers of Anubis.

They patrolled the area in a pattern. Soriya stuck to the shadows, watching their every movement. Satisfied with their absence, she inched forward and slipped on loose stones along the path. Pebbles scattered, the footsteps of the others falling silent at the sound.

"Dammit," she cursed under her breath.

Looking up, she saw them. They stepped into the light, spears pointing at her. She had been mistaken about the headdresses. Believing them to be masks meant they were men wearing costumes. These were not men.

And they were not wearing masks.

Blank eyes widened at her presence. They rushed toward her. She hoped to avoid a fight, hoped that by slipping into the temple she could avoid detection to save her friend.

Gilgamesh.

His screams rejuvenated her sense of urgency. So did the four jackals surrounding her with weapons at the ready.

"Great," Soriya groaned, standing to meet them. "I don't have time for this."

Staffs snapped the air and she ducked between them, pulling one forward. The follower of Anubis staggered off balance and she slammed her fist into his waiting jaw. It hit like the stone surrounding the temple walls and she followed it up with a stiff kick to the gut that sent the creature reeling. He fell, and was quickly replaced by his brethren.

Pain shot up her right arm, a lucky shot from the closest jackal re-opening her wound from the onna-bugeisha. Blood dripped from his spear and she screamed at his pleasure over the assault. She leaped at him; the ribbons of Kali shot down her left side, whipping around his feet, and toppled him over. When he did, Soriya was waiting, dropping all her weight on his chest. Ribs snapped beneath her heels, then she used her momentum to jump back, flipping through the air to avoid the spears of the other two jackals.

More arrived. Two, then four, their cries surrounding her. Drowning out Gilgamesh's screams. Soriya closed her eyes, refusing to back down, refusing to surrender despite the odds.

Fists flew through the air, cries of rage slipping from her lips as she danced in a field of death and decay. The followers of Anubis kept coming, each in turn falling to her desperation.

When Soriya stopped, when she took a moment to breathe and calm her pounding chest, she realized she was the last one standing in the chamber. Blood dripped from her right arm. She felt it join a puddle running down her legs through fresh cuts along her jeans.

The jackals lay unconscious on the floor, their blank eyes closed to the world. The wider room flowed into the temple's center, torches increasing along the left wall down a length of corridor.

The central chamber.

"I'm coming, Gil," she muttered, feeling hot blood mix with spittle along her lips. She wiped it away and charged toward her friend's growing screams.

CHAPTER SEVEN

Soriya stopped outside the central chamber. Patrols ran along the outskirts, sporadic despite the fisticuffs outside. She had been quick enough to silence the jackals keeping her from her friend. That was all the luck she could ask for.

She found more, however, in the distance between patrols. The central chamber, the heart of the immense temple hidden beneath the streets of Portents, was staggering. It could have filled a football stadium in its length but it was the height, arcing up to a central point like a pyramid, that astonished the dark-skinned warrior.

Rafters intersected above, latticing from wall to wall to support the structure. The chamber was one extensive pedestal in the center surrounded by stadium seating. The ribbons of Kali skirted along the wall, grabbing the nearest support beam. Once snagged, it pulled taut and Soriya soared into the air, silent against the cries from the pedestal.

Gilgamesh.

He stood, tied at the ankles and wrists to an enormous apparatus on the platform. He pulled at his bindings, unable to gain an inch away from the device. It stood at fifteen feet tall, a giant Eye of Horus seen by all when the room was at capacity—a dangerous thought if ever Soriya had one. It appeared to be nothing more than a simple stonework statue, connected to a keypad in the shape of a sundial. Large icons decorated the surface, each depression causing short bursts of electricity to charge into the eye and a bright light to grow behind the bound Gilgamesh.

Two figures stood with Gilgamesh on the platform. One, a woman of incredible beauty—and aware of it—remained close to her captive. The other, a tall man wearing a twisted beard and decorative headdress, depressed a third icon on the keypad before moving in front of them.

"The eye is ready," the man said.

Delicate fingers grazed Gilgamesh's bruised and bleeding cheek. "Hear that, my darling? All our time apart and here we come together."

Gilgamesh pulled away, spitting at the ground in disgust. "Of all the gin joints in Portents. Is that it, Ishtar?"

Ishtar? Soriya recognized the name. A spoiled brat of a goddess with intentions to marry a much more arrogant Gilgamesh only to see her love rebuked. In her rage she swore vengeance, even promising to crack open the gates of Hell so the dead could overtake the living. It may have taken centuries, but she appeared close to completing that revenge on the world and the man at the center of her anger.

"Your connection is fresh, my love."

"And yours is stale," Gilgamesh snapped. "Like your fashion sense."

A heavy slap sent him reeling. "Don't be cruel, boy. Who set you on this path? Who provided you with this gift in the first place?"

"You took everything from me, you witch. Then offered me a curse, one I should have avoided."

"Yet didn't," she said. "You're not the first."

"I'll be the last."

"That might actually be true." Ishtar shrugged, stepping over to the keypad. The decorated priest walked her through the icons quietly, nodding with excitement as the eye whirred and grew brighter behind Gilgamesh.

"What are you doing?"

Ishtar glanced at her companion, who nodded his approval. "The eye will open and we will see your connection. It will reach beyond the veil."

"Calling Anubis home," the man finished, his voice booming before the eye.

"Anubis," Soriya whispered from the rafters. If that happened, if the lord of the afterlife returned to the world, no one would be safe. She needed to act, she needed to end this, but she hesitated. Too many jackals on the perimeter. Too much time for things to go wrong for Gilgamesh. She felt the ribbons tighten along her left side and the stone in her right hand burn with anticipation. Still, she waited.

"Osiris, are you insane?" Gilgamesh screamed, his eyes fighting through a growing pain.

And now Osiris? Of course. Another connection to Anubis and the dead. Some believed Osiris to be the father of Anubis, the true ruler of the underworld. Osiris was resurrected by the Eye of Horus, leaving his throne to his kin.

Looks like daddy misses his boy.

"The eye gives us glimpses. We only catch snippets of the world to be, of the darkness rising in the city and beyond. This world has been tainted by humanity, Gilgamesh. Surely you've discovered that?"

Ishtar sauntered to his side. "Anubis will usher in a new age. The final age for man and the dawn of the new."

"Show us the way."

"Don't hold out on me," Ishtar whispered in her captive's ear.

The eye opened more, sending light pouring out into the chamber. Soriya squinted through the wave of white. Gilgamesh grimaced, electricity charging through the apparatus and into him.

"Don't do this!" he bellowed.

Ishtar sighed and returned to the dial. Her finger hovered over a command then pressed it with finality. "Too late."

Gilgamesh screamed, the power flowing freely from the device into the control panel and back in a recursive loop, growing more powerful with each cycle. The eye widened, the luminous white increasing with his pain. He shook his head, struggling to free himself from his bindings.

Until he couldn't any longer. Until all control and all rational thought departed. Gilgamesh howled into the air, his eyes as white as the Eye of Horus itself.

"She is coming," he said, his voice not his own. Like a recording being played back. "From the shadows she builds an army."

"Who?" Ishtar asked.

Osiris clenched his fists in anger. "Anubis! Tell us of our lord!"

Gilgamesh ignored them. He stared off where his rescuer hid in the rafters. Soriya caught his stare and he locked on, talking to her.

"A pawn," he said. "Useless against the rising tide. When the bell rings, it truly begins. He is returning."

"Anubis," Osiris gasped with anticipation.

"The mentor," Gil continued, "will bring back a great evil with his return. Portents will suffer. We will all suffer."

Gilgamesh closed his eyes and slumped forward. Soriya shook her head, unable to wait any longer. She dropped from the rafters, the ribbon tied like a bungee until it released her on the far side of the platform.

"Especially you for what you've done to my friend," she said to the startled Osiris and Ishtar.

Osiris pointed to her. "Seize her!"

"Really?" Soriya said with a roll of her eyes. Jackals leaped from all sides, yet the young woman jumped over their uncoordinated assault before diving into the fray with fists flying. "You guys deserve an ass-kicking with villain talk like that."

"Soriya…" Gilgamesh muttered.

"I'm coming, Gil," Soriya replied, kicking away two approaching jackals while catching the spear of a third. She wheeled him around, flinging the beast clear from the weapon and the platform. "Just hold on!"

Ishtar rushed to the side of her captive. Delicate hands grazed his skin. "Let it go, lover. Bring him back. Anubis will provide."

Gilgamesh's eyes burned. "You want what he has to offer so badly?"

Ishtar staggered, falling away from the caged man. "Don't…"

"Soriya!" Gil yelled across the vast chamber.

She spun, using the spear to cut down the closest pair of jackals. They were replaced with more, a swarm of beasts flooding the chamber's entrance.

"Just need a few more minutes, Gil." Dozens surrounded her, cutting her off from her friend. "Okay. This might take a bit longer."

Gilgamesh shook his head. "Jump."

"What?"

His eyes burst with light once more, his skin barely able to contain the glow permeating his entire body. "Now!" he shouted. "JUMP NOW!"

She dropped the spear and bounded for the sky. The ribbons snapped to life, spreading wide. Hands reached for her, the jackals unsuccessfully attempting to keep her grounded. Fear filled Osiris and Ishtar, who huddled close together, moving in for a kiss.

A goodbye kiss.

The cloud of light exploded in a wave, the force jolting the room. Soriya watched it approach, the ribbons pulling her back as fast as possible for the rafters above. Not fast enough, however. The Greystone rested before her and she tried to focus on its power, hoping it would be enough to save her.

She never had the chance. The stone was already glowing, the sigil upon its surface one she had never seen.

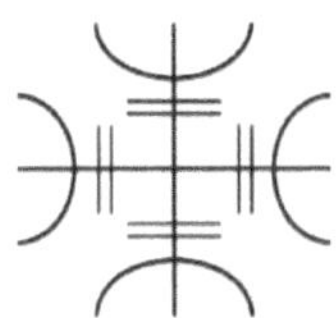

The light split around her as if hitting a protective barrier.

"How?"

When the light finally dimmed, Soriya dropped back to the floor. Bodies littered the ground, the jackals nothing more than bone from the assault. Ishtar and Osiris clung to each other on the platform. Their final embrace carried them across the veil.

No doubt, Anubis waited on the other side to welcome them home.

CHAPTER EIGHT

Blood rushed to his fingers as the chains snapped loose. Soriya held him close, lowering him to the ground from the great Eye of Horus at the temple's center. The dead surrounded them on all sides. His act had saved them, but at a cost.

Gilgamesh fought to stand. Soriya tried to assist until he pushed away from her. He didn't need the help, didn't want the help. Not after what he had done, what he had to do to save them. He feared the light brewing beneath the surface might return, his connection never truly severed from the duty performed over the centuries.

He stopped before Ishtar, the woman who set his destiny in motion. The one who caused so much grief in his existence. She took everything from him—his companion, Enkidu, all choices in life, everything.

"You okay?"

"I'm fine." His fingers ran the breadth of Ishtar's fleshless cheek, offering a silent goodbye.

"That was…well…"

"It had to be done."

"How many, Gil?" she asked, pointing to the door. "How far?"

"The temple. Only the temple," he swore. "Far enough to send a message."

"Hopefully." Soriya staggered, holding her side. Cuts ran along her arms, blood soaking her jeans.

"And you? Are you—?"

"Fantastic," she said with a smirk. "I'd love to hear the trick with overriding the stone though."

She handed him the stone and he cradled it. The mysterious artifact hummed under his wary fingers, light growing then dimming from his caress. He passed the Greystone back and she tucked it against her hip. He offered a sad smile. "We're old friends."

"Care to elaborate?"

He turned for the door. "Soriya."

"And the other thing? Gilgamesh?"

He didn't know what to say, how to tell her the truth. The connection remained. After so many centuries of working as the avatar of Death, his link to the other side continued. He saw death everywhere, no matter the circumstance. Death was integral to his existence and always would be, no matter the sacrifices made for the sake of a normal life.

"They shouldn't have known about me."

"Sounds familiar."

He shook his head. This wasn't about secrets being held back. *To be used in such a manner, to be sought after and hunted as he had?* His presence in the city wasn't common knowledge, especially after his involvement with the Charon and the Medusa coin. Only Soriya was aware he remained. No one else knew, especially of the abilities he hid from the world.

"I'm a danger," he said. "To you. To Portents."

"You're safe now. There's no—"

"No," he snapped. "There will always be someone else. Something else. I was arrogant to think otherwise."

The same crime that plagued his previous life in Uruk. The one that led him back to Ishtar after his failed attempts at immortality—a path that granted him the eternal life he sought but also bound his spirit with Death.

Blaming Ishtar was easy. Putting every fault in her seductive ways kept him clean when he was anything but. His arrogance bought his suffering. His need to be more—to live forever—cost him one life. The curse of his choices continued to cost him even after centuries of sacrifice.

Gilgamesh walked slowly for the exit, leaving behind his rescuer. He kept his head low, his eyes wincing with each glimpse of the dead at his feet.

"Wait," Soriya called. "Gilgamesh! With what's coming…"

She is coming. Out of the shadows she builds an army.

It was coming sooner than he cared to admit. The pain and the death of a war in the streets. He could do nothing to stop the long night ahead. No words could halt the approaching storm.

"You will be better off without having to worry about me as well."

"That's not true, Gil," she said, rushing to his side. "I'm your friend. We can—"

He took her hand. A smile struggled to his face. "Then be my friend and understand why I have to leave."

She shook her head, fighting to find a reason, an excuse to keep him with her, in the city, under her protection. If he waited long enough, she would find one—and he would regret it. The pain in his eyes attested to that.

Finally she nodded, letting him go.

"Goodbye, Greystone."

He left her at the platform's edge, heading for the dim torchlight of the tunnels surrounding the central chamber. Darkness waited beyond—the same darkness, always with him.

Portents was meant to be a chance to change, a new beginning and a way for him to have a life, one shared with the living. A normal life. Now he wondered if such a feat was ever possible, or if it had been yet another lie. Would he ever find a place in the world? Or had his time come and gone and now lay with the dead?

Like those surrounding his heavy footfalls, accompanying him into the shadows of the city.

FOUNDER'S DAY

CHAPTER ONE

The world blurred around Dixon Harris. A red haze fell over everything, his eyes unable to clear. The night had certainly not gone his way.

There was dinner, one he never should have initiated. Pamela was back in town—another promise broken. He continued the streak by answering her call to propose the meal out. The simple affirmative meant more to both of them and he knew it, cursing his inability to say no to her. Cursing the little man downstairs for having such control over his thoughts when it came to the woman that wrecked his first marriage and was working hard on his second.

She held power over him. Her voice, her body. Everything. The same power he held over so many in Portents as the district attorney. The scandal rags had their hooks into his affairs but he countered them for the most part. When his first wife left him, he was a novice at the game.

In more ways than he cared to admit, he remained one.

Dinner was engaging but he stopped it there, the promise of meeting up later offered yet never answered. He needed to forget her, to put her out of his mind, but her number sat at the top of his call history. The image of her lips puckered and waiting for his arrival was too tempting.

So enthralled with his cell phone, Dixon Harris failed to notice the shadow approaching. Not until he felt the prick of a needle in his neck and searing pain race through his body.

Then nothing but darkness.

Ending with the red blur.

Dixon moved to clear his eyes, but his hands were immediately pulled back over his head. Chains clattered along the wall behind him. He kicked out to the same effect, bound on all sides.

His vision cleared; the panic settled over him as he searched the room. Red tinted everything despite his returned eyesight, and he saw that the crimson shined from above. The sound of dripping water echoed throughout the vast space. An altar of stone rested in front of him. Scorch marks lined the walls around him, a half-obscured image of some form of bird charred against the edifice.

"Where?" he asked. "Where the hell am I?"

The panic took over, the chains refusing to bend, refusing to relinquish any power back to him.

"HELP!" His screams filled the hall.

"No one is coming," a voice replied from the darkness.

Dixon quieted instantly; panic escalated to fear and terror. "Who's there?"

Laughter rose to the rafters, bouncing around the high ceilings and the tinted glass skylight. "The sad thing, Dixon, is that with all your so-called friends and that beautiful wife of yours—she's cheating on you by the way—no one even knows you're missing."

Dixon seethed at the shadow's laughter. He pulled at the chains, reaching out to the darkness that hid his captor. "Who the hell do you think you are? Let me go now. You have no idea—"

"I have every idea," the shadow boomed. "But I settled on one."

A knife glinted from the shadows. The chains held Dixon fast, his rage impotent like his every effort.

"No," he pleaded. "Listen. I have money. I can get you whatever you want. Just—"

"This is what I want."

"But I haven't done anything," Dixon yelled. "What the hell could I have done to you to—?"

The shadow stepped from the darkness and Dixon's mouth fell open.

"Oh."

Dixon stopped struggling against the chains binding him to the wall. He stopped protesting, stopped thinking of escape. There was no point. No point in pretending he would see his wife again—or Pamela, or anyone else. This was the end and he earned it.

"I'm sorry," he said to the approaching figure.

The knife struck fast, slipping into his side then again on the other and once more in the center. Precise and practiced. Blood poured from each blow but he did not cry out; he stayed silent in the face of his death.

His killer appreciated it. "Apology accepted."

CHAPTER TWO

Two dead. Another case added to a growing pile. Detective Samantha Myers didn't mind—that was the job. It kept her thinking, kept her moving. And it kept her near her partner, Greg Loren.

He bitched the entire way. Two dead in a warehouse fire, the place burned right off the map without any accelerants. Everything about the case—from the victims to the lack of clues at the scene—led them to believe it was something else.

That was the best way Myers explained things when it came to their work, and to their partnership. If a case couldn't be explained, it meant *something else* was in the mix.

But did Loren care? Was he concerned about the killer, the man they spent three days tracking before he surfaced on a CCTV cam outside the warehouse the night after the fire? Was he worried about whatever the hell this guy held secret from the world as they approached his apartment building?

No. He was too busy bitching about her driving.

"I'm just saying if you had taken King's Lane then—"

"I drive the car, Loren," Myers snapped, slamming the driver's side door behind her. Loren followed her for the front stoop. He had nitpicked her driving all night. Last week it was what she ate in the office while finishing reports. The week before that was her lack of gloves even with the temperatures starting to take a nosedive for the winter.

She wasn't any better, if she was being honest. She hassled him on any number of fronts. His uncombed hair, his thickening beard, and the way he snapped that damn gum in her ear when he felt like getting her attention.

New partners. Growing pains, right?

"I could drive if you—"

She raised a finger and he fell silent. She reached for the door to the apartment complex on the border of Lowtown and Tolliver's Grove. "Arrest the murderer, then bitch."

"Love it when a plan comes together," Loren said, slipping inside with his gun in hand.

The image caught across the street from the warehouse fire brought a new energy around the case. Tip lines blew up; dozens of statements were taken, yet few offered little in the way of assistance. All it took was one, though, and it fell into place like everything else when it came to a case: with time, patience, and a modicum of good fortune. Finally they had a name to go with a face.

Bartleby Kindt.

"How did you find this place again?" Loren asked in a whisper, the pair heading for the second floor apartment on the far side of the building.

"City records."

Loren stopped in the stairwell, holding her up with a glare. "Myers?"

She rolled her eyes at the unspoken accusation. Months of working together did little to help her credibility with the man, who came to learn about her ability to hack into personnel files for fun pretty early in their relationship.

"I made friends with the clerk, Loren."

"Friends?"

She grinned at the tinge of jealousy. "He has four cats at home and a model of every iteration of the Enterprise on his desk. It's a big desk."

Loren continued up the stairs. "Sounds like someone that needs a friend."

"Exactly," Myers replied. "Kindt is on public assistance. Section 8 housing."

"Which the city tracks. And your new friend—"

"Helped out in a pinch."

"Because of your love of *Star Trek*."

She shrugged. "The needs of the many and all that shit. Come on already."

His laughter followed them down the hall. Working with Loren took some getting used to for Myers. The crappy habits were one thing, but his commitment to the work was something else. He held a passion she had never seen during her time in New York, or working the day shift under Mathers—and not in the disgustingly sweaty way that still gave her nightmares.

She couldn't deny it: Loren was good police.

Kindt's apartment sat at the end of the hall, next to the back stairwell. Myers checked her phone to confirm the number with the one on the door before moving to knock. Loren stopped her.

"Myers, listen," he whispered. "Hang on a sec."

"Loren?"

"There's something…"

"Yeah, I know. Something about this guy. You've said."

"I didn't know how to mention it before. I know how you are when it comes to certain things in this city but—"

"Certain things, Loren?" Myers said, hands to her hips. "You mean like the time the coroner turned out to be a freaking Charon bent on sucking my damn soul out of my chest?"

"As an example, yes."

"I think I've been pretty open-minded about the weird crap I've seen."

"You have," Loren mumbled, rubbing his neck. "And I should have mentioned it right off with the fire—"

"Let me guess," Myers interrupted. "Fiery flatulence? Give the man a burrito and the entire block goes up in flames?"

"No, Myers, he's—"

"Crap," a voice rang out from the back stairs. Both detectives turned at the sound, weapons drawn and aimed at the bulky man juggling two brown paper grocery bags. They fell from his hands, landing perfectly on the ground at his feet.

"Mr. Kindt," Myers started, showing her badge. "Police. We have a few—"

"Myers…"

Kindt exhaled hard and smoke escaped from his flared nostrils. His eyes screamed at them and a light grew from his open mouth.

"Loren," Myers muttered. "He's *breathing* fire, Loren."

"Move!" Loren pushed her aside before diving to the other side of the hall. A stream of fire filled the hall, the heat from the instant blaze forcing Myers to hug the wall. When it died down, she peered around the small alcove offered by the apartment door.

Kindt was gone, the sound of footsteps rushing down the back stairwell echoing. Loren joined her, offering a hand. She grabbed hold and stood.

"Okay," Myers said, taking a breath. "What the hell--?"

"Dragon."

"An actual dragon?" Myers shook her head. "You want me to believe that man was a *dragon*?"

"At this point? Probably."

"So now what?" She moved for the grocery bags, stopping at the sound of more steps. "Loren?"

"I've got this," he yelled, rushing after the killer.

"Don't," she tried to say, glimpsing the man's groceries and the objects within. "Loren, don't! He'll—"

"I'll be fine, Myers," Loren shouted before the door slammed behind him, leaving her to the corridor's silence. Small flames flickered along the hall, the remnants of Kindt's presence. Myers lifted the grocery bags and started for the apartment.

"You've got this. A damn dragon and you've got this," she grumbled. "I hate this city."

CHAPTER THREE

What the hell are you doing?
"Chasing after a fire-breathing dragon."
Think about that for a second.

Loren raced through the streets of Lowtown, the frumpy form of Bartleby Kindt unable to shake the determined detective. Traffic blared around them, the evening commute still trying to make it home. Even in this area, a known haven for killers and drug enthusiasts, rush hour traffic still existed during the week.

They should have questioned Bartleby later, when they were sure he was home. Instead, they were arguing. Not actual arguing—those typically came to a point and Loren had none to offer. More like bickering. Why were they always bickering?

The same reason he ran down the street without his partner. With his injuries finally behind him, Loren pushed harder into the crosswind, rushing down the avenues to close the gap on Kindt. Was he trying to prove something to himself? Possibly. He hoped as much because the other explanation was downright childish.

Quit trying to impress Myers.

"Fine," he yelled, turning into the closest alley. He skidded to a halt at the sight of Bartleby Kindt waiting for him. Loren reached for his gun. "All right, Kindt, that's—"

Kindt screamed, fire blasting the alley's length. Loren dove into two pedestrians walking by, driving all three to the ground as the inferno raged overhead.

"What the hell, buddy?" one of the fallen asked, pushing Loren off. The other prodded him, noticing the detective's sidearm.

"Dude," he muttered, pulling his friend along. "Let's go."

"Weirdo," the first said. Neither made a comment about the plume of rising smoke or the sudden blast of heat from Kindt's fiery breath.

"You're welcome," Loren said. He dusted off his pants—not that anyone noticed his faded jeans decorated by stains and holes.

Bartleby stood in the alley, waiting for him. "It was an accident with those two guys! They jumped me and I—"

"Not really feeling like an accident right now, Kindt," Loren replied. "And those two guys ended up corpses so they can't hear your apology either."

He didn't stick around for more ridicule. There was pain in his eyes, true regret, but Loren could do nothing for him. The man murdered two people. Accident or not, truth or not, Bartleby Kindt had to be taken into custody.

Loren ran the length of the alley, finding his target a block north, moving for a nearby bus. Cars blared and Loren stopped short before he reached the street, his toes almost crushed from an impatient sedan. As the light clicked over, Loren burst across the street, making up for lost time.

Kindt, seeing Loren closing the gap, left the bus and ducked into another narrow passage. There was no getting away this time. Loren rounded the corner, his gun raised.

The alley was empty.

"Where the hell—?" A loud rustling rose through the air. Loren peered up into the night sky. The silhouette of Bartleby Kindt soared high over the streets, two large wings spread wide from his back. Loren smacked his forehead with his palm, then slammed his sidearm into his holster.

"Dragon. Right. Idiot."

It took the better part of an hour for Loren to get back to the apartment. Traffic made it difficult to pass through Lowtown and he ended up lost on Furth and Damascus. He tried heading toward the Knoll but it circled around where the expressway met the area going in the wrong direction.

Maybe it's a good thing Myers drives.

He promised to get to know the city better. It would be his fresh start, his new beginning. He was starting to hate thinking of it that way, his rank amateur behavior costing him the collar and his night.

Slowly climbing the stairs to the second floor, Loren considered Myers' reaction. He never should have left her in the first place—the whole thing had been against protocol, with the added bonus of a complete lack of results.

The door to Kindt's apartment lay ajar. Loren, hand to his sidearm, pushed it open farther. Myers waved from the couch, a copy of *Entertainment Weekly* on her lap. Bartleby Kindt sat in the recliner next to her, sporting a pair of handcuffs and a black eye.

"How?" Loren said from the doorway. "Myers?"

"He circled back," she answered, flipping through the magazine before tossing it to the coffee table.

"And you?"

"We chatted," she said with a shrug. "He saw the light."

Loren grinned at the man's puffed up cheek and bloodshot eye. "The light? Or your right?"

"Possibly both."

"How did you know he would come back?"

"Formula in the grocery bags."

"What?"

Myers pointed to the two bags on the kitchen counter. Then she cocked her head to the hallway leading to the two bedrooms in back. "Last door on the right, Detective."

He eyed her and started down the hall, then opened the door to the bedroom and stood within the frame. A nightlight beamed stars to the ceiling and a mobile spun over a white painted crib in the room's center. The little boy within sucked his thumb, busily dreaming the night away—completely unaware of the world around him. Loren offered a sad smile, watching the infant's chest rise and fall in a slow rhythm.

Lucky him.

"I'll handle the dossier next time, genius," she called. "Maybe lead with the whole breathes fire thing."

"Probably a good idea."

CHAPTER FOUR

The interrogation door swung shut behind them, the remorseful eyes of Bartleby Kindt following their departure. Loren watched the grown man bury his head in his hands, wondering if there was some other way, some other path they could have taken.

Unfortunately, the courts would handle things from here. Kindt lawyered up, his guilt all but written on the sheets of loose-leaf tucked under Loren's arm. The case was airtight but Kindt's proclamation of self-defense might hold water with the jury.

Myers led the way through the first floor of the Central Precinct. She nodded to the guard and asked about the man's kids.

Frank? Is his name Frank? Or Chris? Loren shook his head, offering a nod and a smirk to the man before following his partner to the waiting stairs and their home on the second floor.

How she managed to know everything about everyone was astonishing to him. So was his complete inability to even capture a person's name despite that he'd worked with Frank—or Chris—for years.

"It's Curtis. Curtis Bell," Myers said on their way up the stairs.

"How the hell—?"

"Smoke was coming out of your ears," Myers said. "And you make this weird pouty lipped face when you're trying to remember a name you never knew in the first place."

"Liar."

She rolled her eyes then stopped. "So are we really leaving Smaug in Holding? Just like that?"

"*Lord of the Rings* and a *Star Trek* reference in one shift? I'm starting to worry about you, Myers."

"You should," she said, shoving her hands into her pockets. "All I'm saying is a normal, everyday murder would be a nice change of pace."

"I'll add it to your Christmas list."

Loren jammed his key into the door and turned the handle. It failed to budge and he squeezed harder pushing against the wood. Myers cleared her throat and he threw her a thin glare, then backed off to let her take over. She stepped forward, turned the handle and the entrance to their cozy little portion of the Central Precinct opened before them.

"I hate you," Loren muttered.

"You'll get it someday," Myers grinned, tossing her jacket to the floor before collapsing at her desk.

"Doubtful." Loren shook his head, dropping his keys soundly on his desk. Then he started for the filing cabinets crammed into the back corner of the formerly spacious single office. With Myers joining him, Loren spent more time running into furniture and slipping on forgotten reports. Rubbing his latest bruise after crashing into the side of his desk, Loren grabbed two blank sheets from a multi-colored pile.

Myers waited with her hand out when he turned. "Hand them over."

"What?"

She snapped her fingers. "My collar. My paperwork."

"I can fill out the arrest report, Myers."

"Sure you can," Myers said. She circled her desk and snatched the reports from Loren with a smile. "Next time, bag the murderer. You have other things to do anyway, don't you?" She nudged the locked bottom drawer on the left-hand side of his desk. "Super secret work, right?"

He rubbed his neck sheepishly. "Something like that. Thanks."

She hovered over the desk. "Care to share?"

The missing person's reports stumbled upon during the Erikson affair. Mathers assigned them to Loren in the hopes of keeping him out of the investigation, off to the side and forgotten, until Myers called and threw him right into the center of the case.

The reports remained with him. Not officially. Mathers buried them in the cold cases division, split between four overworked and underpaid officers without a clue as to what they were looking at when it came to the stack of reports. *If* reports were even filed, which wasn't the case most of the time.

No, this was Loren's case and he didn't want to share the details with Myers or anyone. Not until he knew more. Not until the truth came out about the individual or group behind the abductions of dozens of special people in the city. Including Hady Ronne.

Loren shook his head, taking his seat to boot up his computer. "It's nothing. Don't worry about it."

"Won't," she replied too quickly. *Genuine concern or something else?*

Myers took a seat and her phone immediately chimed. Instead of reaching for her pocket, she opened the center drawer of her desk and flipped open the device. She peered at the screen before snapping the phone shut and tucking it into her pocket.

"News about the kid?" Loren asked, fighting the urge to ask about the second cell phone—one he didn't know existed.

"Hmmm?" She shook her head. "Sorry. Wrong number." She typed feverishly, a whirlwind compared to the gentle breeze Loren created with his single-finger typing. "Let's see. CPS report is already in the system."

"Damn right it is. He just left the kid alone like that?"

"Babysitter flaked on him."

"No excuse."

"Loren, the kid'll be fine," Myers continued. "There's probably some family out there."

"Probably."

Myers nodded. She took up her pen then dropped it once more on the desk. "You ever think about having any? Kids, I mean?"

"Me?" Loren said, surprised by the query. "I can barely function, Myers." His look thinned, curiosity winning out. "You?"

Myers laughed. "Oh, I'd be a terrible mother. Wife too. Family...let's just say my days of family life are long since gone."

Loren wondered if his own would say the same about him. His sister would. She basically did when he told her he was staying in Portents.

Myers was staring at him.

"Do I have something in my teeth?"

"You've never thought about it?"

"Kids?" Loren tapped along the desk. Reaching inside the center drawer, he pulled out a stick of gum and slipped it between his lips as he turned for the door. "Not in a long time."

She nodded. "Say no more."

"What?"

She pointed to the door and the corkboards behind it. His wife's picture stared back at him. "You're in Beth mode."

"Am not."

"You definitely are."

"Fine," he said, spinning his chair in the opposite direction. Snow fell steadily in tune with the fast approaching season. "She always liked this time of year."

"Winter? Gag me now."

Lights decorated the trees of Heaven's Gate Park and down Evans Avenue. Too early for the holiday season but not for the celebration at the end of the week.

"Founder's Day." Every year the city put on a parade and a number of events downtown in celebration of the founding of the city. A party to commemorate a lie, the truth all but buried and forgotten. For good reason.

"A hundred twenty-five years of Portents," Myers said, disgust in her voice. "How the hell did this city manage that?"

"A very good question," Loren replied. "Plans?"

"Absolutely." She smiled and he waited for her to finish. "A pot of coffee and my Netflix queue. Same as every day."

Loren shook his head. "This is your home now, Myers. You could live in it for one day."

"Coming from you?"

"Point," Loren said. He stood and looked out over the city, the statue of William Rath looming in the square. "I thought I'd hit the parade route."

Myers shivered. "Bitter wind and thousands of crazy people in the streets? My pajamas would be heartbroken."

Loren laughed.

"What's so funny?"

"Just picturing you with rollers in your hair surrounded by cats. You know that clerk at city records might be perfect for you after all."

"Shut your mouth."

Loren reached for his phone. "What was his name again? Maybe you could compare queues? He could bring his cats over for a play date. Could be heavenly."

"Sounds like hell."

A throat cleared from the hall. "I hope I'm not interrupting."

They turned at the sight of Captain Gerrianne Wexler. She filled the frame, broad shouldered with the ability to bench press Loren with ease. Three months at Central, after her transfer from the Ninth to replace Ruiz during his leave of absence, and he was surprised every time she showed up.

Which was too often lately. Wexler enjoyed taking a more active approach to her charges. Updates were constantly required and when it came to the cases Loren and Myers handled; more updates ended up adding to the questions asked.

Questions difficult to answer, to say the least.

Still, Loren respected her. Or tried to at any rate. Thinking and doing had trouble getting on the same page sometimes.

"Captain," they both said in unison.

Wexler squeezed the bridge of her nose. "Would it kill you to wear a decent shirt for a change, Loren? This is work, not comic-con."

"That's debatable with the cosplayers in holding," Loren shot back despite Myers' flaring eyes. A warning to shut up—one typically ignored.

"She's not laughing, Loren."

"She might be," Loren pressed. "A twinge of a grin?"

"Not even a little," Wexler said, ending his rambling. She rubbed her temples in small circular motions.

"Headache, Captain?"

"It's called work, Loren," she snapped. "One increasing every time I walk in here. Between your childish attempts at humor, Mathers' temper tantrums, and this Founder's Day disaster in the making, I have half a mind to call Ruiz and beg him to come back." She drew a deep breath, and the pair waited for the other shoe to drop. She might have been more active with the officers working for her but she still didn't waste time with small talk. "But since I'm stuck in this daycare center, maybe you can put your binky away for a second and do your job."

A file fell from her hand to the desk. "What's this?"

"My next headache. And now yours too."

Loren opened the file and shook his head.

"Loren?" Myers asked.

He tossed it over to her. "A normal, everyday murder."

Her eyes fell on the red label. "Ah, hell."

"You just had to ask for it."

CHAPTER FIVE

Loren was a mess of a human. From his eternal stubble to his shabbily prepared clothing, he looked more like a homeless man than a professional. His attitude rarely helped him in this regard, with his mouth moving faster than his brain. The burden he carried was apparent: the broken and crumpled soul of a man incomplete.

Except when he worked a crime scene.

Call it his natural element—or his staunch professionalism, which it certainly wasn't—or even respect for the deceased, which it probably was. When Greg Loren stood in the midst of a murder scene, he became a different person.

Focused. Finding details no one else noticed. Myers loved to watch it happen. The change, the shift, like a switch in his brain throwing away all the personal crap that weighed him down.

The block was vacant as the hour crept toward midnight. Traffic, both foot and vehicle, had long since ended. The unspoken rule of Portents took effect and Myers appreciated the quiet.

She stood at the base of the courthouse's wide concrete steps. Streetlights beamed down from above but portable spotlights offered a true picture of the scene for the growing number of officers and technicians on hand.

She knew Caldwell Courthouse, where she had appeared on the witness stand a dozen times in the last three months thanks to her work in the department. Nothing worthy of the evening news but enough to keep some bad folks off the streets. The building was a monument to justice and to the city itself. The first of its kind in Portents, frequently used for the tourist crowd on postcards, greeting cards, or depending on your intentions in the city, your final destination before prison.

The body lying along the pillar to the right of the entrance offered its own headline for tomorrow. The white marble contained the final quotes of Wilbur Caldwell, the city's first judge, and ran the length of the column.

Loren paced the outskirts of the scene. From different angles he approached the victim, looking for specifics about the vantage point, about the exact path taken by the killer to and from the area. Then he settled on the body, peeking beneath the thick, black cloak covering the deceased, snapping his gum between his teeth.

Myers muddled through the preliminaries offered by forensics. A male, age forty-three. Approximately 210 pounds—definitely not muscle. Basic information, none of which offered insight. She knew that would come from Loren. It almost always did.

Her view of the scene and her partner was suddenly obstructed by a shadow looming beside her.

"Detective?" Pratchett said, fighting his usual goofy ass grin.

"Pratchett."

"Need anything? Coffee? Wine cooler?"

"Do people still drink those?" Myers turned to the towering officer. "Wait. What the hell are you talking about?"

"I was joking."

"Another failed attempt. Hope the cordon is going better."

Pratchett sighed. "That's why I'm here. Obviously."

"Oh. Obviously."

She peered around, bypassing the smug look on the man's face. The block was cordoned off, four uniforms at every intersection. The lack of traffic made things easy, too easy for Pratchett. A mischievous grin grew along her lips and Pratchett rolled his eyes.

"Listen, I want—" She turned to point down Evans, hoping to extend the cordon out and give her lazy cohort something to do when she caught sight of Wexler heading their way. "You know what? The captain might be a better person to ask."

Pratchett blinked rapidly, shaking his head. "Really?"

"I'm trying here, Pratchett. So go be an umbrella for someone else."

"Somehow that's funnier than wine coolers?"

She patted his arm, pushing him away. "It's in the delivery. Go."

Loren tossed her a look then went back to the body, peering under the cloak. She joined him, grateful Pratchett had sidelined Wexler for the moment.

"What is it?"

"Dixon Harris."

"Dixon…" She stopped. "District Attorney Dixon Harris?"

"That would be the one."

"Holding office in this city is not advisable." Loren threw her a sharp glance and she waved it away. "Sorry."

Loren stood. "Makes the site specifically chosen."

"Courthouse." She agreed. More importantly, the first one. A message? The first of many in terms of victims? "Revenge for a case?"

"Worth looking into," Loren answered, his voice uncertain.

"No blood," Myers continued, pacing around the victim. "Body was moved here."

Loren nodded, pointing to the east. Fredericks Avenue. Side street off Evans. Less lighting. Fewer cameras. Well thought out. "But not dumped. Positioned."

Myers opened the preliminaries, shuffling through to the photos in the back. "Street cams caught him for a second on his way out. Nothing on this guy. His face was covered."

"His? That's something at least."

"Have to be, wouldn't it?" Myers said, the less-than-lean DA between them. "Not a featherweight, this guy."

Wexler joined them. She shook a small bottle, snapping open the lid to down three tablets. She crunched them loudly, joining the chorus with Loren's gum.

"Cause of death?"

"Stabbed," Loren said. "I took a peek."

"Lucky you."

"Don't let Anderson find out you unwrapped his present."

Loren shrugged. "Three clear entries."

He crouched low, delicately pulling back the cloak covering the naked figure of Dixon Harris. Myers knew the man by reputation more than the man himself. Their interactions were brief and biting, usually comprising a fight over a case not going his way. Cops always took the hit on that front and Myers never let him go without a rebuttal or ten. Maybe Loren wasn't the only one that had trouble keeping his mouth shut.

Probably why they fit together so well.

Dixon Harris, while a pain in the ass for the department, was a fine litigator. He held the top spot for the last eight months, working from the dregs of the DA's office. Myers had seen many people do a lot less to get his position. At the moment, she hoped to see a lot less of the nude victim.

Three stab marks to the abdomen from a large blade—a knife but nothing from the kitchen. This one had weight and depth to it. The entry wounds were clean. No struggle. Dixon took the hits without raising a finger.

Wexler brought it home before Loren could go through his findings. "No vital organs were pierced. Not even nicked."

Both looked to her in surprise. "Captain?"

Wexler cocked her head, then pinched the bridge of her nose. "Medical school dropout. Regretting it more and more every day."

Loren nodded. "You're right, though. Each entry was precisely placed to prolong his suffering."

"The killer watched him bleed out," Wexler said.

"Sadistic."

"Part of the ritual?" Loren said, covering the body once more. "Bled out then positioned here for all to see? This was intentional. For us."

"And the robe?"

He fell silent, his eyes distant.

"Loren?" Myers asked.

"I'm not sure," he said, removing his gloves. "I've seen it before."

"I need to start going to your parties, Loren."

"Invitation only, Myers. Sorry."

Wexler groaned. "Banter later. And not in front of the cameras, please."

"Headache won't go away, Captain?" Myers asked as the woman closed her eyes tight.

"It only gets worse," she snapped, shaking her empty aspirin bottle. "Founder's Day is three days away. Parade route runs right down Evans."

"Could be the point," Loren admitted.

"Except we don't know," Wexler said. "So find out, would you? Before we have ten thousand potential victims on this street."

"We'll find him." Myers tucked her notes into the preliminary folder.

"No promises, Myers. Not after that Erikson mess."

Myers nodded. The Erikson mess. Almost four months since leading the case against the worst serial killer in the city's history. A case plagued by poor coordination and a lack of information for the people working under her as lead detective. Her lack of trust remained a sticking point with the bigwigs at the precinct—Wexler among them.

"Right," she muttered. Her partner started down the steps in a hurry. "Loren?"

He stopped at the sidewalk. "You coming or not?"

"Where?"

"After we hit up Harris' office let's see what Anderson can give us."

The coroner's office. The perfect end to the perfect night. "You sure know how to show a lady a good time."

CHAPTER SIX

Gilbert Mitchell never had a care in the world. Born to a modestly wealthy family, he made his mark on politics at an early age with the seed money offered by his dearly departed parents.

Politics came easy. Playing the game between red and blue, right and left, and never missing a beat when switching sides at the appropriate times. Whatever the season, whichever way the political wind blew, Gilbert had his sail ready to carry him further along the stream to his goals.

Life went similarly. An ease at socializing, at making connections, carried over from his work. He met his wife in such a manner. Lost in conversation with a former DA, he almost failed to notice her listening. Or so he played it. Gilbert was adept at drawing a crowd, especially of the fairer sex. His looks helped, his deep voice a strength. More than anything was the confidence behind his opinions. Everyone wanted to hear them and then side with them. It was definitely in their best interest to do so.

The shadow watching Gilbert depart his home always felt that way, at any rate.

He sat in his car across the street, eyes wide on the inconspicuous Cape Cod in Tolliver's Grove. He waited for the right moment, excitement raging down to his fingertips at the sight of the man leaving his home after dinner.

Garbage night. The perfect opportunity.

Despite his relatively low position in the city, Gilbert Mitchell held Mayor Dunn's ear. He carried influence, despite being only a glorified paper pusher. With as much love as Dunn had for him Gilbert could have been more in the administration—deputy mayor even, especially after the untimely death of the last during the unfortunate Erikson debacle. Gilbert could have been anything he wanted, done anything in life.

That was his true power—the same power that won over the woman waving to him from the kitchen window. Leann Daniels, their courtship only lasting a few months before he offered the ring. Leann worked in the DA's office and knew the power players in the city. It was a marriage of convenience for Gilbert. A marriage for knowledge, and he never let the upper hand slip away when he had the chance.

His job of shuffling papers was only a cover. Working with the budget department gave Gilbert access to many things, including the city's lobbyists. More power. More affluence. Gilbert's corruption, the money trading hands in closed-door meetings, paid for his house, for his lifestyle, and possibly for his wife's continued support despite the constant stepping out by both.

It was time for Gilbert Mitchell to pay for his crimes.

The garbage can slammed next to the leaning mailbox. The recycling bin followed, a large wall of bushes blocking Leann's view of her husband.

The shadow exited the car, rushing across the street. Gilbert moved quickly, fixing the trash then starting back to the house. The shadow fell too far behind, afraid of the lingering traffic catching sight of him and the syringe in his grasp.

Gilbert waved to his wife, whose eyes flared. She had spotted the shadow.

Gilbert started to turn, following his wife's terror. The needle struck Gilbert's jugular, his mouth covered to prevent a scream. The man's body went limp, a gloved hand pulling away from the driveway toward the waiting car.

"Gil?" Leann cried, racing from the house.

The shadow cursed. He shuffled Gilbert's limp body inside, the door shutting on his legs. More curses as he corrected the man's position and the door shut soundly.

"Gil, honey, what's…?"

The car peeled out from in front of Gilbert Mitchell's home for the open road. Leann continued to shout from the end of the driveway, her screams drowned out by the roar of the engine.

Too close. He would have to ditch the car. Find a new ride to continue the work. It was all that mattered. Not Gilbert or his crimes. Not Leann and her screams. Only the work.

And the message being sent.

CHAPTER SEVEN

"You don't have to be here."

Loren said the same thing not too long ago. How quickly time flew away from him, yet in an instant dropped him off at the exact moment he hoped never to recall. His visit with Ruiz to question Hady Ronne over missing information related to the deaths of dozens by a mysterious hand.

Her hand, as it turned out.

Loren was on the receiving end of Hady's work, the wounds no longer burning to the touch. Weeks of recovery and months back on the job, however, did little to dilute the memory. From the blinking lights overhead to the bodies stacked inside each room, everything caused Loren to hesitate at the entrance to the coroner's office.

The knob turned, his eyes closed to the act, and he stepped inside. "Let's get this over with."

Footsteps greeted them, the shuffle of papers and the mutters of staffers. Life returned in the coroner's office. A slow process, having to rebuild the entire staff from the ground up. Many questioned what had happened but eventually over the autumn season, the office was brimming with talent again as if the previous incarnation never existed at all.

Lights beamed bright, the walls and floor immaculate. A custodian continued his hard work as they left the main gate for the security station just inside the office. It was a new addition—the building no longer relied on the keycard reader for access to the facility. The human presence of an armed guard helped assuage any future fears of a killer loose on the premises.

For most, at least.

"Cross," Myers called to the guard. She took Loren's badge and handed both over to the strapping young lad's waiting hand. "Drew the short straw?"

"I'm good with it," the guard replied, writing down their information before offering up their visitor's passes.

"Sudoku?"

He laughed, patting the fresh paperback on the desk. "Wife wants me to stay sharp."

Loren stayed silent, following Myers deeper into the facility. The laughter of their exchange faded as she waved to an older gentleman in a lab coat, his thin glasses raised to read the notes on his clipboard. They fell at the sight of her, a smile growing.

"Hey, Al," Myers said. "Anderson in?"

"Room three," the man replied, watching Myers closely. It wasn't until Loren cleared his throat that Al realized someone else was next to the petite detective. "Oh, hey. Loren, right?"

"Yeah."

Myers winced at the momentary silence. "Al's the new assistant coroner."

"Ah." Loren reached out, offering a firm shake. The man took it then reached for a small beeper clipped to his belt. He punched a code along the front.

"I buzzed him. Go on ahead."

"Thanks, Al." They continued, farther down the hall. Loren's pace slowed as they approached the double doors of the autopsy room. He was grateful when she pulled him to the right side of the hall and the door marked by a *3*. She waved to a passing pair of lab techs, calling each by name.

"How the hell do you know all these people?" She shrugged and he skirted in front of her to gauge her reaction. "Did you hack their personnel files?"

She sighed. "You want to do this or what?"

He caught the brief smirk she tried to hide. "Just stay out of my medical files, Myers."

She nodded then reached for the door. She blocked him from entering at first, a wry grin on her lips. "You should get that mole checked out, Loren. You know, the one on your left—"

"All right," he shouted, pushing past her. "Come on."

"Why are you blushing?"

Her laughter followed him into the autopsy room. The bright lights of the hallway cut out as the door closed. Only the overhead light above the metal slab in the room's center illuminated the space. It threw heavy shadows in the corner where a tall, thin waif of a man loomed. His cheeks were sunken, his eyes tucked in deep caverns of darkness. He held a scalpel before him like a flag.

"How did I know it would be you two?" Head Coroner William Anderson asked, stepping firmly into the light. It helped his appearance, making his cheeks full of color, his brown hair thick and neatly trimmed.

Loren peered curiously to Myers. "Looks like we're famous."

"Infamous," Anderson corrected. "Bodies start dropping in dramatic fashion and Greg Loren shows up. Like a damn reaper."

Myers grimaced. "Not exactly the best reference to use, Doc."

He shrugged, uncaring. Crouching to work under the overhead lights, he returned to the naked corpse of Dixon Harris. "Keeps me employed anyway."

"Anything you can tell about the cuts?" Loren asked, hoping to focus on the case. Anything to end their visit as soon as possible.

"They hurt like the dickens. Killer used a blade like the one on the table there."

A hunting knife rested on the instrument tray. A straight blade with deep ridges along one side. Four inches in diameter and a hilt built for a large man.

"You happened to have one lying around to try out?"

"Al did." Anderson's head tilted toward the hall. "Hunting enthusiast."

Loren smiled at Myers, who pushed away from him. "Game hunting, Loren. Get your mind out of the gutter."

He laughed and Anderson sighed, turning to the pair. "Something going on?"

Myers shook her head. "You tell us."

Anderson moved to the wall and turned on the lights. The shadows disappeared and Loren's heart slowed. "Cuts avoided any vital organs."

Loren nodded. "He bled out."

"You're stepping on my material, Detective."

"We wrote it first," Myers said. "Well, Wexler did."

"Did she tell you how they connect to the location where the body was found?"

"The courthouse?" Loren asked, surprised. "He was the DA. Not a stretch to connect the two."

Anderson shook his head. "The pillar."

"Wilbur Caldwell?"

"What about him?" Myers asked.

"He was the first judge of Portents," Loren said.

"I know but—"

"And one of the city's founders," Anderson chimed in.

"What does that have to do with Harris?"

"Considering Caldwell was stabbed to death on those very steps over a century ago?" Anderson remarked. "Probably a bit."

Loren and Myers stood silent, letting the news and the inherently corresponding questions wash over them. Anderson took the moment, returning to the workstation and the single file on the small surface. It was decayed, the paper yellowed and brittle from age. He passed it to Loren.

"The same pattern," the detective muttered, reading the notes from Caldwell's autopsy.

"The same everything," Anderson clarified.

"What the hell is going on?" Myers asked, hoping Loren had an answer. Unfortunately he only had more questions, including the worst one possible.

"And who's next?"

CHAPTER EIGHT

The shadow watched the sleeping Gilbert Mitchell with hate in his heart. The past, usually locked away in his mind, stormed back, forcing him to relive their first meeting.

Those were darker days—a time of loss and suffering when he was nothing more than a broken shell. Once there had been joy and camaraderie. Colleagues that grew into friends, ones there for each other in troubling times.

Men like Gilbert Mitchell and Dixon Harris. The true power brokers in the city of Portents. Men of influence—that was what they held over him.

Influence.

He let them, their game long and practiced. He never noticed it occurring until it was too late. A small favor at first. The passing along of friendly information. Nothing vital, nothing compromising.

But each grew. Simple questions turned to manipulations. Lies jeopardized his professional career. Not that people like Harris or Mitchell cared when their asses weren't the ones in the fire.

By the time the shadow understood the truth of their relationship, their arrangement, he was too far gone. His world had crashed around him and he took to the road to find some semblance of peace. The city, however, called him back. It always called him back.

Gilbert woke with a start, his eyes glazed over. An effect of the drug, one the shadow happily discovered prior to his return. Unlike Harris, however, Gilbert recalled the venue immediately.

This was the shadow's favorite part—the fear. The initial strike of terror from discovering the chains restraining his body. The powerlessness at what came next.

"I hope your recognition means we can skip the prerequisites," the shadow bellowed from the darkness.

"What?" Gilbert asked, confused and startled by the presence. He squinted around the room, unable to focus. His vision, however, cleared with each blink. Definitely stronger and more in shape than Harris, the man in shadow was glad he took extra care to secure the bindings holding him to the altar.

"*Where am I?*" the shadow mocked. "*Oh please, please, this can't be. I'll do anything you want.*" He laughed, his voice a deep growl. "They won't work."

The shadow stepped out of the darkness and Gilbert's eyes flashed.

"Nothing will."

"*You,*" Gilbert said. He slammed his head back against the altar in frustration. "I told them it was a mistake. No matter the advantages that brought you to the table."

"Cutting the red tape on this place?" the shadow said. He leaned over the altar and his bound victim. "The zoning permits, the construction licenses, the contracts? The secrets. The money. Quite a bit for you, wasn't there?"

"I don't—"

"Wasn't there?" he screamed.

Gilbert closed his eyes and swallowed hard. "There would have been—at least, until you and your friend. You cost us everything."

"That is certainly true." The shadow reached behind his back and pulled out the gun, which rested heavy in his hands. His sweaty grip threatened to drop the weapon but he kept it tight to his palm, displaying it for his guest.

"Please," Gilbert muttered.

A finger pressed against his lips. "We're past that point, Gilbert."

"You used to call me Gil," the man pleaded. "Your wife—"

"Is dead!" the shadow yelled. "Her ashes are right over there! Now tell me."

"What?" Gilbert said, sweat and fear overcoming him. "Tell you what?"

"Where is he?" The shadow pulled back the hammer on the pistol.

"I don't—" He stopped as his captor climbed atop the altar and stood over him. The barrel of the gun filled his vision.

"I won't miss," he said. "At this range it will be quick. Painless. Well, almost painless. If you tell me where I can find him."

"And then what?" Gilbert asked, struggling against the chains locking him in place. Fighting for another moment, another way out. "How does this end?"

"It won't matter. Not to you." The shadow leveled the gun once more, finger steady on the trigger. "Now tell me where he is."

CHAPTER NINE

Myers squeezed into the corner booth. Loren took the opposite end of the table. He tossed his jacket in first then settled against the uncomfortable cushion, listening to it groan at his presence. Myers peered around McDuffie's Pub with a dismal expression on her face.

"So this is where people go to die," she said at the sight of the few patrons rummaging around the premises. One man scratched his ass on a stool at the bar. Another couple hooked up in the corner, though couple might have been a stretch at the exchange of money slipping from the young man's hands into the woman's bra.

Loren shook his head. "Seriously, Myers…"

"It's like purgatory's version of Hell," Myers continued, rummaging through a bowl at the end of the table. "Come on in. Grab a stool. We'll be with you in a few millennia. But hey, free peanuts."

"I like it here."

"Red flag number one." She took a swig of the beer. Loren nursed a glass of water, wishing there was a damn lemon on the lip. His companion's eyes flitted toward the window and the small parking lot to the rear of the bar. Her car sat undisturbed but it didn't stop her from checking repeatedly.

They needed to regroup. Their meeting with Anderson failed to clear up the details surfacing from the case, adding new wrinkles and a boatload of questions that needing answering. If Harris' death coincided with Caldwell more than a century earlier, what was the killer trying to say? And why did Loren get the feeling the close proximity of Founder's Day meant more than he cared to admit?

Myers picked at the peanuts, letting him have a moment of silence. The quiet grated on her, but she did her best to litter the floor with shells to fill the empty void of conversation.

Thankfully the bartender and owner of the establishment arrived. Two steaming plates slid before them followed by another round of beverages. "Loaded fries and another pint of Guinness. And well, the less said about this, the better."

"Really?" The pair of over easy eggs and slice of toast combo looked just fine to the detective.

The owner ignored him. "Anything else?"

Loren shook his head. "No, you've summed it up nicely."

Nodding, the man departed. When he started to return to the table, query poised on his lips, Loren shot him a look. The owner, immediately understanding, circled back to his waiting customers.

Loren knew the question, the same one that plagued him for months. The disappearance of the bartender, Dominic. A man Loren called friend since his return to the city. Dominic was one of dozens that had gone missing, reports never filed with the police or buried by department bureaucracy. Both hoped to find answers sooner but there were none coming tonight. Not with Dixon Harris and the ghost of Wilbur Caldwell's murder taking precedent.

"Friend of yours?" Myers asked, watching the unspoken exchange. She tossed a fry in her mouth.

"I'm helping him with something."

"Ah," Myers said. "Super secret work."

The same argument, the split keeping them from a true partnership. The way secrets always did. "Come on, Myers."

"No, it's all right." She took a long sip of her first Guinness, finishing the glass. "You want to tell me, you will. I have plenty to do. Dragons flying around and a lunatic reenacting centuries-old crimes. Plate is full. Least I can take care of this one."

Myers shoveled another handful of fries into her mouth, moaning with pleasure. Loren tried to ignore her, picking at the burnt toast covered in butter. "It's nothing, Myers. If it was something concrete I would…" He stopped, dropping the toast on the plate. "How do I know you haven't hacked into my files already?"

"I wouldn't do that. I don't do that anymore." His glare continued and she rolled her eyes. "What?"

"How old are Anderson's three kids?"

"He has four," she answered matter-of-factly. "Eighteen, thirteen, eleven, and seven. What a lunatic, right?"

He was still waiting, his silence irritating her.

"He told me about them, Loren."

"Sure."

"Eat your eggs," Myers snapped. "Talk about mentally unstable."

"I like breakfast."

"Unnaturally so. You know this, right?"

Loren dropped his fork, the eggs runny and the toast burnt. "Can we…?"

"Please."

Files spun between them. Loren passed one across while opening another and setting it before the ravenous Myers. "I looked into Harris. Not exactly part of the Upright Citizen's Brigade."

"Whatever that is, old timer."

"Ignoring you," he said. "Plenty of shady dealings during his previous positions in the DA's office. A lot of people on both sides of the law wouldn't mind carving him up."

"Any one of them scream ritualistic killer to you?"

"No," he said, holding out the word. "Maybe some possibles."

"Give them to Pratchett."

Loren smiled. "You miss the big lug."

Myers wiped her mouth. "Don't get jealous, Loren. I'm holding out for the nutbag category on this one."

The nutbag category. What Soriya called the true city. The secret hidden beneath the surface of Portents—the freaks and monsters, the myths and legends hidden among them until they decided to make a play for more screen time.

"Wilbur Caldwell." It was the obvious connection to what might be stepping out of the shadows.

Myers nodded. "It obviously means something here. Harris could have ended up anywhere. Shoot him. Shank him. Hell, drown him in pastries but the second the killer decided to display him for all to see he was trying to tell us something."

"Like what?"

The fry dropped from her grip. "History class was not my forte. This is your city."

He never thought so. "Tell me what you've learned, Myers. We'll go from there."

"Fine. Caldwell was murdered by the brother of a wrongfully accused man. Guy was innocent but Caldwell sentenced him to life."

"Mistakes happen."

"Well," she said, pointing to the documents found in the archives. "When the founder of justice in Portents makes a mistake it looks bad. Caldwell buried it under a pile of falsified reports and testimonies."

"Creating his own monster."

"And murderer in the form of the man's brother. None of these guys were saints from what I've read. Or didn't go out like saints anyway."

"Who?"

"Caldwell was one of three." Myers reached into her bag and pulled out a book, its pages folded in various places. "The first judge. The law of Portents. Patrick Hennessey was the first mayor, sworn in by his best bud in the world and the actual founder of the city—"

"William Rath," Loren finished.

"See? You already know this."

"Some." He recognized the book now—one of many he skimmed during his search for the killer at the heart of a case months earlier. Nathaniel Evans. The true founder of Portents. He lorded over the city like a monarch, leading the people to darkness until they finally rebelled and slaughtered their malevolent benefactor. The story of William Rath was falsified, the truth long since forgotten for the sake of the city's future. Was this tied to Evans somehow? Had he missed something from that initial investigation?

"Then you know they all died horribly," Myers said, pulling him back from memory. "All were murdered."

"If you believe the stories."

"You don't?"

Loren shook his head. "Doesn't matter. This guy believes them." He pushed the still full plate away in frustration. "Beth would see it. She loved this crap."

"Maybe Soriya can help," Myers said. "You talk to her yet?"

He hadn't. Loren meant to confront her months ago. Almost had at one point too. But he held back, the question behind the photo Myers found, the one implicating Soriya in the death of his wife still unanswered. Like so many others lately.

"She's busy," Loren deflected. "So are we."

"So no," she muttered. "Got it."

Loren pushed ahead. "If Rath and Hennessey are our next steps, we need to know exactly what happened and where before—"

His phone lit up, vibrating against his pocket. The chorus from "Tonight, Tonight" blasted from Myers' at the same time. Both shared a groan.

"That's never a good sign."

"Never," Loren replied. He answered the phone and she did the same, both quiet as news passed their way. She hung up first, letting Loren take down the details on the back of one of the many files decorating the booth. He dropped the phone.

"Another murder," she said, then pointed to the scribbled note. "That the address?"

He nodded.

"Where is it?"

"Patrick Hennessey's house."

CHAPTER TEN

The cordon stopped them two blocks from the scene. Myers flashed her badge, allowing the car within the perimeter. She promptly put the sedan in park.

Loren had been quiet for much of the ride, thinking about the threat behind the killings, the idea of it being related to the false stories that had been born out of Nathaniel Evans' terror over the city. The founding of Portents had been buried, replaced by heroic figures both real and imagined in a narrative teeming with irony.

Now someone was using that narrative, reenacting the deaths of the so-called founding fathers. But why? And what did it truly mean to the killer?

Myers stepped outside and he followed suit. The silence between them wasn't intentional but he was grateful for the space. Every other partner would take the moment to work out the case verbally, but sometimes the peace brought more clarity than anything said.

The calm ended in front of the stoop and the covered body of their latest victim. He lay across the front doors to the History Museum of Portents. More irony.

"This is Hennessey's house?" Myers whistled. Two officers peered over curious to the noise and she tossed them a nod and a wink.

Loren shook his head. "The city tore down the original home to build the museum. Going on fifty years now, I think. Beth used to bring me on the weekends."

"Cheap date?"

"Work. Always another book to research." Loren noticed the wayward glances from Myers when he said her name. "Sorry."

"It's all right."

"She's been on my mind since this started," Loren said. "Don't know why."

Myers nodded, heading over to the waiting Captain Wexler. "Not your therapist, Loren."

Loren paused, watching her depart. "Thanks?"

Stepping to the stoop, Loren joined Myers and the impatient captain who eyed them. "Problem, Detectives?"

"No, ma'am."

"Surprised to see you here, Captain," Loren said, scanning the scene.

Wexler moved away from the body toward Loren. "And I'm surprised they make onesies in your size, Loren. Shirt and tie. Try it."

"I did once. Not for me," Loren replied, instantly regretting everything about his response.

Wexler leaned close. "It's not *for* you."

Myers smirked as the captain returned to the body. Wexler pinched the bridge of her nose. Her headache returned, compliments of Loren.

Wexler pulled open the body bag; both detectives looking away at the sight of the large bullet hole in the man's skull. "Say hello to Gilbert Mitchell."

"Who is he?" Myers asked, working her way back to the body slowly.

"Works in the mayor's office."

"Oh, great." That was the last thing they needed.

"Exactly," Wexler said, reading his mind. "Dunn's been with the commissioner since the call came in. Needless to say—"

"We're screwed," Myers jumped in, slipping a pair of gloves on with renewed interest.

"Not our concern."

"Loren?"

The body had the same black cloak and hood as Dixon Harris—dumped like the last and positioned for all to see. The courthouse was only four blocks east.

The captain waited for a response.

Loren shook his head. "I mean, it's our case, right? Dunn doesn't like how we handle things someone will take it away."

Wexler understood the implication. She would lose the case as well. Not the best thing to happen on her watch. She took a step back, giving them the scene. Loren was grateful for the reprieve. He felt uncomfortable around the new captain. It might have been their grating personalities or his inability to not say something dickish every time they interacted.

Or he just missed Ruiz.

Myers pulled him back, measuring the bullet wound along his forehead. "So. Gilbert Mitchell."

"Head shot. Close range."

She concurred with a nod. "Body was moved. Positioned here same as the last."

"And the shot?"

"It matches," Myers said.

Wexler chimed in, the answer catching her off guard. "Matches?"

Myers sighed. "Patrick Hennessey was killed outside his front door. Angry electorate."

"Glad we've evolved since then."

"Focus, Loren," Wexler snapped. "You're saying someone is actually recreating these deaths? Why?"

"We're working on that," Loren said.

"Anything from the robe? You said it seemed familiar."

"It does," he said with a nod. From where? A case? Something Beth mentioned in the past during her extensive research into the city? Nothing hit the mark in his memory. Nothing sparked, frustrating him. "It will come to me."

"Hopefully soon," Wexler said, fingers against her temples. Loren's eyes thinned at the veiled threat. "You can give me whatever look you want. Doesn't stop the timeline."

"Founder's Day." Another death along the parade route. Was it planned that way? Or was something else going on?

"Two days, Detectives," Wexler said before heading for the cordon.

"And we're no closer to finding this guy." Loren watched her depart, hands in his pockets. The robe held the key but what did it mean and where had he seen it before?

What the hell am I missing?

CHAPTER ELEVEN

The shadow watched from a distance, enthralled at the drama unfolding before him. There was no denying the surprise he initially felt, the speed at his old friend's arrival to the latest murder scene, but he knew he would come.

Loren never could resist a good murder.

He seemed more alert, stronger than in years. Despite the shabby T-shirt and jeans combination, his casual grizzled look appeared refined. Confidence exuded from the man's stance, in his steps circling the victim.

So unlike before. Loren had fallen so far, weak and broken. The past dominated the detective, the loss of his wife a raw wound constantly picked over by everything seen and everyone met. Only Beth mattered to him, not the present or any hope at a future. They were the same in that regard.

Now, though, he was a lost man found again. Alive and truly living for the first time, when by all rights he should have broken completely and ended his life with a bullet.

It wasn't fair.

The shadow stared angrily from his position across the street, obscured from view. No, Loren needed to suffer, needed to feel the same pain the shadow endured with each day. Every hour, every thought both waking and in sleep.

Instead, Loren laughed and joked with the woman by his side. Another detective, a fresh face to the department, unfamiliar to him. Her connection with Loren was clear. The way they spoke, the stolen glances between the two of them. Loren's persistent smile, something rarely seen in the old days. She excited him, bringing him joy and connecting him to the present.

Guiding him into the future.

An unacceptable twist of fate. There would be no future for Detective Greg Loren, not when all was said and done. And it would be soon. Only one task remained, one victim left to suffer for the sins of the past.

Then Loren's time was up.

CHAPTER TWELVE

Loren dreamed. It was the same dream, haunting him with the sights and scents of the rooftop to his apartment building. Lilacs and lilies filled him, matching the window box she always kept off the front of their home. Their small place in the world for far too short a time.

Beth stood at the ledge, tempting fate over the chasm of darkness. The sun blazed overhead, rising above them.

"Greg."

He kept coming back to this moment, to her. Every night when he closed his eyes, there she was. Her flower printed sundress whipped along the imaginary breeze, her blond locks covering her shoulders and masking part of her sad smile. He didn't want to come back anymore. But he had to understand what it all meant.

"Beth," he called. "Wait."

"You already know," she said. No matter how far he made it in the dream, there was never an answer—never a clear one. Only hints at what was to come. "You can't save them both."

He reached for her, never able to make it to the ledge. His eyes pleaded. "Then what am I supposed to do?"

"Live."

"But Soriya?" he said. "Did she—?"

Beth turned, her arms outstretched and welcoming the darkness.

"No!"

A knock at the door snapped him back. He was sweating, the heat from the dream following him to the waking world. So did the questions, always hanging around without a clue. He tired of them.

Hell, he was tired in general, his sleep having been troubled for months. Ever since Evans and the obsidian tower. Ever since he came back to Portents.

The sun faded from view behind the skyline. Another day lost to a fitful rest. Loren sat up on the edge of the couch. He rubbed his eyes, then ran his hands through his thickening hair. A trim was in order. A hot shower and a shave. A bowl of cereal or some toast. Anything to pluck the image of his dead wife from his thoughts.

The knock returned, louder and more impatient. Loren shuffled the growing number of missing person's reports into a pile. He picked them up and carried them to the closet, popping them on the empty top shelf. He circled back to the table and the image of Soriya. Another problem for another day. It went with the files in the closet and he closed it.

"I'm coming," Loren grunted. His body ached, the strain of the dream reflected in the waking world. He stretched as he meandered to the door, the knock continuing to echo through the apartment. "I said I'm coming!"

He pulled the chain from the door and twisted the deadbolt. The door swung open and he greeted his visitor with a look of anger.

Samantha Myers didn't seem to mind. She held a six-pack of beer in her hand and a number of files tucked under her arm.

"Myers?" Loren asked. "What the hell?"

"Couldn't sleep," she said, entering the apartment with a slight shove. "And I thought why should I be the only one?"

Loren closed the door. "Lucky me."

Myers turned back with a grin. "I had a feeling you would say that."

CHAPTER THIRTEEN

The open fridge was cause for dismay. A bottle of Ginger Ale, two loaves of white bread, half a stick of butter, and two dozen eggs. Myers placed her six-pack of beer inside and removed one of the bottles before closing the door.

"You weren't kidding," she called to Loren. "You do love breakfast."

She stepped into the living room, surveying her partner's home. A single desk lamp, faint in the large space, offered the only light for them. The couch and coffee table rested in the corner by a window overlooking the street. The television hung on the wall opposite, silent and cold from lack of use. The cushions on the couch were ruffled and out of place. His typical sleeping spot, leaving the bedroom he once shared with his wife untouched.

Or so the rumors remained at work. Some Myers pursued, wanting as much information about the reclusive detective as possible. Others trickled down. The problems with Mathers, the fight with a man named Robert Standish leading to his suspension from the force for a time. Most centered on Beth, the blond-haired angel that kept Greg Loren functioning for so long, her death his only focus.

"Myers?"

She stood stock still in the center, continuing her evaluation of the space. The emptiness. The lack of any character, anything that spoke to who Loren was as a person. Who he wanted to portray to the world when company came calling—if any came calling.

Shaking her head, she smiled. "When was the last time you visited a grocery store?"

Loren leaned against the mantel, the mirror behind him layered with dust. "You came to critique my pantry?"

"Not so much," she said, holding out the beer.

"I don't drink."

"It's for me." She tapped the cap. "No bottle opener."

"Right." He took it and headed for the kitchen.

Myers walked the hall, the floorboards creaking under her steps. A single dresser rested against the far wall of the bedroom. One drawer lay open, ratty old shirts barring it from properly closing. Two laundry baskets rested on the floor, overflowing with dirty linens. On the nightstand next to the bed sat a stack of books, the top propped open. Small notations marked the edges of the page, letters and other characters unrecognized by the wandering detective—almost like they held a message in their randomness.

She turned away, noticing a small desk and computer in the second bedroom, dust-covered with cobwebs growing in the corners. She decided not to observe the bathroom if possible.

Loren was waiting at the end of the hall, beer in hand. "Any conclusions, Detective?"

"A few."

He handed her the bottle, then turned toward to the living room and the waiting mantel. "Save them."

"Loren."

"Why are you here, Myers?" He pointed to the files on the table. "This couldn't wait until our shift?"

"And risk another body on the streets?" Myers fell on the couch, feeling the wood frame beneath. "Cold, Loren."

"You know that's not what I meant."

"I do," she replied before taking a swig from her beer. "And I know that I have been up researching this hellhole of a city, our victims, and anything else I can think of for the last eight hours while you've been pretending to get a restful sleep."

Loren sighed, wiping the exhaustion from his eyes without success. "Fine. You found something?"

"I did."

"Myers."

"Right." She shook her head, placing her beer on the floor beside the couch. "Tired, remember?"

"I'm sure the beer helps."

"Not at all." A file skidded from her grasp. Loren scooped it up and paged through it. "I started with the victims."

"Harris and Mitchell."

"It was either that or start to think our only lead was William Rath back from the dead and taking revenge on his founding father buddies only he's a little confused about the date." She laughed, nervous and awkward, the sentiment growing with the silence offered by her partner. "Not even a grin at that insane notion?"

"Not funny," Loren admitted. "Not insane either."

Her beer was back in hand and she took a long swig. "This is why I drink, by the way. When you talk like that, I drink." She finished the beer. "Worst drinking game ever."

"Myers, please."

She let out a deep breath. "Harris and Mitchell. Right. They had similar circles for sure. Friends. Enemies. Rivalries."

"That led nowhere."

"Who's telling the story?"

"Speed it up," Loren said. "I need my morning constitutional."

"It's late afternoon," she clarified before throwing him a look. "And gross."

"Being honest."

"Stop that." She paged through the documents scattered along the table. "Okay. Here."

"What am I looking at?"

"Financials for our civil servants," Myers said, pointing to a number of spreadsheets. "Obtained legally. Warrant and everything."

"Surprising."

"I aim to please."

Loren searched the pages, flipping forward then back again. "A little help?"

"Third page. Halfway down. A recurring charitable donation for the same organization. Same amount each time from both of them. Dozens of payments of $50,000 over a four-year period."

Loren looked puzzled, dropping the financial reports on the coffee table. "Where does an aide to the mayor's office get that much money?"

"Harris was strapped as well. Child support. Alimony. A second nasty divorce on the horizon. The guy was a mess."

Loren pointed to the line item in question. "What does SEC CHU stand for?"

"A dummy corporation they both had a stake in," she said. "But it all led to one thing. Some church."

"A church?" His eyes snapped wide, his hands rushing to his temples. "Shit."

"Loren?"

He raced down the hall and she followed him.

"How the hell did I not see it?" he grumbled, pulling a dirty shirt from the wash and reaching for a pair of jeans from the open drawer. "The damn robe. Everything."

Myers stood in the doorway, watching him dress. When he finally noticed her, his cheeks flushed as he slipped his shirt over his head.

"Grab your coat. We're leaving," he said. The closet door opened. Inside sat a small safe. He punched in the code and the lock clicked. He pulled out his gun and badge, leaving behind his spare. Myers saw it for only a second—a revolver—before the door to the safe closed.

"You've heard of this place?"

"I was almost a member," he said, passing her in the hall. He grabbed her coat and tossed it to her before reaching for his own. "Last place I wanted to see again. But it's been that kind of case."

"What is it?" He didn't answer, his keys clattering in his hand. Myers looked to the fridge and her waiting five beers then shook her head. Snatching up her files, she rushed to catch up with the departing detective, hoping for answers.

"Dammit, Loren," she called after him. "What the hell is the Church of the Second Coming?"

CHAPTER FOURTEEN

The church was still there. Almost two years since the fire consumed the structure's interior and the Church of the Second Coming remained at a corner lot near the Riverfront district. The edifice was intact, the exterior a testament to the era's architectural geniuses. Most windows survived the initial blaze; others shattered during the interim months of emptiness. The skylight above, however, continued to tinge the world in a deep red.

Another place Loren never wanted to revisit. First, the coroner's office, and now this? He was fast becoming sick of this case, especially the current direction it headed. And what it meant for him and his past mistakes.

They had driven him from the city. Taken away his badge, his sense of purpose and dignity. It strained his partnership with Soriya Greystone, who almost died to serve his desire to have his wife back. Remembering who he truly was saved her, and his wife, from suffering a horrible fate.

But his actions destroyed lives as well. Too many lives that night and all thanks to him.

Myers examined the grand hall from behind the glass of the vestibule. "Wow…" she started, having heard the entire tale on the drive over. Loren took his time, with many starts and stops along the way to come to terms with what happened and how to relay the information to his current partner. "I mean…wow."

Loren nodded, leading them into the nave. "The less said, the better."

The pews were torn up and tossed around like kindling. The front half bore scorch marks along the ground, the walls, and everything in between. Myers stayed close to him, their pace slow up the center aisle.

"How?" she tried to ask. "How did they—?"

"Don't ask." No answer came to light. Not to any degree of satisfaction for someone as analytical as a cop. "I'm not even sure. Science. Faith. Or something in between. Take your pick."

"And they just stood up and walked around like nothing had happened? Just like that?"

The altar at the church's front towered over them. Stonework remained untouched by the intensity of the flames. But Loren wasn't seeing the room as it stood now, only how it had been that day—the white sheet covering his wife's body.

"They were back," he whispered.

"Loren?"

"Don't, Myers."

"You said you were almost a member. Did you…?"

He offered a silent nod.

"Oh."

"Soriya stopped me," he said, stepping up to the altar. "Saved me from—"

"What is it?" she asked, following his gaze to the ancient stone in the altar.

"Blood." Crimson marked the top of the stone and the wall behind it, obscuring the image of the white dove on the church's back wall. Chains dangled from the wall, recent additions to the room, while others lay along the floor.

"Lots of blood," Myers said, joining him.

"Looks like we found where Harris and Mitchell were killed."

The amount of blood on the floor near the wall was the likely spot for Harris. His death, undoubtedly the more painful one, took time to bleed out. Mitchell was relatively quick, a bullet to the head.

"I've got a slug here," Myers confirmed, lifting the shell from a small indentation on the stone altar.

The connection between the victims—both city officials in some capacity—led them to the church where they met their end. But why not leave them here? Why go to the trouble of displaying them in public? Why dress them in the black robe, the one worn by only one person in the church during services?

"The Founder."

"Excuse me?"

"It's him, isn't it?" Myers circled the altar. "Think about it. You do all this, build all this, and end up the villain instead of mankind's savior. That's a hard knock on your pride. So you target your business partners, everyone that threw you aside. Even leave your signature with the robe and hood combination."

Her reasoning made a sick kind of sense to him. To see everything lost in an instant, the hard work of a lifetime gone. The mechanisms beneath the altar, the great machine tied to the miracle of resurrection destroyed and never able to be recreated could cause anyone to snap. It made sense but didn't fit. Not with the victims. Not with the messages being sent and the locations used.

"I'm not so sure."

"Why the hell not?"

"He worshipped this place. The Founder. This was his sanctuary. He wouldn't defile it."

"It had already been defiled," Myers replied. "By Soriya."

"And me," Loren added.

Myers noticed the breathless answer, the distant look in his eyes. She pushed for more. "Then who? Another victim? Someone who lost everything in this place?"

His eyes snapped open, like waking for the first time all day. "Someone who is using the robe and hood to draw out the last founder of this church. Dammit."

"You know who this is."

Loren raced for the door. "One of the few people I was lucky enough to call a friend when I needed one the most. All this, Myers? Harris and Mitchell? This is all my fault."

"Where are you going?"

"To follow a lead," he shouted back.

"Wait. I can—"

He stopped, his eyes catching hers. "I have to stop him, Myers. I won't have another death on my conscience."

"Stop who, Loren?"

He wanted to be wrong. He wanted the killer to be The Founder, a faceless ghost of a man with no connection to him. He wanted it to be anyone else. But it wasn't.

"Richard," Loren said. "His name is Richard Crowne."

CHAPTER FIFTEEN

Myers stalked up the road, scanning every shadow she passed. Every sound of rattling bottles from every alley made her fingers inch closer to the butt of her sidearm. Her nerves were up. They always were when she got the call.

Not that it couldn't go simply. The call could have been straightforward. Answer and receive more instructions. Get pissed off, say something stupid, and pay for it with veiled threats. The typical night when her burner phone rang unexpectedly. This time, all that came was a text with an address.

Her travels took her downtown on the border of Lowtown— not exactly a hotspot for cops. Patrols were staggered, the community precincts stretched too thin from too many calls on a nightly basis.

She stopped in front of her destination, eyeing the building warily. *Life Paths*. Some sort of planning service for people unable to learn about the importance of a savings account or those too impetuous to miss a shoe sale. Another industry that fell under "Are you kidding me, this actually exists?" in the phonebook. Probably why the place closed up shop.

Myers stepped inside the office, closing the door. "I'm here."

She hoped the nerves would settle once off the streets but they heightened as the door closed. It would be her first face-to-face with her mysterious benefactor, the synthesized voice on the other end of the phone. The one that found her at her lowest and gave her a second chance. A way to take back control.

While also giving it up fully.

Every query into the identity of the caller went nowhere. Or resulted in them finding out, which did nothing for their trust issues. Still, she needed to know. She had to find out who they were, why they wanted so much information on Loren and Ruiz. What did they care about such a minimal portion of the department? Especially two largely ostracized members?

Myers crept deeper into the office, down the long hall for the conference room at the rear. The office had been closed but most furniture had yet to be removed.

"I'm glad we're finally moving past the robo-voice stage of our relationship," Myers called out, announcing her presence. The last thing she needed was to scare her benefactor. "But we could have done it another time. I'm absolutely beat so how about…"

The conference room was empty. A phone sat at the center of an oblong table. Another damn phone. It started ringing the second she entered the room. A large eye watched her from the far side of the room. Too many eyes on her lately.

Myers put the phone on speaker. "This better be Clooney telling me he's available again."

"Hello, Detective."

The synthesized voice. So much for the trust-building exercise she envisioned.

"We could have done without the Scooby Doo setting. This giant eye makes me think a damn mummy or something is going to jump out at me."

"A necessary precaution."

"Leave the paranoia at home next time and join me out in the world," Myers said, circling the table. "Might help your demeanor."

"And Loren?" the voice boomed.

So much for small talk.

"He trusts me."

"Completely?"

She paused, her hands braced against the table's dusty surface. Every second she held the answer back was another chance to make things right. For her relationship with her new partner. For her time in Portents.

But if the question was asked, the answer was known more often than not. She couldn't take the chance, not with eyes on her from somewhere in the room or nearby. The voice read her face, her movements, every stance, and every blink for signs of honesty.

"He's holding something back," she replied.

"And here I imagined your gruff exterior could win any man's heart," the voice joked, but its attempt failed to come through in the computerized tone. "What is he hiding?"

"I don't—"

"Detective," the voice interrupted. "If there is a mystery with your new partner, you have already sniffed it out. That's why I like you."

"Not creepy at all," she muttered. Of course she had lied when Loren questioned her about his secret work. Of course she broke into his desk and hacked his files. That was who she was.

"Missing persons," she said, lifting the phone and turning off the speaker function. "He's working on a number of missing person's reports buried at the precinct."

"Any leads on these missing souls?"

"Just one from what I've gleaned. Something about a circle of shadows?"

Silence answered her, the voice taking in the information passed behind her partner's back. Betraying his trust, not that he had actually offered it in the first place. And not that she had a choice in the matter. Not really.

The line crackled; the voice returning. "Keep me informed on this matter, Detective."

"Why?" Myers asked. "What does Loren have to do with anything?"

"Everything," the voice replied. "Greg Loren needs to be contained."

She understood too well. "Controlled."

"Don't say it like that." An unspoken joy hid beneath the surface. "You'll hurt my feelings. You wouldn't want that, would you?"

"Of course not," she said, her words sharp. "How should I—?"

"You'll find a way, Detective. You always do."

The line went dead. Myers held the phone to her ear for a long moment, trying to steady her speeding pulse. Anger welled, spreading throughout her body.

"Dammit," she screamed, slamming the phone against the table. The plastic casing smashed, splitting along the poorly crafted hinge. The top half flew across the table, the bottom stayed locked in her hand. She threw the remnants at the giant eye looming over her.

Deep breaths soothed her, the sudden violence helping her work things out. She needed to get out of there, to get back to work.

She pulled out her phone and dialed her partner. She told herself it was for an update on the case, hoping her rationale was true. Hoping the call wasn't about working him, manipulating him further, but she knew it was that too.

And always would be with her benefactor whispering in her ear.

The phone rang until his voicemail picked up. Wherever Loren was, whatever he was doing, he wanted to do it alone. He didn't trust her enough to include her. And she proved why with every move she made.

"Great," she said, heading for the exit. "Just great."

CHAPTER SIXTEEN

Loren stepped out of the cab and watched it depart. The cabbie, dissatisfied at his frequent passenger's meager tip, offered a few less-than-courteous words as the door closed. It had definitely been one of those nights.

A second trip to the DA's office topped the list for the detective. A quick sweep left Loren feeling nothing but cold and tired. The photos lining the halls did nothing to dissuade him from thinking differently. Many of them included former Assistant District Attorney Crowne before his sudden departure from public service.

No one questioned his resignation at the time. No one thought anything of it. Richard Crowne held a spotless record, squeaky clean in the eyes of the public and the press. Not a soul knew what lay beneath the surface. The secrets kept from his office and those closest to him.

Only one person mattered to him through everything—his wife. Jennifer Crowne lost her life, saving her husband from a drive-by shooting. Revenge for doing the job for which he was appointed. He remained a true public servant, and the city took everything from him.

Then it gave it back to him—or one person did. The Founder. The Church of the Second Coming gave Richard a second chance, a new lease on life. It brought Jennifer back to him. Richard tried to do the same for Loren.

And Loren ripped it all away from him, from all the so-called Resurrectionists.

Richard. Why did it have to be you?

He was a friend, one of the few. Loren never held much esteem for those around him, especially after his wife passed. Richard was different. Richard tried to make life better for Loren. Hell, he tried to make Loren better, offering to help him find peace in the return of his own wife. Loren stopped him.

Now Richard was back for revenge.

With the DA's office offering nothing in the way of a clue, a single lead into Richard's whereabouts, Loren moved to his old homestead. He hadn't been to the grand estate in Venture Cove for almost two years. Not since right after he brought down the Church of the Second Coming and Richard disappeared.

He should have done more, looked harder, for his fallen friend. But he wasn't in a much better place. He lost his job, had been suspended from the force, and decided to take Ruiz up on his offer of therapy to work through the loss of his wife, the anger that ate up too many years.

If only Richard had done the same.

The house, once devoid of inhabitants with a *FOR SALE* sign punctuating the pristine front lawn, held a new family. Life pushed forward. The world continued to spin, never dwelling on the past. Unlike him. Unlike Richard.

Why now? Why come back?

Worse, why kill these men at all? Harris and Mitchell may have been shady in their dealings but they helped the Founder build his operation. They put the funding behind the church, allowing the flock their loved ones back. So why kill the only people with the knowledge and wherewithal to make it happen again?

The payments.

Both Mitchell and Harris funneled hundreds of thousands of dollars into the Founder's operation. Money they never actually had, borrowed against public funds and a dozen other illegal sources. They were on the hook for it. Which meant they needed a return of some kind. But the church charged nothing for its miracle.

Not yet, anyway.

"Loren."

His name caught him off guard and he spun to face the new arrival. The man came from behind the brush lining the edge of the former Crowne home, his hands open and spread.

"Richard?"

The man drew back his hood. Not Richard but Loren recognized the thick black tuft of hair decorating the man's chin and his dark eyes. He had seen them on dozens of *WANTED* signs from over a year ago when the Church of the Second Coming went up in flames.

"Richard is not here, Detective," the Founder said. "But I am."

CHAPTER SEVENTEEN

Loren decked him. It was his first reaction upon seeing the man known as the Founder. His right fist pummeled the man's cheek, driving him back.

His second reaction was simple.

Hurt him. Hurt him now.

The Founder staggered along the sidewalk. Cries escaped him, the air spilling from his lungs. A sharp kick to his gut forced the former church leader to curl into a fetal position as Loren laid into his midsection.

"You son of a bitch!" Loren screamed, no longer caring about discretion. Lights flickered from the homes across the street and behind him. People raised curtains to peek at what was happening. Still he continued, his voice billowing down the palatial avenue in the cove. "You have any idea the pain you've caused the people of this city? How dare you show up? How—?"

The Founder spit blood along the curbside. Loren stopped, catching his breath. The horror of his actions took him back to darker times. Days better left forgotten. Days that never needed to be repeated.

"Dammit."

"Finished?" the Founder groaned, rolling along the ground. His bloodshot left eye glared at Loren. "I imagine I deserve much worse."

"You do," Loren said. He held out a hand and helped him to his feet. "But not like this."

Loren kept a tight grip on the Founder's wrist, pulling his arm behind his back as gently as possible.

"What are you doing?" the Founder asked.

Loren pulled out his handcuffs. "Arresting you. You can file brutality charges against me, I don't care, but you're wanted for grave robbing and a dozen other charges."

"Good," the bleeding man replied as the cuffs closed.

"Good?" Loren noticed the man's dingy clothes. The shagginess of his beard where once it had been trimmed with pride. Uncut hair. And a smell that probably wasn't sublime before but now contained the distinct addition of urine. "You're running."

"Hiding mostly," the Founder admitted. "Waiting for you."

"You know he's coming for you."

"Richard? Yes. Since I found out about Harris. It was only a matter of time."

"Harris *and* Mitchell," Loren pressed. He saw that more people stood at their windows. More lights in the neighboring homes. "They backed the church."

The Founder nodded. "Made it all possible. As did Richard later on. Permits, licenses. Keeping it off the books. Keeping me hidden to do the work."

"Bringing the dead back was only the first step, wasn't it?" There was too much money being invested to not expect some form of return from the church. From the Founder's great miracles. "You were going to extort those people."

"And they would have given us anything," the Founder said. "Willingly. All to keep their loved ones with them. Even you."

He was right. Damn him. "Richard didn't know, did he?"

"No."

"He does now." That much was clear. That was why Richard was striking out at the church that had been his salvation. He found out about phase two of the plan, the extortion of the grieved.

"He's unstable, Detective," the Founder said. "A danger to everyone."

"You made him that way."

"And you."

Loren shook his head. "He's still my friend."

"He might not see it that way."

He shouldn't, though Loren hoped for better. Loren took his second chance away. The grieving widower understood Richard's anger, the decision to pull down the church with the help of Soriya being one of the toughest he ever made.

But it was the right one.

Loren pushed the man against a nearby parked car. "You won't have to worry about it. There's a cozy cell at Central with your name on it."

He patted him down, reaching into his right pants pocket to retrieve a set of keys.

"What are you doing? I'm not armed."

"No car." Loren dangled the keys, clicking the alarm button. A sedan down the block lit up, blaring the horn. Loren clicked the button one more time and silenced the vehicle.

The Founder looked astonished. "Really? In this day and age?"

"I'm unique," Loren said with a shrug. He escorted the cuffed man down the sidewalk. The Mercedes was exquisite, the stark black exterior shining under the streetlight. *Of course he owns a luxury sedan. Don't all villains drive the best cars?* "Though this might change my mind."

Loren shoved him in the passenger seat then circled around. Slipping behind the wheel, he turned the key in the ignition and the engine roared to life. "Oh yeah. Definitely might have to change my mind."

The car coasted down the block and Loren turned back toward the city. The Founder stayed quiet beside the distracted detective. As much as he needed to live in the moment, Loren couldn't help thinking about the past. How his decision broke a man he once called friend. Two people were dead because of his actions in the Church of the Second Coming.

It was his fault as much as Richard Crowne's.

Their trip took them to the city's outskirts, away from the lights of the cove to desolate country homes. Olcott Curve lay ahead and then downtown. Central would be glad to book a scumbag like the Founder, but what next? What happened when Loren finally caught up with Richard? Someone else to carry away in handcuffs, or would it end worse for one of them? Would either be able to walk away from this?

"Detective!" The Founder yelled. A car sped right for them.

"What the hell?"

Loren jerked the wheel to avoid a head-on collision, sending the sedan careening for the side of the road.

The Mercedes slammed into the ditch at forty-five miles per hour.

Vision blurred, head aching from the crash, Loren tried to push the airbag away to get a better view of the man in the passenger seat. He could hear the moans from the Founder. He was still alive but his breathing sounded off. Labored.

The sound of the door opening made it worse. Hands wrapped around the Founder's shoulders and Loren watched with bleary eyes as he was pulled from the wreckage. Even through the blur, he recognized the man's abductor.

"Wait," Loren said, his voice muffled and coarse. "Richard…"

Richard Crowne peered inside, his eyes black as night. "I'm sorry, Greg. It's not your turn. Not yet."

CHAPTER EIGHTEEN

When the call came, her heart stopped. The phone blared in her coat pocket and she immediately silenced the ringer, staring at the name on the screen.

Loren.

Did he know?

She knew the chances of that were slim to none. Her entrance into the apartment went unseen, her study of the place on her previous visit thorough enough to notice the lack of any security measures other than the deadbolt on the door. One easily subverted thanks to the lessons of her father.

The safe was another matter but she circumvented the combination lock quickly. The door swung along the incline thanks to the off-kilter dresser. She stared at the object within, hesitant after so much confidence to obtain the gun.

Loren's gun.

Her gloved hand encircled the revolver, pulling it free from the safe and stuffing the weapon in her coat pocket. She closed the safe and rushed for the exit, taking care to make sure everything stayed in place.

She answered the call on the fifth ring.

"I'm on my way."

The car veered to the side of the road on the lone stretch along Olcott Curve. She rarely came out this far—the city limits were a natural border. A car, black and sleek from the back end, lay crumpled in the ditch on the opposite side of the road. She didn't recognize the luxury vehicle but recalled the squad car to the right and the tall lug that came with it.

John Pratchett examined Loren's forehead. Myers waved after parking, reaching into her pocket to make sure the revolver was secure. Satisfied, she opened the door letting the cool night air fill her lungs and moved to join them.

"What the hell happened?"

Pratchett pointed to the crashed sedan. "There was an—"

"Not you," Myers snapped, pushing in front of him. "Him. Why was I not your first call? No offense to Goliath over here."

"He's fine," Pratchett said with a glare.

Loren smiled, immediately wincing. He had a gash along his forehead and another down the side of his face from the impact. His last bout of stitches barely in the rearview and here he was looking at another set.

"Pratchett says I'm fine."

"I'd ask to see his medical license."

The towering officer laid bandages over the wounds, applying each lightly. "I've seen worse."

"With your driving, you were probably at fault," Myers replied. She drew in a deep breath, her hands gripping her hips. "Dammit, Pratchett."

"He's going to be fine, Detective."

Loren slid from the squad car and patted the man on the shoulder. "Thanks."

Pratchett nodded, packing up his gear. "You should get checked out though."

"I will."

Both stared at him.

"I will!"

Pratchett stepped away, waved on by the impatient Myers. She led her partner to her car, watching the squad car's flashing lights as the officer started for the city. As soon as he was out of sight, she turned to Loren.

"Why not now?"

Loren sighed. "A stay at the hospital means more reports. More reports puts Wexler up my ass and an internal review on the schedule. Richard is the priority right now."

"What happened?"

"He took him," Loren said. He grazed his cheek, holding back a scream. "Richard took the Founder."

"Where? The church?"

Loren shook his head. "I put a patrol there after our visit. Nothing."

Where else? Where could Richard Crowne go and not be spotted, not be recognized in Portents? She snapped her fingers. "William Rath."

"What?"

"Not where he is now, but where he's going to be."

Loren slowly came around. The link between the victims and their predecessors from the city's founding days. "William Rath."

"He burned to death," Myers continued. The last founder. The last victim to be imitated and reflected by Richard Crowne.

"That's right," Loren echoed. "Burned to death by the same constituents that proclaimed him a saint."

"Their savior."

"Where?" Loren asked.

"Town hall."

Loren shook his head. "The original town hall is a broken-down pub near the docks."

"Not public enough for him."

"But the current town hall…"

Myers agreed. "Plenty of witnesses."

"But when?"

"Loren." He winced, trying to hide the pain from the crash. He pushed it aside, refusing to share it with her. Refusing to trust her completely.

Of course, her own secrets shadowed that connection as well. Including the revolver in her pocket.

"He hates him, Myers," Loren said, lost in the memory of his former friend. "More than anything he wants revenge. It will be public. Exposed."

"Founder's Day is tomorrow."

"The parade." Loren nodded. "He's going to be at town hall tomorrow during the parade."

"Worse," Myers corrected, heading for the driver's side door. "He's going to burn the place down for all to see."

CHAPTER NINETEEN

The crowd cheered at the parade in full swing. Thousands gathered along the street as floats maneuvered down the center. Marching bands from local high schools filled the air, the loud percussion and brass instruments ringing in the celebration.

Loren hoped to glimpse the community's civic pride. An instance of someone dressed as William Rath or the float retelling the region's initial settlement and the first winter that almost wiped them out. Their own myths and legends brought to life by the citizens of Portents that grew from those stories.

Instead he looped around Town Hall Pub once more, then ducked inside for a quick inspection of the premises. There would be no mingling with others, no chance for a day off, not with the well-kept secrets surrounding the parade. No, Loren had one task and one focus: Find Richard Crowne before everything went to hell.

Distractions remained. The gashes along his brow and cheek offered up their own version of a drum beat inside his skull. The painkillers helped, but he kept the dosage down to stay alert, unwilling to dull his senses when he needed them most. As if the pain wasn't enough, he was forced to listen to Myers' anger from across the street at the courthouse thanks to his Bluetooth headset.

"We should have backup," Myers grumbled.

"You said that already." His hand hovered over his sidearm. He paused at each branched hall, waiting for someone to jump out. But he was alone, except for Myers' constant reminders about his decision.

"Yet here I am repeating myself. Why is that?"

Loren stopped at the front doors of Town Hall. Myers sat, tucked behind the pillar etched with the quotes of Wilbur Caldwell.

He gave her the all-clear sign and she tossed her own colorful response.

"Cute," he said before heading outside for another lap around the building. "Backup puts more people at risk. Or it sends Richard running."

"Not if what you believe is true. That he has to be here," she said. "But this isn't about stopping a murder, is it, Loren?"

He hesitated. Richard had the Founder. He could end his life at any moment, yet they were still reacting to his movements instead of trying to stop him from killing again. Was he doing enough?

"He's my friend, Myers."

"He's a killer," Myers said. "You can't save him."

"I have to try." Loren turned down the left hand side of the building, the cold whipping through him. "Anything?"

"I'm freezing my ass off," Myers started, the same as she had with each update. "I'm missing *Storage Wars* and I'm surrounded by shiny, happy people as far as the eye can see."

Loren sighed. "What am I missing?"

"You're too close to this, Loren."

He shook his head. Was she right? Was he too busy trying to save his friend that he was unwilling to catch a killer?

"I'm involved, Myers, but my judgment is crystal clear. He said..." Loren entered the building. Offices surrounded him; the hall was lined with photos of administrations and staffers both past and present. Including those of Richard Crowne. Richard celebrating holidays and victories with his colleagues and friends. Richard Crowne living and loving life. "He said I'm next."

Everything clicked in that moment.

"Dammit, Myers," he snapped, running for the exit. "He's not here. He won't be here. This isn't about the Founder or Founder's Day or any of it. This is about the founding of Richard Crowne."

The wind slammed into him, crackling raging from his headset. Loren pushed through it for the front door and the departing parade.

"Think about it," he continued. "The courthouse wasn't about Caldwell. How Harris died was smoke and mirrors. Like we thought, a calling card for the Founder. The courthouse mattered because of the man behind the act. It was where Richard first worked as a law clerk for Judge Mattis."

He closed his eyes, leaning against the building. How could he have been so blind to it all? The story of the founders, of their deaths, distracted him from the real tale being told. The story of Richard Crowne.

"Hennessey's house," Loren said, the wheels spinning faster in his mind. "The city holds a gala there after the Founder's Day parade every year. Richard met his wife there once upon a time."

What about the Founder then? What about the connection to William Rath? Did one exist or was it only to draw out the cloaked figure from their shared past? What was Richard's next move? What was he trying to tell Loren?

"Dammit. He's using the Founder as bait. For me. I know where he's going to be."

Silence continued on the headset. Loren waited, hoping to hear the grumbling of his partner. Static remained.

"Myers?"

"I wondered when you would get there."

Loren staggered back. Myers' voice had been replaced by another, the voice calm and collected but the threat inherent behind each word.

"Richard?" Loren asked, his head pounding. He started down the steps of town hall. "Where's Myers?"

"Occupied, Greg," Richard replied. "I didn't think that robed bastard would be incentive enough. And I thought I'd spare her your self-righteousness."

Stragglers from the parade barred his path and Loren shuffled through the departing crowds for the courthouse steps.

"Richard," he shouted over the throng of people. "Don't do this. We can—"

"See you soon, old friend."

The line went dead. Loren yanked the headset from his ear. He took the steps two at a time, running against the wind for the white pillars before the courthouse.

Behind the pillar sat two cell phones, her sidearm, and an empty syringe. Loren peered around the surrounding area frantically, but there was no sign of her or her abductor.

Samantha Myers was gone.

CHAPTER TWENTY

Her neck stung like hell. As far as first responses to waking up in a strange place, Myers thought she did pretty well. She struggled to snap out of the haze of the sedative still working through her system.

Crickets chirped outside, the lights and sounds of the city no longer present. Neither were the ten thousand cheering spectators to the Founder's Day parade. Myers took that as a good sign and not a fatal one.

Daylight faded. The wind slipping in through tired, old windows chilled her skin. Her coat was missing, along with her phones. Splinters ran from the wood on the chair beneath her strapped arms. The ropes were tight, allowing her little movement and no chance to slip free.

Not that Richard Crowne would ever give her that chance. That was not why she was there, the realization coming too late from Loren.

A figure rested on an adjacent chair. A cloak covered his face, the same black getup worn by the first two victims. It didn't take a genius to figure out his identity. Concern came from what was done to him. An empty syringe rested between them and a small dab of blood dripping along the man's right arm, the sleeve of the cloak rolled up to deliver the concoction.

Whatever the injection held left the man known as the Founder moaning. Myers couldn't tell if it came from pain or a gag hidden under the thick hood.

As her vision continued to clear, she saw her captor on the far side of the room. Richard Crowne stood before a wall mirror just off the kitchen. He fixed his tie in place, his suit jacket pressed and cleared of all wrinkles. Like he was heading for work, just like any other day of the week.

"Seriously?" Myers asked, pulling against the ropes before surrendering to catch her breath.

"Welcome back," Richard said. The tie lay crooked and he corrected the knot. "I apologize for the accommodations. I didn't have time to dust."

"I'm sure you're all torn up about it," Myers said. "Let us go, Crowne. You don't have to do this. No one else has to die."

"I disagree," Richard replied. He reached for his jacket and slipped it on, a long breath leaving him. It signified a return to form—who he was, before he lost everything.

Except the cabin. There was a cabin in his portfolio, used during the summer or when the city became too much for them. A place to escape, just him and his wife. Well preserved and kept intact, unlike everything else in his world. He tried to reclaim a little piece of it before the end.

"I used to love coming here," Richard said, catching her thoughts with a smile. "I bought it for my wife after we married. Our way to leave the world behind. But you can't ever really escape, can you?"

His eyes were distant, tinged with regret. "Crowne?"

Richard chuckled, leaning along the back of a chair overlooking the woods at the rear of the property. "I was sitting right here. This very spot. Lost in memory. That's all I was able to do back then. Sit and think about Jennifer. About my life. Then he came."

Myers cocked her head to the adjacent chair. "Him?"

Richard slammed his hand against the furniture. "Stop looking at him! He means nothing to this!" Richard's chest heaved and he let out a slow breath. "Not anymore."

"Okay, okay," Myers said. "Who?"

"Greg. Or whatever pet name you've developed for him."

She opened her mouth and he silenced her with a wave.

"I've seen the looks. The stray glances," he spat. "You can deny them all you want but it doesn't matter. I know."

"I don't—"

"He came and he saved me that day. Right here. Greg pulled me into the case, promised me he would catch Jennifer's killer and he did. Justice was served because of him. He gave me my life back but it wasn't enough. Not without her."

"That's when the church reached out to you? The Church of the Second Coming?"

Richard nodded. "I had it all again. Joy. Happiness. And he…he was my friend. He called me a friend. I tried to help him and he took it all away. He took everything from me!"

Rage burned in his eyes, anger seething to his fingertips as they squeezed the chair. Struggling was useless; the chair had been unwilling to give under her pressure.

"What are you going to do with me, Crowne?"

Richard circled around the chair, crouching before her. "I'm going to take you away from him. I'm going to take *everything* away from him."

"Like he did to you." Myers watched the light glow along his pupils. The joy at his final revenge. "And him? The Founder? What did you do to him?"

Richard grinned. He reached to the small tray beside her chair and retrieved the pair of gloves next to the empty syringe. He put them on, the leather stretching with his fingers. "Killed him. He simply refuses to accept his fate."

"That's not… William Rath was burned to death."

"It was silly, I know. Stories I learned in history class. But they carried weight. They inspired me—these tales of great men and the secrets they carried. Powerful men who held the world in their hands, yet it was never enough for them. They craved more, compromising more with each desire attained.

"Using their fates seemed almost poetic. He ruined it, though." Richard slapped the Founder's hood. The cloaked figure gurgled beneath his death shroud. The well-dressed murderer laughed. "The sedative… Well, how was I to know he'd have an allergic reaction to it?"

"A reaction?"

"More than he deserves, I agree. A simple death compared to the pain I had planned for him." Richard lifted the gun beside the syringe, Loren's revolver, the one she had in her pocket. Richard aimed, cocking back the hammer, and fired once at the Founder's head.

The cloaked man fell back, the chair crumpling under his weight.

Richard stood over his latest victim, a wry grin spreading. "There. Much more satisfying."

"But not enough for you, is it, you son of a bitch?" Myers seethed, struggling harder against the ropes.

Richard shook his head and put the gun away. He reached behind the couch and lifted a large drum of gasoline.

"No," he said, flames flickering behind his eyes. "Not yet."

CHAPTER TWENTY-ONE

The pale moon sat in the sky overhead yet the world blazed before Greg Loren. Richard Crowne's cabin, the last vestige of his life in the city of Portents, was on fire.

"Just like Rath," Loren muttered, parking Myers' car. "Dammit."

Wood sparked, snapping and crackling, the entire structure threatening to collapse. Loren rushed toward the home, realizing his illusion of Richard Crowne recovering from this was shattered. He had brought Richard to this point—so broken and lost that he would set fire to his prized possession, the place that made him happiest when his wife was still living. Where Loren first met the man he would come to call a friend.

Loren slammed through the door, covering his mouth and nose with his shirt as a makeshift filter. "Myers!" The flames rose in response, everything catching, the fire spreading in all directions. "Sam!"

The heat was dizzying, and his injuries from the previous night didn't help matters. Loren staggered deeper into the burning home, searching through the burning refuse that was a man's life, hoping for some sign of life.

Then he saw her. She lay along the floor, unconscious. Pieces of a chair were tied to her arms and legs, the rest shattered into shards strewn about the room. Her arms reached out, inching for the door. The attempt to reach the fresh air outdoors had been too much for her.

"Sam," he whispered. He picked her up, her delicate frame almost toppling him. Fighting through the pain and the spreading blaze, Loren held tight to his partner and raced for the door. Her eyes fluttered, fighting to stay with him. "Hang on, Myers. Just hang on."

Loren bashed open the door, then kicked it aside once more as it ricocheted back. He didn't rest, didn't breathe until they reached a large maple tree at the end of the property line beside the driveway and Myers' car.

"Myers?" he called, resting her against the tree trunk. He pulled off his jacket, wrapping it around her. Her eyes were closed again, her body shivering despite the heat pulsing from it. "Come on, Myers. Don't even think about—"

Her body spasmed, her head dipping toward the ground. Coughing in long hacks to remove the smoke from her infested lungs, Myers struggled to breathe. Hard, ineffectual gulps forced more coughs. Loren patted her back for support.

She knocked his hand away, her eyes finally clearing and the spasms lessening. Words fell short though and instead, she pointed for the woods. Her gaze, hard and cold, told him the story behind her gesture.

Loren stood and started for the thin dark path through the brush. The heat from the fire left him, the cold night air covering him in shadows. The moon, tucked behind the clouds overhead, beamed tiny streams of light down upon the widening path into the woods.

The sound of animals scurrying and crickets chirping filled his senses. Any other night the noise would have been peaceful, but each shift brought new dread. Loren held his pistol against his side, crunching leaves beneath his approach, terrified of the path's darkness.

And the ending to come.

The woods opened up, the trees fading behind him. A clearing stretched out in all directions before dropping sharply over a cliff. The edge of Portents. Beyond the cliff were open fields and undeveloped land desperate to be turned into a suburb. But for now, it remained open and barren beyond the grass and the brush.

Except for the man standing at the cliff's edge.

"Richard."

"Greg." He smiled, a revolver glinting under the thin streams of light overhead. He wore a suit, was clean-shaven and proud—a man reborn from the flames of his former life. Loren stopped as

Richard turned the gun on him, a gloved finger hovering over the trigger. "Not another step."

"I only want to talk," Loren said. "This doesn't have to end with more death."

"That's all that is left for us, Greg," Richard said. "You know that."

For so long Loren tried to find him, to help him through the second loss of his wife. He wanted to be there for him the way Richard was for him. With a smile, a handshake, whatever it took to keep him from this point.

At the edge.

"I refuse to believe that," Loren said. "Not after everything. Not after all we've suffered."

"We? Like you know about suffering!"

"Richard, please—"

"You blind yourself to it," Richard continued, the gun swinging wildly yet always on Loren. "But it is always there. You're just like them. Trying to lift everyone else as you keep sinking."

"That's not true."

"Except for me. You couldn't stand my happiness. You took my wife away from me, Greg."

"They would have done the same."

"They wouldn't," Richard yelled, squeezing the revolver. "I wouldn't let them take her from me."

"You're not a killer, Richard. You don't have to be a killer."

"There's nothing else for me, Greg. Just this." Richard cocked the hammer, filling the chamber. He pointed the weapon at Loren's chest.

Loren raised his sidearm, following suit. "Don't do this, Richard."

Both men hesitated. Loren's fear, his hope for a peaceful solution clouding his reasoning. But Richard? What stopped him? Why not take his revenge?

Because who was left after Loren was dead?

No one.

Loren lowered his pistol and dropped it in the grass. He took a small step forward. "That's what you want, isn't it? Me to end this for you? I won't. I'm your friend."

"Stay back!" Richard shouted.

"Let me help you, Richard. You can come back from this. Let me try. Please."

Tears stung the man's eyes. "You would too, wouldn't you? Even after all this? But you can't. She was all I had. There's no light for me anymore, Greg. Only darkness."

"Richard…"

He turned the gun on himself and pulled the trigger. The revolver fell into the tall grass and Richard Crowne's body teetered to the edge. Loren reached out for him, catching nothing but emptiness in the moonlight.

Richard's body sailed over the edge into the chasm's shadows. Loren watched his friend fall.

Forever lost to the darkness below.

CHAPTER TWENTY-TWO

Loren pushed the brush aside, staggering through the woods. The cabin fire crackled to the left. The structure had collapsed with smoke billowing high into the night air. The dark cloud spread rapidly, the wind blowing toward the city in the distance.

It was quiet, peaceful outside the crowded thoroughfares of Portents. There was a lot to love about the home—when it had been a home. Now the haven crumbled; the final reminder to a life long since lost—long before a bullet ended it, at any rate.

He stood before the flames, the darkness at his back. He watched the world burn and wondered if there was another way, a better way. For Portents. For Richard. For himself.

Silence answered him.

Loren shuffled back to the driveway, pushing away from the blaze. The maple tree at the end was vacant.

"Myers," he whispered. He drew his gun once more, circling the tree. "Sam?"

A thick branch swung out and he leaped back, narrowly avoiding impact against his recently healed ribs.

Myers' eyes flashed at the sight of Loren.

"Myers!"

She dropped the remnants of her weapon and shook her head. "Christ, wasn't sure it was—"

"I got that," Loren replied, holstering his sidearm. He reached out for her, helping her back to the trunk to rest. "Easy now. Easy."

Myers fought for breath, her breathing still ragged from smoke inhalation. He should have left a phone for her or called for backup immediately. He didn't, couldn't, though. Not with Richard involved. Not with the chance at saving him, at pulling him back from the edge. But he still went over, falling into darkness.

"You going to be all right?" he asked, taking a seat beside her.

Myers nodded, coughing. "Yeah. Eventually. Thanks to you. Not that I wouldn't have been fine."

Always the pain in the ass. Always. Loren smiled. "Right." The fire burned across the yard, snapping and sending tiny sparks flitting overhead. The last embers of Richard Crowne's life faded against the night sky. "The Founder?"

Myers fell silent. Loren understood. He never saw the body, never had a chance to save him. Not with the fire raging. Not with the world burning around them. Myers pointed to the woods. "Crowne?"

"I..." What could he say? What would be enough? Nothing ever would. Richard tried to save him and in return, Loren destroyed his every dream. Even in revenge, Loren stopped him in the end. He may as well have pulled the trigger.

A hand fell on his shoulder. "I know he was your friend."

Loren stared at the woods and the dark path to the cliff. The emptiness and the silence. "I don't have many friends left in the world, Myers." Then he turned to her with a smile, patting her hand. "I'm glad I didn't lose another one."

"Loren," she said. "Greg—"

He stood, letting her hand fall back into her lap. Opening the door to her car, he grabbed a small bag with the items lost during her abduction. He tossed them into her waiting hand.

"Call it in, will you? I..." He started for the open road and the quiet of the night.

"I will," Myers said, struggling to stand and fighting back another coughing fit. "I'll take care of it, Loren."

"Thanks."

"And then what?"

He looked up into the darkness surrounding them, the cold air struggling against the raging fire. "We go on. Same as we always do. And try to find a better way than those we leave behind."

CHAPTER TWENTY-THREE

Myers leaned against the tree and waited. The fire burned bright before her, the cabin in the woods outside Portents lost behind the flames. Smoke plumed above, spreading like a beacon against the night. Wood creaked, screaming for relief, before collapsing from the strain.

Loren sauntered down the road, his head heavy from the night's events. His trust surprised her—the solidifying of their partnership. He saved her, risked everything to rush into the flames to pull her free. He called her friend, a rarity. There was only her father and after him, only the lessons taught.

Control.

When Loren left her sight, she took a deep breath. It caused her to cough in great heaves, the remnants of smoke escaping. Myers, her chest burning from the flames, left the collapsing structure for the woods. The first steps pained her and she struggled to stay upright. With each passing moment, though, her resolve increased. Her need took over and she left the pain behind.

The cliff lay ahead and she stopped short of the precipice. Through the thickening darkness, the ever-increasing shadows surrounding the wide chasm, she could see him at the bottom.

Richard Crowne.

His dead eyes pierced the shadows, reflecting the soft glint of moonlight peeking from the clouds overhead. Regret, loss, and sadness filled those eyes and she stared at them, unable to look away.

Her death meant nothing to Richard, other than the pain it would cause Loren. And it would, she saw that now. Loren cared for her deeper than she imagined.

Not that his feelings mattered. Not with what she had to do.

She flipped open her phone, the burner Loren never questioned, and held firm to the number seven until it dialed the saved contact. The ringing boomed in her ear but she paid little attention. She was focused on the body below and then on something else that shone under the moonlight.

The gun.

It lay in the brush near the cliff's edge, lost and forgotten by Loren after his friend fell. Myers slipped a glove on her right hand and lifted the gun from the wet grass.

Loren's gun.

The murder weapon.

Shoving it in her pocket, Myers stood and waited until the phone clicked over. The voice at the other end said nothing, not needing to as Myers returned to the edge and stared into the abyss.

We need Loren contained.

Controlled.

"I have what we need."

She hung up without further explanation, the audible sneer from the other end enough to make her stomach lurch. Loren trusted her, put his faith in her. Saved her life. Selfless and brilliant, her partner.

Myers closed her eyes and spread her arms, the edge looming ahead. Her actions took her closer and closer, yet she didn't stop, didn't hesitate to continue. She had no choice. Not really.

Regret followed her—regret over things done and those yet to occur. She continued to walk, unable to find any light. Unable to believe light was possible in a place like Portents. Regret raged through her every breath, filling her every fiber.

Then she swallowed it down and started back to the burning home and the shadowy path ahead.

ABOUT THE AUTHOR

Lou Paduano is the author of the Greystone series of urban fantasy adventures, which follow Detective Greg Loren and Soriya Greystone as they hunt myths, monsters, and legends in the city of Portents.

He is also the author of the conspiracy thriller series, The DSA, a serialized tale about a clandestine government agency trying to discover the true power behind humanity's future.

He lives in Grand Island, New York with his wife and three daughters. Sign up for his e-mail list for free content as well as updates on future releases at loupaduano.com.

AVAILABLE NOW

BOOK ONE - SIGNS OF PORTENTS

Portents is a city like no other—and one that Detective Greg Loren can't wait to escape. Since his wife's death years earlier, Loren has looked forward to the moment he can leave the city of Portents for good—and never look back.

But fate has another plan for Loren. Called back to duty, Loren finds himself embroiled in a series of murders that has shaken the city. Together with Soriya Greystone, a young woman with unearthly powers, Loren must work quickly to find the otherworldly being that is killing citizens of Portents one at a time. Loren is tasked with deciphering the mysterious signs left at each of the crime scenes…even if it means traveling to worlds not his own to do so.

BOOK TWO - TALES FROM PORTENTS

Six tales of monsters, the dead rising, and the terrors of Portents.

The beasts Detective Loren and Soriya Greystone battled in Signs of Portents were just a hint of what lurks in the city. Tales from Portents explores the city's immersive history, including stories of Loren's descent after his wife's death—and his opportunity to have her rise from the grave. Among the pages, Soriya battles gremlins, navigates lessons with Mentor, and meets the werewolf Luchik. Follow new characters with expansive histories as they come face to face with the horrors of Portents—both human and otherwise.

AVAILABLE NOW

BOOK THREE - THE MEDUSA COIN

Death has come to the city of Portents.

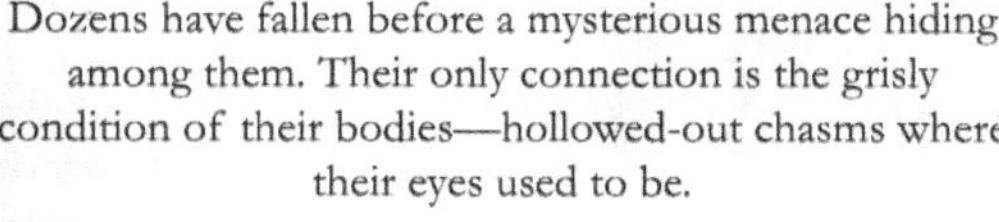

Dozens have fallen before a mysterious menace hiding among them. Their only connection is the grisly condition of their bodies—hollowed-out chasms where their eyes used to be.

Setting aside the aging case on his wife's murder, Detective Greg Loren has returned to the city with the task of stopping the bearer of the Medusa coin—an artifact with power over Death himself—from continuing to slaughter the people of Portents.

Soriya, no longer able to control the enigmatic Greystone, grapples with the decision to forge ahead in the case on her own, leaving Loren behind. But without the two counterbalancing each other, Death may be the force that levels them both.

GREYSTONE CONTINUES IN…

The war for Portents begins.

Soriya Greystone faces threats on all sides as the city turns on her, accusing her of multiple murders. Even Loren stands against her, the secrets between them too much for him to bear.

But their conflict is only a distraction from the threat building behind the scenes. A dark light is rising and with her comes an army of darkness.

The Heads of Cerberus have returned.

Portents and the Bypass at her heart will fall unless Soriya and Loren can face their darkest secrets and stand together—one last time.